Hallmark
PUBLISHING

RESCUING
Harmony Ranch

A feel-good romance
from Hallmark Publishing

USA *TODAY* BESTSELLING AUTHOR
Jennie Marts

This book is dedicated to Todd, my
real-life Hallmark hero.
Thanks for always believing in me.

Chapter One

IT SEEMED FITTING THAT JOCELYN Stone's cell phone died just as the driver pulled up in front of the gate leading into Harmony Ranch.

Perfect. I lose my connection to the present just as I step into the past.

"This is as close as I can get you," the driver said, clicking the trunk open.

"This is fine." Jocelyn stepped from the car, the fine brown dust of the dirt driveway settling on her black high-heeled boots. It had been years since she'd been back to Colorado, back to the small ranch where she'd spent so much time with her grandmother. She inhaled a deep breath. The spring mountain air was so full of memories, she had to grab hold of the door to keep from stumbling back.

The air felt different here, drier and cleaner, and steeped with the smell of pine trees and freshly mown grass. A slight breeze lifted her bangs, and Jocelyn caught the scent of lilacs from the long stand of trees lining the yard of Gram's Victorian home.

The soft scent of the pond and the earthy smell of

the horses in the corral spurred recollections of her childhood and all the time she'd spent here. She'd learned how to ride, how to make soap, and how to milk a cow.

And this is where she'd first fallen in love. She could almost feel the scratchy wool blanket covering the seat of the truck where Mack had taught her to drive...and the scent of hay in the barn where they'd shared their first kiss.

Stop. This trip was *not* about Mack Talbot and going down memory lane. This was about helping her grandmother. She took another deep breath and resolved to put the past behind her.

Yeah, right. The past was all around her, compressing in like the walls of a trash compactor. Which was exactly what she needed to do—compress those memories into a small little cube and tuck them away. She could think about them later. Or never. Yeah, *never* sounded good.

She grabbed her backpack and the designer purse she'd bought with the first paycheck she'd earned at her marketing firm in New York. She'd spent the last four months working her tail off trying to nab a new account and put herself in the running for a swanky promotion. A promotion that might now be in jeopardy.

This trip couldn't have come at a worse time. Her company had been trying to win the account of Midtown Perk, an up-and-coming coffee house scheduled to open that fall. Jocelyn had already put in countless hours creating a marketing campaign that she hoped would blow away both the client and her boss, Andrea, and make her the clear front-runner for the Director of Creative Services position.

Fortunately, Andrea had agreed to give Jocelyn two weeks' leave—provided that she'd continue to work on the client's portfolio—when she'd called her that morning to say she had a family emergency and needed to fly out to Colorado that day.

She still couldn't believe she'd secured that flight. It had maxed out her credit card, but there wasn't anything she wouldn't do for her grandmother. Heaven knew Molly Stone had done enough for her growing up. It was too bad they couldn't count on Mom for help—she'd been holding a silly grudge against Gram for years. Jocelyn didn't know what the argument was about. She doubted her mom even remembered after all this time. It most likely had something to do with her deadbeat dad, who had walked out of her life when she was twelve years old. But as the only daughter of an only daughter, her mom and her grandmother were all the family she had. So when Gram had called to tell her she'd broken her leg in a car accident and needed help, Jocelyn had booked the flight without hesitation.

She'd hauled out her suitcase and had started throwing everything she could think of into it before they'd even hung up the phone. Which was evident by the way the driver was dragging the brute of a bag over the edge of the trunk.

It hit the ground with a thunk, one of the ends of the orange tape declaring the bag "Heavy" hanging limply from the side. She'd been thankful the gate attendant hadn't charged her a fee for the bag; it had topped the scale at fifty-one point two pounds. But now, as she regarded the long walk up the dirt driveway, she wished she'd been more discerning in her packing choices. This wasn't the city. Did she really think she'd need two pencil skirts and four silk blouses when most days on the ranch called for nothing fancier than jeans and a T-shirt?

"What is this place?" the driver asked, shielding her eyes from the sun as she peered down the driveway where two girls clad in prairie dresses and sunbonnets walked toward the large white barn.

"It's a living history museum and ranch. It's a real working farm with horses and cows, but it's also a historic site that's been preserved so visitors can see what it looked like in its original state in the early 1900s. The staff and volunteers wear period dress and do programs about what life was like during that time."

"Oh, wow. That's neat."

"Yeah, it's pretty cool. Every effort is made to keep everything really authentic to what the original homesteaders would have had. They do a lot of demonstrations and hands-on activities so visitors can experience what daily life was like for the people who once lived here. My grandmother owns it. She's been running it since the Sixties." She lifted her chin. Gram was an amazing woman, and Jocelyn couldn't help bragging a little about all the things she'd accomplished and built here.

The driver nodded. "I live in Colorado Springs, but I'm gonna bring my kids to check it out this summer."

"You should. And thanks again for bringing me all the way up here." Jocelyn had flown into Colorado Springs, but the small town of Harmony Creek was close to thirty minutes into the mountains above the city. She'd been lucky to find someone willing to bring her all the way up.

The driver shrugged and passed Jocelyn her card.

"I don't mind. It was a gorgeous drive. Call me when you're ready to go back to the airport, and I'll bring you back down." She waved before getting back into the car.

Jocelyn pushed through the gate, hauling the suitcase behind her. Her grandmother had given it to her for her sixteenth birthday, but it was still in great shape. Probably because she never went anywhere.

The bag lurched to a stop as the wheels caught on a row of rocks. *Gah.* She leaned back as she tried to yank it over. The bag tipped to the side as the handle broke loose in her hand.

She fell back, right into the hard body of a man. And quite a man, judging from the strong muscled arms that wrapped around her.

"Whoa. You okay, there?" he asked, his voice a deep-toned bass in her ear.

She pushed to her feet, holding his arm to steady herself. She turned as the scent of him swirled around her, a masculine blend of musky aftershave, earth, and wood smoke. And something else, something familiar.

She blinked as she took in the sight of the man who had caught her. He was tall, well over six feet, with shoulders that seemed almost as broad as the barn in the background behind him. Her gaze traveled up from his square-toed cowboy boots, over his jean-clad legs, and the burgundy thermal shirt that stretched over his chest to the trimmed black beard covering his chin. His hair was dark and thick, a lock of bangs hanging over amused blue eyes—eyes that she knew as well as her own.

Her breath caught in her throat, and all she could whisper was, "Mack?"

"Hey, Joss."

"Is it really you?" She blinked again. What was he doing here? Her gaze raked back over his shoulders. "You've gotten so...big."

He raised an eyebrow at her.

Her face flushed with heat. "Okay, that sounded weird. But I just mean, I haven't seen you in years. And the last time I did, you did *not* look like...*this*." She pressed her hand to her leg to keep from reaching up again. What was wrong with her?

"You mean like a scrawny seventeen-year-old kid?"

"I wouldn't say scrawny—more like lean and wiry."

"Huh," he grunted. "You mean scrawny."

"Well, you're not scrawny now." The last time she'd seen him, he'd only had half an inch on her five-foot-eight frame. Now, even in her heeled boots, she had to peer up at him. "When did you get so tall?"

He pushed back his shoulders, making him seem even larger. "The year after you left, I had a growth spurt, grew another six inches by the time I hit eighteen. I marked it on the board in the barn so if you ever came back, you could see that I beat you."

A pain twisted her heart at his words. That was the year her mom had gotten into the fight with Gram and had moved them to New York. Jocelyn had spent her senior year in the city, and hadn't made it back to the ranch since.

She'd wanted to. She and Mack had been dating for years by then, and they'd devised a wildly romantic plan to keep in touch. Both of them had planned on her coming back to Harmony for good after they graduated. They'd talked of getting married and eventually taking over the ranch.

But Mack hadn't followed through on his side of the deal. Instead, by the next spring, he'd taken up with Ashley Deeds, another girl from their school. And she was the one he'd married.

Once Jocelyn had heard about that, she hadn't wanted to come back.

She tried to push away the memory with a forced laugh. "Oh gosh, I forgot about our competition to see who would get taller."

"How could you forget? Seemed like we had a competition for everything—who could swim the farthest, who could milk a cow the fastest, who could find the most eggs from the chickens."

"Don't forget who could bake the best cookies. I definitely won that one."

"That remains to be seen. My cooking skills have gotten better."

She shook her head, surprised at how easily they fell back into their easy banter. "Why did we do that? What made us compete over every little thing?"

He shrugged. "I think it started that summer your parents got divorced. Maybe you felt like you had something to prove."

It was her turn to raise an eyebrow. It was her parents' divorce and the lack of financial stability it had caused that had finally forced her and her mom to move in with Gram the summer she'd turned fourteen. The same summer she started to notice new feelings for the cute boy she'd spent the last four summers with, catching crawdads and running around the ranch. "Wow," she said. "That was deep. Especially since we haven't seen each other in over a decade."

She still held the suitcase handle in her hand, and

she twisted the faux leather in her fingers, not sure what to say next. She hadn't meant to bring up the fact that she hadn't been home in so long. What if he asked her why she hadn't come back? No way was she ready to go there.

For a minute though, it had felt like old times, teasing and joking around, and he seemed genuinely glad to see her. Now, she just felt self-conscious and uncomfortable, the memories of being ignored and forgotten swirling through her.

She forced her hands to still.

It was a long time ago. We were just kids, she reminded herself as she tried to steer their conversation away from their personal lives. "Let's go back to talking about something less awkward—like your muscles." *Yeah, much less awkward to talk about those.* She needed to just stop talking. "What kind of workout are you doing? Kickboxing? Free weights?"

He huffed again. "I don't *work out*. I just work." He nodded his head to the blacksmith shop, a smaller wooden barn set off to the side of the larger one.

"What? Here? You work here?" He'd gone on to work at Harmony Ranch without her?

She'd done her best to put him out of her mind, to not let herself imagine what might have been, but in the few weak moments she'd let herself think about him, she'd always assumed he'd left Harmony Creek to go off and live the perfect life with Ashley.

He stared at her as if she'd just sprouted horns. "Yeah. I apprenticed here after high school, then took over the shop from my grandfather. How do you not know this? Don't you talk to your grandmother?"

Her back bristled. *Not about you. Never about you.*

Not since her grandmother had told her he'd married Ashley, and Jocelyn had declared she didn't want to hear another thing about Mack Talbot. *Ever.* "Of course I talk to her. I just talked to her this morning when she called to tell me she'd been in a car accident. Why do you think I'm here?"

He leveled her with a cool stare. "I would not presume to know why you do anything, Jocelyn."

Ouch. His comment felt a little salty. What was that about? She lifted her chin. "Well, what does your wife think of being back on the ranch again?" Two could play at that game.

"What wife?" He laughed, an actual chuckle. "You mean Ashley? Dang, you are out of touch. We were married for less than a year."

Less than a year? Jocelyn couldn't believe it. She'd assumed they had a house, a dog, and several little Macks and Ashleys running around. Her gaze flicked to his empty ring finger, and she was a little embarrassed at the way her heart perked up at knowing he wasn't married anymore.

"We lasted about nine months, right up until my grandfather got sick and left me the smithy shop, and I told her I was planning to stay in Harmony Creek. Then she hightailed it out of here faster than an ornery bronc at a rodeo, and I moved back into the caretaker's cottage with my grandparents."

Oh no. She lowered her eyes. "I'm so sorry."

"Don't be. We never should have gotten married in the first place. We were too young. And we got married for the wrong reasons."

The wrong reasons? What did that mean? "I meant

I'm sorry to hear about your grandfather. I didn't know he was sick."

"He's not. Not anymore. He kicked the cancer, but decided to retire anyway. By that time, Ashley and I were already divorced."

"That's good. I mean about the cancer, not the divorce." Her cheeks warmed again. Where had all their easy banter gone? Their conversation now felt as painful and prickly as a peeved porcupine.

A grin tugged at the corner of Mack's lips. "Grandpa accredits his recovery to his steady diet of bacon and eggs, buttermilk, and the shot of pickle juice he takes every Sunday night. He claims it cleans his gut and his palate and sets him right with the Lord to take on a new week."

Jocelyn wrinkled her nose as she laughed. "How does a shot of pickle juice set anything right?"

Mack laughed with her. "I don't know. Personally, I'm going to give modern medicine the credit, but you know there's no arguing with Hank Talbot. Which is why I still live in the caretaker's cottage, and he and my grandma moved into a little apartment in town."

"Oh. I guess I'd heard that they moved into town a few years ago, but I didn't know you were still living at the ranch." Which meant he'd be in the house directly behind the one she'd be staying in—almost close enough to touch.

No. No touching. No even *thinking* about touching Mack Talbot. She was here to help her grandmother, not rekindle an old flame that had been snuffed out years ago.

She lifted her chin, determined to appear nonchalant—like this easy chatting about their past wasn't affecting her at all. If he was going to act like every-thing was fine between them, then so would she. Even though a million questions ran through her head. The biggest one was, *Why?*

But now wasn't the time for questions, for digging up past hurts. Now was the time to focus on her grand-mother. "Speaking of grandparents, I should probably head over to see Gram."

"I've already been instructed to bring you to the hospital as soon as you arrived."

"Oh, you don't have to do that." His offer was kind, but spending more time with him felt like just extend-ing the awkwardness.

"How do you plan to get there, then? Walk?" He glanced down at her boots. "Not in those heels."

"I'll have you know I've walked all over New York in these heels." Although the boots *were* starting to get a little uncomfortable. And being back on the ranch had her wanting to slip on her sneakers and explore the sweet-smelling pastures beyond the fences and the cool shadows of the trails leading up the mountain be-hind the barn. "I figured I could use Gram's car while I was here."

"Good luck with that. Her car was totaled in the ac-cident."

"Oh, no. I was in such a rush when she called me this morning that I don't really even know what hap-pened."

"Spring thunderstorm and wet roads are what hap-pened. She was a mile south of town when she must have hydroplaned and lost control of the car. Tire tracks show her skidding off the shoulder and into the ditch."

She brought her free hand up to cover her mouth. "Poor Gram. She must have been so scared."

"Lucky for her that Taurus was a beast and took the brunt of the crash, or she could have been hurt much worse."

Mack nodded toward her suitcase. "Why don't I carry that up to the house, and then we can head to the hospital?"

She held the handle out. "This broke off. But I can get it." She leaned down and tried to lift the suitcase by the sides. Dang. It was too heavy. She blew up her bangs and got behind the bag to push it forward.

Mack shook his head as he stuffed the broken handle in his pocket. "I got this. You want your backpack inside, too?" He put the backpack on his shoulder, then easily lifted the suitcase in his arms as if it weighed nothing. "If you're ready, you can head over to my truck. I'll put this stuff inside and meet you there in a minute." He nodded to the blue pickup sitting in the shade by the blacksmith barn.

The sight of the truck brought a swirl of memories spinning through her stomach. "Isn't that your grandpa's truck? The one you taught me to drive in?"

"Same one. But it's mine now. Can't you tell? I added a new sticker."

The truck had always had an American flag sticker in the back windshield and a *Support Our Troops* bumper sticker. Jocelyn squinted at the bumper and could barely make out the decal in the shape of an anvil and a hammer. "Yeah, you really went crazy. It looks totally different now." She shook her head. "I can't believe you're still driving it. Or that it still runs."

He shrugged. "Not everything has to be new and

different. Some things are made to last. Especially if they are built strong to begin with. And if you take good care of them." He kept his gaze on hers for just a beat too long.

She wondered if his words held more than one meaning. But then his gaze shifted to over her shoulder as he gestured to the truck. "Hope you don't mind dogs. Mine is already waiting in the pickup. His name is Savage, and I'd approach him carefully. He's quite a beast."

A beast? She started toward the truck, bracing herself for the growling teeth of a pit bull or a snarling Rottweiler.

Could her day get *any* better? Her phone was dead and her suitcase had broken, landing her in the arms of the one person she'd hoped to avoid during this quick trip home. And now she was going to get mauled by a mangy mutt.

Welcome home to Harmony Creek. The place she'd had her heart broken.

Chapter Two

J OCELYN'S PULSE RACED AS SHE prepared herself to face down the beastly brute. She gripped the strap of her purse, steeling herself as she peered through the window.

A laugh bubbled out of her throat as the sinister creature turned his head and gazed back at her—through the saddest, sweetest big brown basset hound eyes she'd ever seen. She opened the truck door, and the dog lifted his head. His large tongue flopped out of his mouth and reached to lick her hand.

"Oh you *are* scary, aren't you?" she cooed, letting him sniff the back of her hand before she scratched his wrinkly neck. Apparently Mack still had his witty sense of humor, because the frightening beast he'd warned her about had five-inch legs, and if he were any calmer, he'd be asleep.

"All right, cutie," she told him, giving his side a gentle nudge. "Scootch over so I can get in here."

The dog dropped his head to the seat and wouldn't budge.

By the time Mack walked over, she'd worked up a

sweat as she cooed and cajoled and flat-out pleaded, but the dog hadn't moved an inch. "He won't scoot over," she told him.

Mack awarded her efforts with an amused glance. "Oh yeah, I'm all too familiar with that game. So if you want to make it to the hospital before midnight, you'd better just get in on my side."

She gulped. "And ride in the middle?" With her leg and shoulder pressed against Mack's? The sweat on her back from trying to move the dog just inched farther up her spine.

Mack shrugged. "I can give you another ten minutes to try to convince him to move, but I've argued with that dog before. And have rarely come out the victor. He's even more stubborn than me."

She raised an eyebrow. "That's hard to believe. I remember you once ate an entire earthworm just because someone said they didn't believe you could."

"Yeah, I know. That's what I mean."

She glanced from the dog back to Mack. Savage let out a long groan as he melted deeper into the seat. It didn't look like she was going to win this battle. "Fine. I'll sit in the middle." She followed Mack around to his side of the truck. As he opened the door for her, she was all too aware of him as she slid past his body and into the cab. Her heart pounded as she scooted across the seat and up against the dog's squat frame.

Savage lifted his head and rested it on her leg, looking up at her with soulful brown eyes. "Don't try to butter me up now." She pressed her lips together and glared down at him—for all of three and a half seconds—which is about how long it took those sad puppy dog eyes to win her over and have her reaching out to scratch his neck.

He rolled to his side in doggy bliss, then sprawled his head upside down on her lap, one floppy ear covering the end of his nose. His long pink tongue drooped out the side of his mouth as he gazed adoringly up at her.

"Come on Savage. Have some dignity," Mack told him. "You could at least *try* to play hard to get." Mack shook his head in mock disgust, but a grin played at the corner of his lips as he started the truck.

She smiled with him, but as they drove, his words rankled her a little. Is that what Mack had been doing their senior year when he'd ignored her efforts to communicate with him? Had *her* leaving triggered something in him that brought up memories of his mom abandoning him when he was younger? Had she opened old wounds that made him decide to play hard to get, or some other kind of game to make her prove how much she cared about him?

If he was, he'd definitely won that round, but he'd taken the game a little too far when he'd gotten married.

It was a long time ago, she reminded herself. They'd been kids. Their plans to get married and someday take over the ranch had been the daydreams of lovestruck teenagers. And besides, *she* was the one who'd moved away. She couldn't expect him to wait for her forever. Except a small part of her had expected exactly that—because she hadn't just been a love-struck teenage girl. She'd really loved him.

Too late now. They'd both obviously moved on. She swallowed back the hurt and kept her focus on the dog. "I never pictured you as a basset hound kind of guy."

He huffed. "Me either. Although it's not exactly like I *chose* him. I just made the unfortunate mistake of petting him and being nice to him one day."

"And what? He followed you home?"

"Not exactly. He belonged to a couple of out-of-state tourists who had stopped to sightsee at the ranch. I was walking through the parking lot and saw him sitting by their car. I felt sorry for him and brought him a dish of water and gave him a little attention. Next thing I know, the tourists took off, leaving the dog, half a bag of food, and a note that claimed they were bored with his droopy demeanor. They said I took better care of him than they ever had."

Jocelyn put her hand to her mouth. "You mean they just abandoned their dog? To some stranger in a parking lot?"

"Yep."

"So what did you do?"

He let out a soft chuckle. "I became the new owner of a boring basset hound who has short legs, a drooling problem, and is completely averse to any kind of training." He snuck a glance at the dog. "But he does kind of grow on you." He reached across her lap to give the dog's head an affectionate pet.

She nudged his shoulder, trying to ignore the battalion of butterflies that had just taken off in her belly as his arm brushed across her leg. "You always were an old softy. And it doesn't surprise me a bit. I remember Eeyore was always your favorite."

He shook his head as he cringed. "Oh dang—I forgot how you made me watch Winnie the Pooh like five times that one summer. Or at least I've tried to block it from my memory. Although I probably know half those songs by heart."

"We watched that shoot 'em up car chase movie just as many times. And Winnie the Pooh was my favorite. You said you liked it too."

"No, I just liked *you*," he muttered, not quite under his breath.

She blinked. Had he really just said that? There was no question that he'd liked her back then—they'd been inseparable and he'd professed his love for her. So was his comment meant to be an opening to talk about their past? She couldn't imagine he'd want to bring it up right now, just as they were pulling into a spot in the hospital parking lot.

"Molly's gonna be so happy to see you," Mack said, effectively changing the subject before opening his door and exiting the truck. *And* cutting off her opportunity to ask.

Mack held the door for Jocelyn and closed his eyes for just a second as he inhaled the scent of her—expensive perfume mixed with shampoo, something floral and feminine, different but still so familiar. Even though Molly had warned him she was coming, he couldn't believe Jocelyn Stone was here, climbing out of his truck, his dog's hair clinging to her fancy purse.

He'd thought about this moment for so many years, imagining what he'd say or how she would react. He hadn't ever imagined a scenario of her stumbling into him and his being so completely dumbstruck that the opening five minutes of the first conversation they'd had in years consisted mainly of his grunting, nodding, and fielding comments about how much he'd grown. He wanted to smack his palm against his head for admitting that he'd chronicled his tallest height on their old chart in the barn.

Inhaling a deep breath, he tried to get it together as he followed Jocelyn into the hospital.

"Are you sure Savage is going to be okay in the truck?" she asked, narrowing her eyes in concern.

He nodded. "He's more than okay. It's one of his favorite places. Sometimes we get back to the ranch, and he'll just hang out in the truck for another hour after we get home. Personally, I think it may have something to do with his aversion to exercise, but I could be wrong."

She raised her eyebrows. "Are you saying your dog is too lazy to get out of the truck?"

"No, *you're* saying that. But I'm not disagreeing with you."

"Hmmph. That would be a first," she quipped.

"What? We've been known to agree on things before. Not many."

"Okay." She laughed as she pointed toward him. "*That* we can agree on."

Her laugh did something funny to his stomach. Even after all this time, she still made him feel like an awkward geeky teenager. And it didn't help that she still looked as gorgeous as ever. Different, especially since he was used to seeing her in cutoff shorts and Converse sneakers, not designer jeans, high-heeled boots, and whatever she called that flowy silk top that probably cost more than his whole drawer full of T-shirts. She looked put together and like a true city girl, but he'd caught a few glimpses of the goofy girl he'd known.

She'd been adorable as a teenager: tall and gangly with long legs, long blonde hair that was usually trying to break free of her ponytail, a great smile, a big laugh, and a light spray of freckles across her nose. Her teenage cuteness had turned into a woman's beauty. Her hair wasn't quite as long now and had turned a darker blonde, and her freckles had lightened, barely visible, but she still had the great smile, and her laugh was bringing up memories that he'd spent the last ten years trying to forget.

Jocelyn's easy smile fell as they approached the open door of her grandmother's room. Molly was asleep in the bed, her arms tucked under the blankets. A purple bruise colored her cheekbone and edged around her eye.

Mack's grandmother, Loretta Talbot, had been Molly's best friend for most of their lives, and he'd rushed her to the hospital as soon as they'd heard about the accident, so he'd known how Molly looked, but he probably should have prepared Jocelyn.

She stopped in the doorway, one hand covering her mouth, the other gripping his arm. "Oh, gosh. She looks so small in that hospital bed," she whispered.

Molly Stone *was* a small woman—barely over five feet—but her bold personality made her seem bigger.

"She's okay," he assured her. "Just a little banged up."

"It's my leg that's broken, not my hearing," Molly said, cracking open an eye. "And the sight of my favorite granddaughter is the best medicine I can get, so quit standing there gawking at me and get over here and give your Gram a hug."

Jocelyn rushed to her side, then leaned over the bed and gently pulled her grandma into her arms. The moment was so tender, Mack had to look away. He might not have seen her in a long time, but he knew how much Molly had done for Jocelyn as a kid and how much her grandmother meant to her.

Mack's grandmother had been reading in the chair on the other side of the bed. She smiled warmly as she stood and set her book aside. "I'm so glad to see you, Joss," she said, hurrying around the end of the bed to give Jocelyn a hug. She wasn't much bigger than Molly, and Jocelyn's chin rested on her silver curl-covered head. "It was good of you to come. How was the flight? Are you tired out?" She leaned back to peer up at Jocelyn. "You look beautiful as ever. I love that blouse. So pretty."

To her credit, Jocelyn took his grandmother's mishmash of questions and comments in stride as she smiled affectionately down at her. "Of course I came. And my flight was fine, and no, I'm not tired. I grabbed a nap on the plane, which is why I'm a wrinkled mess."

Mack didn't think she looked wrinkled at all. Although he almost wished she did. It might've been easier if she'd been a hot mess instead of this stunning, stylish woman. He raked his fingers through his hair, trying to remember if he'd even run a comb through it after he'd gotten out of the shower that morning.

"Thanks for bringing her over, Mack," Molly said, reaching for his hand.

"Happy to do it." He gave her hand a quick squeeze

and smiled, then leaned against the wall next to the chair Loretta dropped back into.

"Now that everyone has hugged and hello'd, tell me about you," Jocelyn said, turning back to Molly. "How are you feeling? Really?" She reached out and lightly touched her grandmother's cheek below the bruise.

"I'm fine, honey. Nothing to worry about."

"Mack said you slid off the road. What happened?"

"I'll tell you what happened," Mack's grandmother said. "Your grandma thought she needed to take a casserole out to the Jenkins house in the middle of a spring thunderstorm."

Molly frowned at her friend. "It was barely raining when I left the house. And I always drop off a casserole when a new baby arrives in Harmony Creek. The family would be insulted if I didn't."

"You don't need to do everything and go everywhere at a hundred miles an hour all the time. Have you considered that if you hadn't been racing around like a cat with its tail on fire, you might not have hydroplaned on the wet road and landed your car in the ditch?"

Molly tilted her head, ignoring her friend's admonitions. "I wonder what happened to that spaghetti casserole. It's one of my favorite recipes."

Mack's grandmother threw up her hands. "It's probably splattered all over the floor of your totaled car."

"That's a shame," Molly muttered. "I spent an hour on that sauce."

"All I'm saying is that it's okay to slow down once in a while and take it easy."

"Take it easy?" Molly huffed. "I'll take it easy when

I'm dead. For now, I've got things to do and places to be."

Her friend peered at her over the top of her glasses. "Oh yeah? Was the hospital one of those places? Cause that's where you ended up." She glanced at Jocelyn. "At least this might slow your grandma down a little."

I doubt it, Mack thought. Molly had been an unstoppable force for as long as he could remember.

Jocelyn held up her hand like a referee. "How about you two stop bickering like an old married couple and someone tell me what the doctors are saying?"

Molly shrugged again. "The obvious—that I broke my leg and I'm bruised up. Although one of them had the audacity to call me old."

"The nerve," Jocelyn murmured, a grin tugging at the corners of her lips.

"As if," Molly scoffed. "I'm barely a day over eighty."

"So besides insulting your youth, what did they actually say about your health and your recovery?"

Molly waved her hand away. "Some hogwash about resting. And keeping off my leg for at least a month."

Jocelyn folded her arms over her chest. "Well then, that's the hogwash you need to do."

Molly shook her head. "But I can't. I don't *have* a month to take it easy. I've got the Spring Festival in less than a week, and the whole town is counting on it."

"Then the whole town can wait. Your health is way more important than the community of Harmony Creek getting their funnel cake fix."

"It's more than just funnel cakes," Molly said, pushing her bottom lip out in an indignant pout.

"Look Gram, I know the festival is important to

you," Jocelyn said, resting her hand on Molly's leg. "But you're important to *me*." Her voice caught, and she pressed her lips together to keep from crying.

Mack's chest tightened at seeing her emotion, and he pushed his shoulders into the wall to keep from going to her. He hadn't seen her in close to a decade, but he still couldn't handle seeing her cry.

"I need you to take care of yourself," Jocelyn told her. "Harmony Creek will understand if we have to postpone the festival for a few months. Or even if we have to skip it this year."

Molly's face drained of color. "We can't *skip* it. We can't even postpone it for a day. We *have* to have the festival. And it has to be the best one this town has ever seen." Molly reached for Jocelyn's hand. "Please honey, this is why I called you, why I *begged* you to come."

"You begged me to come for the *festival*? I thought you called me to help take care of you."

Molly huffed again. "I can take care of myself. But I can't make the festival happen from a hospital bed and hobbling around on crutches. I need you to take it over."

"Take it *over*?" Jocelyn's eyes widened, and her mouth gaped open as if Molly had just asked her to plan the royal wedding. "Gram, I've got a job, a life in New York. You know I'm trying to land this promotion. I can't just drop everything to organize the Harmony Creek spring festival."

"You don't have to organize it. I've done all the legwork." She glanced down at her propped up foot. "No pun intended. But I need someone I can trust who knows the festival to step in and make sure it goes well."

"You *can* trust me, but I haven't been to the event in ten years."

"But you'd been to every one for the ten years before that." She squeezed Jocelyn's hand. "I know you're busy, and I'm not asking you to give up your job. But I really need you, honey. I wouldn't be asking you at all if it weren't really important to me."

Jocelyn let out a sigh. Mack could see that she was wavering. "My boss did give me the next two weeks off, so I'll be here anyway. I guess if I work in the evenings *and* if you agree to be a model patient and do everything the doctor tells you to do, I could probably work on the promotion *and* oversee the festival."

Two weeks? Mack swallowed, and his stomach did a funny flip. Jocelyn Stone was going to be within arm's reach for the next two weeks? Wait, *not* arm's reach, at least not his arms, but a stone's throw away. He wasn't sure he could handle seeing the woman who'd broken his heart walking around the ranch where they'd shared so many memories, every day for two weeks.

A look of relief washed over Molly's face. "Oh, thank you. And I will be the best patient you can imagine."

Jocelyn raised an eyebrow.

"I will. You'll see. This means everything to me." She clasped Jocelyn's hand tighter. "But you have to *promise*—promise me you'll take over the festival."

"Okay. Okay. I promise. But I can't guarantee it will be as big as you normally do."

"It has to be *bigger*. This is the 50th anniversary of Harmony Ranch. It has to be the biggest celebration yet. Loretta and I have been working our collective tushes off to bring in new attractions and to find more ways to raise money. We even talked about doing a 5K run this year. We've been planning it for months."

Mack didn't like the panic rising in Molly's voice. He glanced from her to his grandmother, then back at Molly, whose free hand was gripping the side of the hospital bed. Something was up. He'd caught the look the two older women had just shared.

Jocelyn must have noticed, too. She narrowed her eyes at her grandmother. "All right. There's obviously something more going on here than just corn dogs and a mini marathon. This really has you upset. So time to fess up. What's really going on here?"

"I'm sure I have no idea what you mean."

"Cut the innocent act, Grandma. Just tell us what's happening."

"We just want the festival to be really nice," Mack's grandmother started to say, but Molly held up her hand, cutting the other woman off.

"It's no use, Loretta. We might as well tell them the truth."

Mack leaned forward, tension twisting his gut. He didn't like the sound of this. He was used to Molly and his granny cracking jokes and being silly. This note of seriousness between them had him worried. "Yeah, I think I'd like to know what's going on, too."

"Yes. You should," his grandmother said. "Since it concerns you, too."

Jocelyn snuck him a worried glance before plopping herself on the end of the hospital bed. "Spill it."

Molly said, "Well, you see, it takes a lot to run a ranch and a historic site like we have. It's special, unique. And I manage. I'm not saying I don't. Especially now that Mack's come on board. He's been a huge help." She granted Mack a loving smile.

He appreciated the gesture, but had a feeling it was more of a stalling tactic than a compliment to his work. "And?"

"And, well..." She turned back to Jocelyn. "You know we went through a bit of a rough patch when your Grandpa died. And we had some setbacks a few years ago—had to replace the furnace and buy that new tractor. Which was all okay, we've been through rough patches before, and we just borrowed a little, or in this case, a lot, from the bank to get us through until things turned around. And they always do. And I've been paying this last loan back just fine, but the problem is that it comes due this year. This month, to be exact."

Jocelyn furrowed her brow. "But that seems good if you're at the end of it. Sounds like you can get out from under the payments then."

Molly cut her eyes to the bedsheet in front of her. "No, it's not good. You don't understand. That last one is a balloon payment. And it's a doozy."

Mack scrubbed a hand across his jaw. He'd known something was up with those two, the way they'd had their heads together so much lately, always whispering about something or other. He'd just figured the two of them were scheming to matchmake some poor unsuspecting couple in Harmony Creek. Ever since they'd cunningly brought together Paul Jenkins and Sally Thompson, the first of the wedded couples, they'd considered themselves matchmaking mavens. They'd taken credit for half a dozen of the latest weddings in town.

He usually rolled his eyes and tried to ignore their Cupid conversations, but right now, he dang sure would have preferred some romantic meddling to financial woes at the ranch. Especially since his livelihood was tied to it. "Just how big a doozy are we talking about?"

Molly shrunk smaller against the hospital pillow. "Pretty big."

"*How* big?"

She twisted the sheet between her fingers, lowering her voice to a whisper. "Twenty-four thousand dollars big."

"Twenty-four thousand dollars?" Jocelyn choked, her eyes growing wide. "Holy Frappuccinos."

"That wasn't what I was going to say," Mack said, leaning forward. "Why didn't you tell me? As the caretaker, I think I have a right to know this kind of thing."

Jocelyn whipped her head towards him. "Wait. What? You're the caretaker?" She turned back to her grandma. "When did this happen?"

"A few years ago. I was going to tell you, but you always say you don't want to hear about anything concerning Mack." She clapped her hand over her mouth and shrugged at her granddaughter. "Sorry."

Interesting. Why didn't Jocelyn want to hear anything about him? Because she still had feelings for him? His heart did a little stutter at the thought. Or because she didn't? And was that why she didn't know about his divorce or his grandfather's illness—because she'd told her grandmother not to talk about him?

He'd have to ponder this later. Right now, they had

more pressing concerns. Like how they were going to come up with twenty-four thousand dollars in the next few weeks. "Let's stay focused. What do you have in place for the festival so far?"

"I told you, Loretta and I have done a lot of the work, and we've made tons of notes and all the contact information for the vendors and such are in the big binder I've got sitting on the kitchen table. Everything is there. We just need you to keep things organized, help set it all up, train the gate people, count the money, and try to come up with a couple of additional ideas for making some more cash."

"Oh, that's all," Jocelyn said, shaking her head.

"And I can still help once they let me out of here."

"None of that sounds like it involves resting or staying off your leg."

"I can still make phone calls and work on schedules. I'm not totally useless," Molly countered, her voice sounding a little miffed.

"No one has ever accused you of being useless," Jocelyn told her. "But you still need to take care of yourself. And that's why I came. To help you. Let me look at my schedule. Maybe I can take a little more time off." She frowned as she pulled her phone from her pocket, then scowled at the dead screen. Digging in her bag, she found a charger and plugged it and her phone into the outlet on the wall behind her grandmother's head.

"I've got this if you need to get back to New York," Mack told her. "I've been helping put on this festival for years, and I'm sure I can handle what needs to be done."

"But this year is different," Molly said. "It's bigger

and more complicated than it's ever been before. And it *has* to go well. For the ranch to survive, we need to knock it out of the park. There are jobs and livelihoods at stake here—including yours and mine." She directed the last comment to Mack but included them both in the next. "You've both got great skills to bring to the table, but you're going to have to work together. You're going to need each other."

He glanced from Molly to Jocelyn. "You know you can count on me."

"Me too," Jocelyn said, pushing her shoulders back. "I'm not going anywhere."

He pressed his lips together to keep from smiling. But he wondered if her firm stance came from the resolve to help her grandmother or the competitive spirit she'd always had with him.

She rubbed her hands together. "I guess now we just have to figure out how to put on one heck of a great spring festival. Which is where my skills as a marketer come in handy. I'll come up with a whole social media package—Facebook, Instagram, Twitter. So first of all, we need a better name—something that sounds bigger, flashier, more exciting."

"It's a living history museum," Mack reminded her, bristling a little at her take-charge demeanor. He was the caretaker. She'd been here all of five minutes. "We focus on the past. Which means we don't do flashy. Or any of that social media insta-whatever business."

"You're going to need that insta-whatever business to drive new people to the festival," she said, dismissing his remarks. "Now let's put our heads together. What else could we call this to make it sound bigger, different than years before, but also the same? How about the Harmony Creek Jamboree? Oh, how about the Harmony Hullaballoo?"

Mack's eyebrows drew together in a frown. "I am not calling this thing a hullaballoo."

She grinned at him, a move that didn't help his crusty response. "Okay, maybe hullabaloo is a little much. But what about Spring Fling? Or Spring Spree? A shindig? A wingding? A soirée?"

He shook his head. "Now you're just trying to annoy me."

"I like shindig," Molly said. "And a wingding sounds like a heck of a good time."

Jocelyn flashed him another impish grin. "See, it's working." She turned back to Molly. "Did you already have a logo? Signage? Brochures to put around town?"

Molly shook her head. "We just have the same sign we hoist up every year. And everyone in town knows it's held the last weekend of May. But we did make a little flyer." She gestured to Loretta. "Do you have a picture of this year's flyer on your phone?"

Loretta nodded and found the right screen, then passed the phone to Jocelyn. Mack took a step forward and leaned over Jocelyn's shoulder to peer down at the picture. It was designed to look like parchment paper and had a young girl in period dress running alongside a hoop that she was pushing with a stick, her pigtails flying behind her.

"Okay, I like this," Jocelyn said, tapping her finger to her chin. "How about we use this and call it the Harmony Creek Hoopla?" She glanced around, waiting for their reaction.

The two older ladies smiled.

"I like it," Molly said.

"So do I," Mack's grandmother agreed.

They turned to him. He raised one shoulder in a shrug. "I don't hate it."

"Yay," Jocelyn said. "I can start working on a media package tonight. We can get flyers and signage and put them up all over town and hang some in the next few towns around us too. And my social media strategy might bring up some folks from Colorado Springs, as well."

"Sounds like we've got a plan." Molly's shoulders relaxed a little.

"I'll look at the stuff you've put together and run some numbers," Jocelyn said. "How much do you typically make in profits from the festival?"

"Oh, well..." Molly's tension returned, and she looked down at her hands, evading her granddaughter's eyes. "Um, usually about four or five thousand."

"Four or five thousand dollars? And this year we need to bring in twenty-four?"

"That one year we made sixty-five hundred," Mack's grandmother reminded them. "Remember? That was the year we hired the petting zoo. They brought a camel. *And* we had kettle corn."

"Sounds great," Mack muttered. "We just need another camel and a kettle corn stand. And maybe an elephant and a giraffe. No problem."

Jocelyn stood up off the bed and pushed her shoulders back. "Sounds to me like we've got a *hoop*-lot of work to do. And less than a week to do it. We'd better get out of here if we're gonna get started."

Chapter Three

SAVAGE WAS STILL LOUNGED ACROSS the passenger seat when Jocelyn and Mack made their way back to the pickup. Resigned to the middle, Jocelyn slid past Mack when he opened the door for her and scooted onto the seat. The basset hound lifted his head, then dropped it onto her leg. She scratched his chin, and he let out a blissful sigh as if he were telling her he'd been waiting for her and this very moment to make his life complete.

The drive back to Harmony Ranch didn't take long. Jocelyn didn't talk about the festival—she was still trying to wrap her mind around how much money they needed to raise, and how little time they had to do it. Instead, she and Mack made small talk about how the town of Harmony Creek had changed as they drove past new businesses and old ones that had been shut down.

"This place hasn't changed a bit," Jocelyn said as she climbed from the truck and surveyed the ranch. Everything about it still matched the photograph she carried in her mind. Rows of tall pine trees surrounded the meadow. Cottonwoods interspersed with the evergreens that circled the small pond. It sat at the ranch's center, surrounded by the three historic homes, a small general store and gift shop, the chicken coop, and the large garden plot full of freshly turned soil.

The massive white barn stood sentinel over the ranch, home to several horses and cows, and the center of so many memories of learning to ride, of helping her grandfather bucket-feed a calf...and of kissing Mack in the rafters above the stalls. She could almost smell the earthy scent of dust and feel the scratchy hay that always found a way into her clothes. Two corrals branched out from either side of the barn, one holding the horses still used to pull plows and wagons, the other holding a few cows and several sheep and goats.

Molly's home, an old Victorian, sat at the side of the property, a small stone path leading toward the caretaker's cottage and the blacksmith shop set a little ways behind it. In between those homes and the pond sat a large grassy meadow where the spring festival had been held for the last several decades. And where Jocelyn and Mack needed to throw the biggest festival yet.

But what if they failed?

Failure wasn't an option. They couldn't lose Harmony Ranch. They just had to make it work.

"We've updated a few things and had to replace some stuff that broke, but most of it should be just like the last time you were here," Mack said. "That's the allure, and the magic, of the place—it doesn't change. Visitors can count on it being the same every time they visit. I think it's like visiting an old friend.

And the connection to the past inspires comfort in a lot of folks—makes them remember simpler times."

That allure of nostalgia and memories swirled around her as she inhaled a deep breath. "Gram's lilacs are as beautiful as ever," she noted, pointing to the long row of bushes lining the back edge of the home's property. "I love the way they seem to announce spring is here. Every time I smell lilacs, I always think about being here in the spring and summer. I just love them."

Mack nodded. "I remember. Back when you used to just come for the summer, it was always one of the first things you did when you got here—filled a big mason jar with water and stuffed it full of lilac sprigs. Then when you lived here, you always filled the house with them. I can picture you perfectly, standing at the bushes, a clipper in your hand, and your arms full of flowers."

She smiled at the memory. "Gramps always had the clippers and some mason jars sitting on the table so I could fill them up as soon as I arrived." She blinked back the sudden well of tears filling her eyes. "I miss him."

"I know you do," Mack said. His gaze stayed trained on the ranch. "So do I."

"I miss everything about this place," she whispered, hoping he knew she meant him too, even though she couldn't bring herself to say it out loud.

He turned to her, gazing down into her eyes, conveying a message that maybe he couldn't say either. That he missed her too? Or just that he understood the grief of losing the man who had touched both their lives. "Well, we'd better get you inside."

She swallowed the emotion as she followed him up

the steps and into the house. Then she gasped as the scent of lilacs filled her nose, and she saw the large jar of purple flowers in the middle of the kitchen table. A set of shears and a few smaller jars were lined up on the counter.

Her throat burned as she stepped up to the table and leaned her face into the gorgeous blooms. "They smell amazing," she whispered, and felt like the flowers were a heavenly gift wrapped in memories of her grandfather. "But who did this? No one even knew I was coming. Gram was already in the hospital when she called me."

Mack shrugged as he stuffed his hands in the front pockets of his jeans and averted his eyes.

Her eyes widened. "You? You did this?"

He shrugged again. "I just thought you'd like it."

"I love it," she said, throwing her arms around his neck. "It's perfect. Thank you."

"It's not a big deal. It took me five minutes."

"It's a big deal to me. It's everything to me." She stepped back, a little embarrassed by her impulsiveness, and looked up at his face. "You look different, but still so much the same. I like the beard."

"You look exactly the same." He lifted a strand of her hair and then released it. "Except your hair is shorter. And fancier. No ponytail."

The brief touch of his fingers in her hair had her wanting to close her eyes and lean into him, to savor the feel of him again. After all these years, she hadn't expected the feelings to still be so strong.

His eyes darkened, narrowed as his gaze dropped to her lips. She caught her breath as her body froze. Was he going to kiss her? Did she want to kiss him?

No. She'd been back less than a day and hadn't seen this man, the one who shattered her heart, in years. She should be backing away, thinking this through and putting a stop to it before someone, like her, got hurt again. But instead, she drew just the smallest bit nearer.

A loud rap sounded on the door, as if her good sense had been locked out and was knocking to be let back in. She sucked in a quick breath as she took a step back.

"Hellooo?" a voice called through the screen.

She was imagining things, she told herself. Of course Mack wasn't going to kiss her.

Mack strode toward the door, opening it for an elderly woman to walk in. She wore a pair of beige polyester capri pants, beige orthopedic shoes, a light blue collared shirt, and a beige cardigan, even though the day was warm. She must have recently been to the salon because her short hair looked like white cotton candy in a cloud of soft silvery curls around her head.

The expression on her face was anything but soft as she marched past Mack, a casserole dish cradled in a nest of hot pads and tea towels held in her arms. She plonked the dish onto the counter, then turned back to face Mack. "I see those weeds out next to the entrance gate still haven't been taken care of."

"Nice to see you, Mrs. Crandle," Mack said, an amused smile on his face. "And I've already told you, those aren't weeds, they're wildflowers."

"Hmmph. They look like weeds to me."

Mack appeared to be used to this argument and didn't seem bothered by it at all as he gestured toward

Jocelyn. "Mrs. Crandle, you remember Jocelyn, Molly's granddaughter?"

"Of course I remember Jocelyn. I'm old, not stupid."

Hmm. And still just as cheery as ever, Jocelyn thought.

"How are you, Mrs. Crandle?" she asked, stepping forward to shake the woman's hand.

"I just told you, I'm old," she replied, shaking Jocelyn's hand, then glanced down at her body with a grimace of disgust. "My bones ache, my joints hurt, and I've got a bunion that turns my big toe as crooked as those politicians in Washington. But I got out of bed today, and I'm still breathing, so I can't really complain."

Jocelyn nodded, trying to think of a fitting response to anything the older woman had just said.

Mack saved her by pointing toward the casserole dish. "I sure hope that's your famous macaroni and cheese. It smells delicious."

"It is. And it's still hot. I figured you all would need something to eat with Molly out of commission. How's she doing? Have you been to see her yet?"

Jocelyn nodded. "Yes, we just got back from the hospital. She's in good spirits, but she broke her leg and she's bruised up and sore."

"I imagine so. Well, give her my best," she said as she collected the towels from around the dish. "I suppose now with Molly in the hospital, they'll have to cancel that horrible spring festival."

Jocelyn stiffened. "Horrible?"

"Yes. I hate that thing. Every year hordes of people show up, parking in front of my house and blocking my driveway. It's nuts with the traffic and the noise."

Jocelyn's heart sank. How could they make the festival a success if even the locals didn't support it?

"It used to drive my little Charlie crazy, barking his head off at every person who walked by the window," Mrs. Crandle continued. She stared down at her hands. "My Charlie is gone now. But that dang traffic is still going on. Makes my head hurt just to think about it."

"I was so sorry to hear about Charlie. He was such a sweet dog." Jocelyn had fond memories of the little white Westie.

"Yes, he was," Mrs. Crandle said, her shoulders loosening as she softened a little. "Thank you for your sweet note and the lovely flowers you sent after I lost him. They meant a lot."

Jocelyn smiled, her heart breaking for the woman who'd lost her precious companion. "I'm glad. I wish I could have done more."

"It was enough."

"I hate to be the bearer of bad news, but I have to tell you the festival *hasn't* been cancelled. In fact, this is the 50th anniversary of the ranch, so this year's festival is going to be bigger than ever."

"Bigger?" the older woman croaked.

"Yep. Mack and I are taking it on, and we promised my grandma it would be the best and most successful spring festival yet." She didn't want to give away Gram's financial difficulties. "So maybe you should think about taking a trip that weekend. Or just be prepared for lots of people. Because we are hoping for double the normal traffic." Or triple, if they were really going to make the money her grandmother needed to save the ranch.

"*Double*? That's just great," Mrs. Crandle grumbled. "Is it too late to take back my macaroni and cheese?"

"Not a chance," Mack said, putting an arm around the older woman's shoulder and leading her toward the door. "But we will do our best to make sure you aren't impacted any more than necessary. And remember, it's just one weekend, and it's for a good cause."

"Fine," she said. "Just make sure you get my casserole dish back to me."

"Will do," he said, opening the front door and ushering her out. "And thanks again. That was real nice of you to think of us. I know we'll enjoy that mac and cheese."

"Bye," Jocelyn called, crossing the room to stand next to Mack. "Thank you so much."

They watched the woman march across the driveway and toward the front gate. Mack grinned as she bent to pull one of the wildflowers from the ground, then he pushed the door shut. "She's a little salty, but she's sweet on the inside. And she does make amazing mac and cheese."

Jocelyn's stomach growled. She hadn't realized how hungry she was. "Good, because I'm starving. I'm grabbing a plate now. You ready for some too?"

"Sure. Might as well. My big plans for supper tonight included a ham sandwich and reading the new issue of the *Blacksmith Quarterly* magazine."

"Wow. You really know how to live it up. *Blacksmith Quarterly and* a ham sandwich? On a Wednesday night, even?"

He shrugged. "I know it's crazy, but that's just how I roll."

She laughed as she got out two glasses and filled

them with ice water. He took plates from the cupboard and silverware from the drawer to set the table. As she moved the pasta dish to the table and then dropped into the chair across from him, she shook her head. "It's funny how comfortable we both are in the kitchen of a home neither of us lives in."

He shrugged as he dished out heaping spoonfuls of pasta onto their plates, the melted gooey cheese clinging to the spoon. "I might as well have lived here, for all the time I've spent here. And Molly never moves much. And hardly gets rid of anything."

"Yeah, I think I spied a women's magazine from the nineties in the stack by her chair. I'm sure it had some great article in it she wanted to keep." She took a bite of the macaroni and cheese and let out a groan. "Oh my gosh, this is delicious. And it's still warm." She shoved another bite into her mouth, then pulled over the thick binder from the other end of the table. "So, this is the famous festival binder, huh?" She scanned over the details as she flipped through the pages.

"Yep. That's got all of Molly and my grandma's notes in it, plus all the contact info for the vendors and the schedules of activities. It's quite a production."

"I remember."

He shook his head. "It's grown quite a bit since you last attended. We've added a pie auction, an obstacle course, and more blacksmith demonstrations."

"I'll bet those are well-attended. Have you ever taught any classes on blacksmithing?"

"Not during the festival."

"Maybe that's an extra idea to bring in some added revenue—teach classes and have visitors pay to make one small item that they get to keep. You could offer several short time slots during the day. What do you think?"

"I think it's a great idea. I'm not sure how much interest there would be, or what the liability would entail, but I can check into it. And I do have an apprentice who could teach some too if enough people were interested."

"Yes. We've got our first new idea." She grinned and made a note in the binder. "Now we can tell Gram that we at least came up with something different." She tapped her finger to her chin. "How about the concert and sweetheart dance? Do you still do that at the end of the night?"

He nodded. "That's the grand finale. And we always get a good turnout. We've got a local band scheduled, and they're pretty good."

That was encouraging, at least. And was there any way to make it even better? "Maybe we could think of something extra we could sell at the dance—like a signature dessert or a special memento to commemorate the anniversary."

"Good idea. I'll see if I can think of something."

"There's a lot of details, but we can totally do this. I'll enter all this stuff into my phone and set up notifications for us throughout the weekend." She stretched for her purse, but couldn't reach it. "Can you pass me my bag? I seem to be a little encumbered at the moment." She pointed to her feet.

Mack leaned back to peer under the table and smirked at the sight of his dog sprawled across Jocelyn's ankles. "I told you he was a beast. Just kick him off your feet."

"I wouldn't dare. I think he's adorable."

"I think he has a crush on you. Although I've never seen him so taken with anyone else. It's usually *my* feet that he's inconveniently sprawled across."

Jocelyn's heart warmed. "I'll take that as a compliment."

"You should. He doesn't usually make friends so quickly. And he's pretty stingy with passing out affection, so I'm telling you that dog digs you."

"Well, I dig him too."

"That's good, because you're going to be stuck with him for a long time. Once he settles into a comfy spot on your feet, he doesn't budge for hours."

He pushed her purse toward her, but the base of it hit the placemat and tipped over, spilling the contents. Tissues, a makeup bag, her sunglasses, and two packages of peanut butter cups slid across the table. Her keys and two lip gloss tubes rolled off the side and hit the floor, followed by one of the packages of peanut butter cups.

"Shoot, sorry," Mack said, scrambling to grab the loose items. He picked up one of the candy packages. "You still have a passion for peanut butter? You used to eat that stuff every day. Peanut butter sandwiches at lunch, spoonfuls of peanut butter for a snack, and I don't think I've ever seen you pass up a peanut butter cookie. And you always asked Molly for peanut butter cups when she went to the store."

She shrugged, unable to stop the grin sneaking across her face, but reluctant to admit that she'd had peanut butter and honey on toast for breakfast that morning. "Yes, I still love peanut butter. But I can think of worse vices to have."

"True. And I hate to tell you, but you might have

just been thrown over for a new love in the eyes of my dog." He laughed as he gestured to where Savage had lumbered out from under the table to sniff the package of peanut butter cups. "Sorry, buddy." He grabbed the package from the floor and held it out to her.

"It's understandable," she said. "There are plenty of former crushes that I would definitely choose a peanut butter cup over." She held the pack up. "Want to split this with me?"

"Sure."

She opened the package and handed him one of the paper-wrapped cups. Lifting the remaining cup to her lips, she took a bite and made an appreciative sound. "How can you *not* love these? They're amazing."

Mack ate his in two bites. "They are good. I haven't had one in a long time. But whenever I do, they always make me think of you." He held her gaze for just a beat too long.

Long enough for her to wonder if thinking of her was a good thing he relished, or a bad thing he avoided. She popped the second half into her mouth and shoved the contents of her bag back into her purse. Pulling her phone from the depths, she tried to resume their earlier conversation before they'd gone off on a tangent of her peanut butter fetish and his dog's crush on her. "We should exchange numbers so I can shoot you all the calendar invites and notifications I enter."

Mack shook his head. "I don't think so."

Chapter Four

J OCELYN JERKED HER HEAD BACK, swallowing at
the hurt in her throat. *Wow.* He must still be
pretty mad at her if he didn't even want her to
have his number. "Oh, okay. We don't have to. I can
always have Gram call you if we need to talk about
something."

"I didn't mean that. I'm good with exchanging numbers," he told her, then recited his number for her to
enter. "But it's not going to do any good to send me
whatever you just said." He pulled an old-school flip
phone from his pocket and waved it at her. "I don't
think I can get them on this."

"Why are you carrying your grandma's phone?"

He cocked an eyebrow. "This is *my* phone."

Her eyes widened. "Like your *original* phone? From
when you were a kid? Because I don't think they even
make those anymore."

"It's not *that* old. And it still works just fine."

"As what? A life-alert signal?" It felt so natural to
be teasing him again—just like old times. "Have you

contacted *Antiques Roadshow*? They might offer you some money for that thing."

"Wow. You're hilarious."

She squinted at the piece of duct tape stretched across the base. "Can you even get the internet on that thing?"

He shook his head. "No. But why would I need to? It's a phone. And it serves the purpose of making and receiving calls just fine. Although sometimes not if I'm on the south side of the barn. But nobody ever really needs to get ahold of me that badly anyway."

She shook her head. "Geez, you are stuck in the past."

"I don't consider myself stuck. This is where I choose to be." He pushed the phone back into his pocket. "Not everything new and shiny is better. Sometimes the old stuff starts off stronger. Which is why it lasts longer."

Did he mean *them*? Was that a thinly veiled comment on their relationship? Or about his feelings for her? Or was he still just defending his ancient cell phone?

She peered around the room, looking for a way to change the subject. She wasn't ready to dive into their past. Spotting her broken suitcase by the door, she groaned as she gestured toward it. "Not that bad boy. I think it's seen its last leg. I'm not sure how I'm even going to get it upstairs."

He pushed back from the table. "I'll take it up for you. Then I should probably get going. Send me a text, and then I'll have your number. And before you say anything, *yes,* my old phone still gets and sends text messages," he told her, as he hefted the suitcase onto one shoulder and carried it up the stairs.

The second level of the home held three small bedrooms. Two were used as guest rooms and one had always been the sewing room. Gram's room was on the main level, which was fortunate, since she'd be dealing with the frustration of wearing a cast.

Jocelyn peeked her head into the first room and was relieved to see it looked the same—the sewing machine against the window, stacks of discarded fabric on the end of the old ironing board, and piles of fat squares and quilting implements spilling from the old dresser. The fresh scent of starch hung in the air.

"There's a lot of memories in this room. Gram taught me how to sew in here. I still remember the first thing I made. It was a hot pad," she told Mack.

"Yeah? Was it any good?"

"No. It was terrible. The stitches were all wonky. But it was this gorgeous fabric with blue roses on it, and I thought it was beautiful. I learned later that it was this expensive fabric Gram had bought for a quilt, but she let me use it and never said anything. And of course she raved over what a great job I did on it."

"She would." Mack carried her bag into the last room on the right. Even though she hadn't lived here in years, she still considered it *her* room.

"Speaking of memories," she said, stepping into the room and getting hit with a swell of nostalgia like a wave in the ocean knocking her to her knees. She ran a hand over the soft fabric of the faded pink and white quilt that was still spread across the bed. "Gram made me this quilt for my sixteenth birthday. I wanted to bring it with me when we moved to New York, but my mom made me leave it here."

Mack nodded and set the suitcase on the end of the bed. "Sorry about the small accommodations."

"Are you kidding? This is luxuriously spacious compared to what I'm used to in New York."

He peered around the small dormer room. "How could this be considered spacious? What do you normally live in? A shoebox?"

"Close. I live in a walk-in closet."

He frowned and studied her as if he couldn't quite tell if she was joshing him.

"I'm totally serious. My bedroom is literally the walk-in closet of one of my roommates' bedrooms. She's a friend I met in college, and she travels a lot for work. So when she's gone, I get to sleep in her bed. But when she's home, I sleep on a futon in the closet."

He stared at her. "What about all your stuff?"

"It's in there too. It's amazing what you can do with a double closet rod and a good storage system."

"And dare I ask how much you pay to live in a closet?"

She told him the ridiculously high amount she shelled out for her tiny piece of real estate and the privilege to live in the city.

He jerked back. "Are you kidding me? You could rent a five bedroom house for that here. With a yard. And maybe even a pool." He shook his head. "And you were supposed to be the smart one."

Hopefully her smarts would land her the promotion she needed to finally move out and be able to afford her own room. She shrugged. "It's the price you pay to live in New York."

"Seems like a pretty steep price. Is it worth it?"

"Yes. Of course." Although being back in Colorado on the ranch with its wide open spaces and panoramic views of the mountains cast a slim shadow of doubt in her mind.

He patted her suitcase. "I'll leave you to get unpacked then. Although from what you've just been telling me and from the weight of that bag, I can't imagine there's much you didn't bring with you."

"Very funny." She pushed off the bed and pulled her phone from her pocket. "Before you go, will you take a selfie with me? I want to send it to Gram." She held the phone out at arm's length and leaned in next to him.

He twisted his mouth into a snarling grimace, and she snapped a pic.

"Oh that's a good one. I'm posting that to Insta with the caption, 'Sighted a grizzly bear in Colorado'," she teased.

"We don't have grizzlies in Colorado," he corrected her.

She shook her head, smiling. "Man, you're tough."

He grunted, his mouth wrinkling into a frown. "I don't really do 'selfies'."

"Fine, then we'll just take a picture." She held the phone up again and tapped it with her thumb. "Of ourselves." She nudged him in his stone-hard abs.

That earned the smallest of smiles from him, and she grabbed the shot. Although she knew what would *really* make him smile. "Do you remember that time we tried to ride one of the cows and I fell off, right into that huge mud puddle?"

His lips curved into a grin, then he let out a laugh.

She tapped the screen several times and caught it all. And it was worth the humiliating reminder of that day just to get a shot of him laughing.

Except he was *still* cracking up.

"Okay, okay. It wasn't *that* funny."

"Oh, yes. It was. I can still see your face. You were so mad." He pressed a hand to his stomach. "Man, I haven't thought about that night in years."

"Glad I could remind you." She put the phone back in her pocket. "We did have some good times, didn't we?"

His smile disappeared. "Yeah, we did. A lot of them." His eyes cut to the antique dresser he stood next to, and he ran his finger over a scratch in the wood. "That's why it made it awful hard to understand why you never came back."

She jerked her head back. It was hard for *him* to understand why she never came back? How hard did he think it was on *her* to hear he'd gotten married? "I *couldn't* come back," she stated, louder than she'd intended. "My mom and Gram had another falling out, and I wasn't allowed to come. Plus, I was only seventeen. It's not like I could jump on a bus and come out on my own." Although she'd wanted to and had been ready to try.

"It was a long time ago." He tapped the side of the door jamb as he took another step back through the door and into the hallway. "It doesn't matter now," he said, then turned and walked away.

❀❀❀

"Savage. Here boy," Mack hollered into the front yard the next morning. *Where did that mutt get to?* He'd put him outside twenty minutes ago, and the dog was usually waiting on the front stoop when he came back and opened the door.

He walked a few steps into the yard, whistled, then called the dog's name again. *Nothing.* A tiny edge of panic churned in his stomach. This wasn't like the basset. He was nothing if not predictable.

"Hey, Mack," a voice called from the direction of Molly's front porch. Jocelyn's head poked around the corner of the porch. "Do you happen to be missing a canine with a hangdog face and a penchant for pancakes?"

"Ayup," he said, blowing out a sigh of relief as he hurried toward the Victorian.

"Well you better come and get him before all the pancakes are gone."

He rounded the porch and took the steps two at a time. Jocelyn had already gone back inside, but had left the front door ajar, and he stepped inside to the delicious scent of vanilla and maple syrup. A platter full of fluffy pancakes sat on the counter, and his traitorous dog lay sprawled across the kitchen floor.

Savage lifted his head and groaned by way of greeting. Mack knelt down and scrubbed his hand over the dog's wrinkly neck. "You scared the heck out of me, you silly mutt." He peered up at Jocelyn. "He doesn't usually take off like that. He's always waiting by the door when I open it."

"I'm sorry," Jocelyn said. "I should've called you. I was in the kitchen making breakfast when I heard him scratching at the door. He came right in and made himself at home when I opened the door, so I figured he must come over and visit Gram often." She was dressed in cropped jeans and a pastel pink T-shirt that read, "A Bookworm is my Patronus." Her feet were bare, and her toes gleamed with glossy hot pink polish. She looked cute—younger, and more the way he remembered her—without her designer clothes and with her hair pulled into a messy ponytail on top of her head.

"No, he's much more of a homebody. And he doesn't often leave my side for very long." He scratched his chin, feeling a little bewildered at his dog's unusual actions. "He must *really* like you."

He isn't the only one.

Mack had tossed and turned the night before, thinking about Jocelyn and replaying their last conversation in his head from the night before. They'd been getting along so well, they were laughing and joking around, and then he'd gone and opened his big fat mouth. He shouldn't have brought up the fact that she hadn't come back. Even though it had been all he'd been thinking about. It was great having Joss back in her old room, but it also brought up all the old feelings of hurt and betrayal. And all the questions about why she hadn't returned.

Although her reaction to his statement brought up even more questions. Why did she act surprised by his comment? And how did she think she had the right to get defensive?

More to the point, why did hanging out in her grandmother's kitchen with her again feel so dang right? And why was he feeling jealous of all the affection she was doling out to his four-footed friend?

"Aww, sweet puppy," she murmured as she rubbed the dog's belly with her foot. He groaned again and rolled over to give her more space to rub. "That's the best compliment I've had all week. I'll take it. And I really like him. He's good company."

"Do you have a dog back home? In your spacious closet apartment?"

She shook her head. "No. For obvious reasons. But it stinks, because I love dogs and would love to have one. But with my job, and living in an apartment, it's just too hard." She held up a plate. "You up for a short stack?"

His stomach growled in response, and he nodded as he washed his hands then took a seat at the counter. "Sure. They smell delicious."

She filled a plate with several pancakes then pushed the butter and syrup toward him. "Coffee?"

"Yes, thanks," he said, the butter he slathered on already melting into the still-warm pancakes. "Just black is good." He drizzled syrup over the stack and then moaned as he took a bite. "Dang. These are good. You didn't used to be able to cook."

"You didn't used to drink coffee." She handed him the cup, then picked up her own and took a sip.

He shrugged and nodded to the cup in her hands. "You didn't either."

"I still don't much. I like the flavored creamer much more than I like the coffee. But I do enjoy a cup in the morning."

"I thought everyone in New York was addicted to their caffeine and spent half their paychecks on expensive coffee drinks."

She shrugged. "Some do. I prefer fruit smoothies. And my company is really forward-thinking so they have their own coffee shop and cafeteria."

"Sounds fancy."

"It probably is. A little. But no fancy cup of coffee compares to the way this one tasted as I sat out on the porch this morning and enjoyed the view of the mountains."

She had a point. And it made him feel a little better about her that she recognized the fact. She wasn't totally lost. The girl he once knew was in there somewhere. She just wasn't "his girl" anymore. "You been up long?"

"Oh yeah. For hours. Time change and all. I called Gram first thing, and she's in good spirits, but the doctor said they may keep her one more night, just because of the concussion. She wasn't pleased, but at least there won't be staff and visitors to oversee today. You're still just open on the weekends, right?"

He nodded. "Friday through Sunday through the spring, then we'll go to Thursday through Monday once summer hits. We talked about adding another day this year, but the farm and museum are still such a small operation that the revenue just didn't support adding the extra volunteers and employees. Although I do have some staff coming in today to help set up for the festival, so you might see some people around."

"Oh good. That was on my list. I spent the last few hours working on festival stuff, and I went through Gram's binder again and divided the remaining tasks into four groups. I figured I'd tackle the booths and the publicity and marketing stuff, and you could work on setting up the grounds and the food vendors. How does that sound?"

"Sure."

"Good. I already created a Facebook event page this

morning, sent out some invites, and set up some small ads for it. I created a few graphics and several tweets to use with the hashtag HarmonyHoopla. I tested a few tweets this morning, but I've scheduled several more, plus some extra Facebook posts to go out over the next few days. Did you know Gram didn't even have an Instagram for this place? I had to create one. But it's going to take weeks to grow a following, so I just posted on my account for now."

His head spun with all the terminology and details she was describing.

Jocelyn picked up a small notebook and leaned against the counter as she scanned her notes. "I can email you some graphics to post on your social media too. Although I tried to follow you on Instagram and Twitter this morning and couldn't find you. I figured you must use something clever like YeOldeBlacksmith or ForgedInHarmony or TheBeardedBlacksmith or something."

"Those do sound clever, and I appreciate the nod to my skilled creativeness, but I'm not actually using *any* of those names, or any like them, because I don't *have* any social media accounts."

"What?" Her eyes widened as she almost dropped her notebook. "How can you not have *any* social media accounts? Not even Facebook?"

"I know. It's hard to imagine that someone could continue to breathe and survive and actually live without social media." He arched an amused eyebrow, and his lips curved with the slightest grin. "But I somehow manage."

"How do you keep in touch with people? With the world? With the news and latest happenings?"

"First of all, if you're getting your news from so-cial media, you've got bigger concerns than my lack of tweets. And second of all, there aren't that many people who I really care about staying in touch with. And if I want to talk to them, I call them. Or send them an email. Or stop by their house."

She shook her head. "I'm glad to hear you at least have email. But seriously, you need to have at least *one* social media account. Just to stay connected to the world."

He took her shoulders and turned her to face out the windows overlooking the farm. "*That* is my world. And I'm connected to it by being present in it every day. You should try it. Put your phone away and just enjoy life without worrying about posting a silly picture of what you ate or where you walked or updating the world on the last semi-clever thing you thought about."

She sighed as she shook her head. "I don't have that luxury. Social media is my *job*. My livelihood de-pends on those posts and those silly pictures, and I get paid to share those semi-clever things I think."

He ducked his head. "Sorry. That last one was a bit of a low blow."

"You might think this is stupid. But it's real to me. And social media is often the only way that people have to stay connected. It might seem like it's all about pic-tures of food or people posting silly duck-faced poses, but it's also a way for people to share their lives and to feel tied to the world. And to other people." She pulled her phone from her pocket and held it up. "This *is* the future." She pointed out the window. "And as lovely as it is, *that* is still the past."

Her words rankled him like a spur stuck under a

saddle. "Well, just like you, *that* is my livelihood. So I'm going to get out there and do some actual work and not post a single picture or status report about it. And the work will still get done." He whistled for the dog as he headed toward the door.

"Maybe you shouldn't knock what you haven't even tried," she called to his retreating back.

He turned his head, narrowing his eyes in a cool stare and getting off one last quip before he walked out. "I could say the same to you."

Chapter Five

J OCELYN SHIFTED FROM ONE FOOT to the other as she stood outside the door to the blacksmith shop. She raised her hand. Should she knock? Or just go in? She could hear music coming from inside the shop, a classic country station, so she was sure Mack was in there. Plus, she'd seen him go in thirty minutes before.

Not that she was watching for him. She'd actually been quite miffed when he'd walked out earlier. But she'd distracted herself from thoughts of him by staying busy the rest of the morning. She'd logged several work hours tackling the coffee house campaign and answering emails, then spent some time making calls and creating new signage for the festival. It was only her growling stomach that told her it was time to stop for lunch.

She'd planned to make a sandwich and figured it was the neighborly thing to do to see if Mack wanted one too. Yeah, right, especially since her neighbor was a six-foot-something bearded hunk.

Stop it, she scolded herself. Her history with Mack was just that—*history.* It was part of their past.

But hadn't Mack told her he *liked* things from the past? Maybe. It felt like they lived in such completely different worlds, and he didn't seem interested in any part of hers. Which might account for why he hadn't tried to contact her after she'd left.

They'd promised to write to each other, but he hadn't kept up his end of that promise. She'd sent him scads of letters, but he hadn't written her once. It felt like he'd forgotten her as soon as she'd left. Which made his comment the night before feel odd—how could he be upset with her for not coming back when he hadn't given her any indication that he'd wanted her to?

She'd wanted to ask him *why* ever since she'd been back—why he hadn't written her, even once. But there never seemed to be the right time to ask. And maybe she didn't really want to hear the answer. Especially if it was that he really had forgotten about her and moved on.

Hearing that would devastate her, and she wasn't ready for him to trample on her heart. Again.

Stop stalling and just go in.

She carefully pushed the door open enough to poke her head in, and spotted Mack. He stood in front of the forge, a rod of iron in his hand. Pulling the rod from the coals, he set it on the anvil, hammered the white-hot end to a point, then stuck it back into the fire. He wore a faded T-shirt with the sleeves ripped off, and he'd tied a leather apron around his khaki Carhartt pants. The navy thermal shirt he'd been wearing earlier hung over the side of the workbench across the room.

Jocelyn slipped inside the door and watched him work. His concentration was on the task in front of him as he took the rod back out and shaped one side of it into a curved curl. The air smelled of smoke and coal and iron. She breathed in the slightly acrid scent that was also filled with memories of time spent in this shop with Mack as he was learning the craft from his grandfather, Hank Talbot.

Hank had been the ranch's blacksmith since Gram had first started giving tours of the living history museum. Jocelyn remembered him as a tall, broad-shouldered man who had a big laugh and kind eyes.

The sharp clang of the hammer against the anvil rang out through the shop as Mack molded and shaped the iron piece he was working on. Savage lay in the dirt several feet away. He must have smelled or sensed her, because he pushed to his feet and loped toward her, his big ears flopping in the dust as he ran.

She knelt to give him a cuddle, then wiggled her fingers at Mack in a small wave. "Hey. Sorry, didn't want to interrupt."

"You're not. I was just fooling around with an idea."

"Yeah?" She took a few tentative steps closer.

"Yeah, I'm just finishing it." He held the piece with a pair of tongs and dunked it into the barrel of water sitting next to the forge. It hit the water with a hiss, and steam rose into the air. He swirled it around for several seconds, then took it out and wiped it with a rag from the workbench.

"I'm always amazed that you can touch it so quickly after it's been in the fire," she said.

"Yeah, that amazes a lot of people. It doesn't take

long to cool it." He passed her the piece. "What do you think of this?"

The iron was heavy in her hands. She looked down at what was once a rod of iron and was now forged into the shape of a heart. "Aww. I love it. Are you giving me your heart?"

Her joke fell flat as he returned his focus to his work, picking up a hammer and another rod of steel. "I already did that," he said, not quite under his breath. "And you broke it."

She balked at his muttered comment. "You broke mine too."

He jerked his head back. "*Me*?"

Before she could say another word, she was interrupted by the chiming of her phone. This conversation with Mack felt important, but it was her boss's ringtone, and ignoring her calls didn't feel like the best way to secure the promotion she so desperately wanted. She offered Mack an apologetic look. "I'm sorry. It's my boss."

"You should take it," he said with a half shrug before turning to his workbench and wrecking her chances of getting a good read on his expression. Was he upset or nonchalant?

She tapped the screen and held the phone to her ear. "Hello, Andrea."

"Jocelyn. Good. I'm glad I caught you. I just got off the phone with the coffee house clients, and they had a couple of thoughts on the briefs you'd proposed."

Her stomach clenched. *Good thoughts or bad thoughts*? "Sure. Yeah, of course," she said, doing her best to sound positive and accommodating. "What are they thinking?"

"Nothing too crazy. They had a few tweaks and recently updated some of their color schemes, and were hoping you could incorporate their new palette into your campaign."

Whew. "Sure. That's easy. What are their tweaks?"

She watched Mack methodically clean and return his tools to their spots around the workbench as she listened to the rundown of ideas the client had pitched. "Those all sound great. I'll make the changes," she told Andrea when she'd finished.

"I'm anxious to see the completed product," her boss said.

Me too. "It's going to be great," she said with more confidence than she felt. There were a couple of other employees who were also gunning for the promotion, so she was up against some stiff competition.

She said goodbye and pushed the phone back into her pocket. "Sorry about that," she told Mack.

"Don't be. It's your job." He leaned his hip against the workbench, their earlier animosity seemingly forgotten, or purposely put away in the same manner he'd tidied up his tools. "What are you working on?"

"I'm creating a big marketing campaign for a new coffee house that's opening in Midtown, but what I'm really working on is getting a promotion. I've spent the last several months putting in tons of extra hours and taking on more work, all in hopes of securing the new title and the raise that goes with it."

He dipped his chin. "Impressive. But isn't that a little hard to do from here?"

"Yeah. But I'm figuring it out. I'm still working while I'm here. I'm just doing it remotely. Gram doesn't often ask for help, so when she called and said she needed me, I knew I would move heaven and earth, and add a bigger balance to my credit card, to get here."

He smiled and something in Jocelyn eased. She liked that she could still make him smile. And she loved the way his face softened with the easy curve of his lips. "Speaking of your grandmother asking for help, I had another idea for the festival."

"Oh great. I worked on it this morning, too. This thing feels like almost more pressure than my promotion. I really want it, but if I don't get this one, I can always try again. But we only get one chance with this event. If we don't knock it out of the park, Gram could lose everything."

"We've got this," he assured her, pushing away from the bench and taking a step toward her. "Like you said, we'll figure it out."

She lifted her chin. "Dang right we will. So what was your idea?"

He pointed to the heart she still held in her hand. "You said you were looking for something to sell at the dance. I thought maybe you could tie some sprigs of lilacs or flowers to something like this. We could charge twenty bucks for them and hope the guys will shell out the dough to buy them for their sweethearts."

She gave a slow shake of her head. "Well, Mack Talbot, you do surprise me. Under that tough exterior, you're just a big romantic at heart."

He furrowed his brows. "You've known me since we were ten years old. That shouldn't really surprise you."

A hint of a smile played at her lips. "No, actually it doesn't." She held up the heart. "And I think this is a fabulous idea. How many can you make?"

He shrugged. "How many do you want? That didn't take me long."

"If you can make me five or ten to start, I can decorate them with different flowers and color schemes, then post pictures of them on the event page. I can try to get some preorders going while you make more."

"Good idea. I can make them this afternoon. But first I need to fix a hinge from one of the gates that got bent." He stuck the twisted piece of iron into the coals, then gave her a sidelong glance. "You want to help me?"

"Sure. What can I do?"

"You remember how to double strike?"

She grinned, recalling the method of taking turns striking the hot iron like Hank had taught them when they were younger. She held out her hand. "Pass me a sledgehammer."

He lifted one of the smaller hammers from the many sizes hanging from his workbench.

She shook her head. "No way."

He eyed her bicep. "You sure? This is the one you used to use."

"Maybe. But I'm much stronger now."

"Much?" he teased.

"*So* much," she said, forming her arm into a muscle. "Dude, I work out. Forty minutes of cardio five times a week, and I take a kickboxing class on Tuesdays and Thursdays."

"I'm impressed." He passed her a bigger hammer. "But we'll see if your fancy kickboxing class helps you to keep up with me."

"You're on," she said, taking the hammer. It felt

good to be back on solid footing with him, joking around and teasing each other.

He passed her a pair of black safety goggles. "Here. Put these on."

She nodded and pulled on the goggles as she repeated Hank's old adage that he'd drilled into them as kids. "Safety first." She laughed as Mack said the words at the same time she did.

He slid a pair of black-framed glasses on his face, then pulled the hinge from the fire and set it on the anvil. "You ready?"

She hefted the hammer to her shoulder and planted her feet in a fighter's stance. "Ready."

His eyes crinkled with his smile as he lifted a much larger sledge and banged the first strike.

Jocelyn struck the hinge next, trying to hit the center of the orange glow.

"Nice," Mack said, hitting it again.

They went back and forth, forming a rhythm as they took turns striking the iron. Their tempo increased as Mack brought his hammer down faster and faster.

Jocelyn set her jaw and narrowed her eyes, all her focus on keeping pace with Mack's steadily increasing swings. The double strike was not just about speed, but also about accuracy and rhythm, and she was determined to keep up with Mack.

Another swing. Another. Her shoulder ached from the intensity of the bangs and the swifter swings, but she wasn't giving up. No way.

Just as her arm felt like it might fall off, Mack's swing missed the hinge and hit the side of the anvil.

She opened her mouth to tease him that she'd won. But Mack's attention was drawn to the door, and she lowered the hammer as she caught sight of the young woman standing inside the door holding a picnic basket. She wore a white blouse with full sleeves and a long blue cotton skirt with a white apron tied around her waist. Her hair was pulled up in a bun, and her face was free of makeup, but instead of looking washed out, she looked fresh-faced and pretty, like a gorgeous extra off the set of *Little House on the Prairie*.

"Hey, Sophie," Mack said, setting his sledgehammer down and taking off his glasses.

"I didn't mean to interrupt," the woman said. "I just figured you'd be about ready for lunch." She raised the basket in front of her. "I brought fried chicken."

Who the heck was Sophie? And why was she bringing Mack fried chicken? Jocelyn set her sledgehammer down and took off her safety goggles. She fought the urge to smooth her hair.

"Hi, I'm Sophie," the woman said, smiling at Jocelyn. "Are you a new apprentice?"

Mack laughed, and Jocelyn gave him the stink eye. He lifted one shoulder. "Oh, come on. Admit it. You'd be a terrible apprentice. You've never let me tell you what to do."

The man had a point. She turned her attention back to Sophie. "I'm Jocelyn Stone."

"She's Molly's granddaughter," Mack explained. "She's here to help out with the festival since Molly's in the hospital."

"And to help take care of my grandma."

"Good luck with *that*. Molly doesn't let anyone take care of her," Sophie said, crossing the workshop. "It's nice to meet you, though. I don't think I've heard much about you."

Jocelyn's back bristled at the familiar way Sophie spoke of her grandmother, like she somehow knew her better than her own granddaughter. And she also didn't like the way the other woman took a spot next to Mack and laid a proprietary hand on his arm.

"Sophie is one of the docents," Mack told her. "She's been volunteering here for the last several years. And this year, we hired her on as one of the seasonal staff."

"I thought the staff didn't work today." Jocelyn's tone was chillier than she'd intended. Why was she sounding snotty to this woman? It wasn't like her.

"We don't usually," Sophie explained. "But I've been putting in extra hours to help get ready for the festival. We all have. But Mack works so hard, he forgets to eat, so I've been packing us a picnic lunch on Thursdays so we can brainstorm and plan for the weekend ahead."

Jocelyn did plenty of planning meetings with her boss, but she'd never considered bringing a picnic. *Calm down,* she told the green-eyed monster threatening to rear its ugly head. Even though Jocelyn had history on the ranch, she hadn't been here in years and had no right to disrupt their routine. "What a nice thing to do," she said, forcing her lips into a smile and her tone to stay even.

"You're welcome to join us," Sophie said.

"Sure. I do love fried chicken," Jocelyn told her, and noticed the way Mack's eyebrows raised.

"Great," Sophie said, grabbing the picnic basket and heading for the door. "It's a beautiful day. I thought we'd eat outside."

Jocelyn followed them out, quickly smoothing her hair and trying not to notice Mack's hand on the small of Sophie's back as he took the picnic basket from her.

She stepped into the sunshine, then stopped as she caught sight of the blue-and-white-checked blanket neatly laid in the grass outside the shop. It was set with two place settings, two bottles of iced tea, and a clear container of pink watermelon wedges. A small jar of purple wildflowers sat in the middle of the plates, giving the whole arrangement a cozy romantic feel.

Savage trundled out behind Jocelyn and plopped onto the corner of the blanket with a sigh.

"Oh gosh," she said, pressing a hand to her stomach. "You know, I'm suddenly not feeling so great. I think I'm going to head back to the house and let you two enjoy this."

Mack's mouth turned down in a frown. "Are you all right?"

She waved away his concern. "Really, I'm fine. But I don't want to ruin this nice lunch Sophie has obviously gone to great effort to put together."

"It's no trouble," Sophie said, with genuine feeling, which only made the odd ache in Jocelyn's stomach hurt more. "We have plenty of food."

The word "we" twisted the ache that much more. "Please, enjoy your lunch. I need to make some calls for work anyway. I'll just catch up with you all later."

She turned and hurried toward the house before either of them could offer her another chance to stay.

Jocelyn pulled a loaf of bread from the pantry, then slammed the door shut. She stomped toward the counter, tossing the bread onto it. The bag slid into the jars of peanut butter and grape jelly already sitting there.

This is ridiculous. Why am I angry? He can have lunch with anyone he wants.

She yanked two pieces of bread from the bag and slathered a thick layer of peanut butter on one, then gobbed jelly on the other. Smashing them together, she shoved the sandwich into her mouth and tore off a bite.

Get a grip. Sophie had seemed nice. And Mack hadn't been surprised by the picnic blanket spread, which could only mean this was their usual lunch routine.

The bite of sandwich sunk like a stone in her stomach. Was she missing the obvious here? Were they a couple? She thought back to the way Sophie had laid her hand on Mack's arm and the way he'd touched her back as they'd exited the blacksmith shop. Why *wouldn't* Mack have a girlfriend? He was a good-looking guy. And this was a small town. He was probably on the top of the list of eligible bachelors.

She needed to get her mind off the bearded blacksmith and his bachelorhood. Grabbing her laptop, she took it and the rest of her sandwich to the kitchen table. She had plenty of work to do, and with the promotion looming, now wasn't the time to slack off or let herself get distracted by some guy. Even if that guy had stolen her heart a decade ago and still had a smile that sent butterflies racing around her stomach like they were in the Daytona 500.

Three hours later, she looked up at the sound of a knock on the front door. She'd made great progress, spending a few more hours on stuff for her job, and the last hour working on marketing for the festival.

"Joss? You home?" Mack's voice came from the next room.

"I'm in here," she answered, setting her laptop down and pushing up from the big wingback chair in the sunroom she'd moved into an hour before. She stood and stretched as Mack appeared in the doorway. "What's up?"

"I finished a bunch of those hearts," he said. "I left them in a box on the table. And I was going to take a walk, stretch my legs a bit. Thought I'd see if you wanted to go along, and I could show you the progress of what we've set up for the festival so far."

"Sure, sounds good." She stuffed her feet into her sneakers and followed him outside. Savage was waiting on the porch, his head hanging forlornly over the edge of the steps. She bent to give his head a scratch and got a lick to her hand in return.

They wandered the grounds of the farm. Mack showed Jocelyn where they'd already set up the area for the food vendors and craft booths. "We'll do games throughout the afternoon in the middle grassy area," he said. "Gunny sack races, three-legged races, the stick and hoop races, and the ever-popular watermelon seed-spitting contests. We'll do the tug-of-war after the races, then have the pie auction." He pointed to the grassy edge behind the barn. "We'll have the hayrack rides over there, then the barbeque and the big dance in the barn will finish out the night."

"Sounds like such a fun day."

"If it all goes according to plan."

"It will."

They stopped at the edge of the pond, and he bent

to pick up a couple of flat stones. He passed one to her. "Can you still skip this?"

She huffed. "Of course I can. And if you recall, I could always skip farther than you."

"But I've been practicing," he said, sending a rock skipping over the calm water. "Just to keep up my skills. I can't imagine there's a lot of opportunity for rock-skipping in New York."

"I've still got skills," she told him, and flung the rock he'd handed her. It landed with a plop in the lake. *Shoot.* "Pass me another one. That rock must have been a dud."

His smile was amused as he handed her another rock. "Uh huh. I'm sure it was the rock's fault."

"I might be a little rusty, but I've still got this." She tried again, and this time the rock sailed over the water, skipping three times before it sank. *Yes.*

Mack lobbed another rock. It flew smoothly over the water, skipping four times. "Ha. Top that."

She swung her arm in an exaggerated circle. "Just warming up my pitchin' arm."

"You're gonna need to get it really warm to beat my last turn." He tossed another rock and got five skips this time. "Oh no, you're going down now, Stone."

She scrunched up her face in concentration, staring at the lake and willing the rock to go in the trajectory she pictured. Sliding her arm sideways, she released the rock and it skimmed across the water. She counted each skip. "One, two, three, four...oh no." She groaned and hung her head as her rock sank on the fourth skip.

Mack shrugged. "Better luck next time."

She pushed her shoulders back. "I still beat you at double strike this morning."

"That didn't count. I was distracted."

I'll bet. "Yeah, sorry I missed out on lunch."

"Sorry you weren't feeling well. Although that did seem to come on rather sudden. You all right now?"

"Oh, sure." She kept her tone even and searched the ground as if looking for another rock to skip. "That was a pretty nice picnic Sophie set out for you."

"Yeah, she's a great girl. And a good cook. Her fried chicken is amazing."

"And she's pretty, too."

He turned his head and gave her a side-eye. "Do I detect a hint of jealousy?"

She reared back. "What? Me? Jealous? No, I didn't say that."

"You didn't have to." He nudged her with his elbow. "Your face says it all. You're jealous."

First he'd beat her at skipping rocks, now this. She narrowed her eyes as her gaze went from the lake to his feet and back again. He was standing right on the edge of the water. All it would take was one little push. And it wouldn't be the first time one of them had bumped the other into this pond. She raised her hands, but he caught them in his.

"You weren't thinking of pushing me into the lake, were you, Joss?"

She batted her lashes at him. "Who, me?" she asked in her best innocent voice.

"Yeah, you," he said, chuckling as he pulled her toward him, then swept her legs out from under her and lifted her to his chest. "I think I still owe you a dunk in this lake from the last time you got me." He took another step forward and moved as if to swing her into the water.

"You wouldn't dare." She clung to his neck as she shrieked with laughter. "If you toss me in, I'm bringing you with me."

"That's what you think." He laughed with her as he swung her forward again. But this time, his boot slipped on the slick rocks, and he lost his footing.

Jocelyn felt the momentum shift and held tighter as they pitched forward. They both yelled as they plunged forward and hit the water with a splash.

She sputtered as she broke the surface. "Gah, it's freezing." She splashed water toward Mack as she swam to the edge. "I can't believe you tossed me in."

He laughed as he shook the water from his hair. "I can't believe I fell in. I swear I did not mean to do that."

"And I didn't mean to do *this*," she said, turning to splash more water at him as she tried to climb up the bank. Her sneakers slid in the muddy silt and she fell forward, her hands sinking into the mud. She couldn't help but laugh as he playfully splashed her back. Turning back around, she slipped again and fell to her bottom as she shot another spray of water toward him. "Take that."

"How in tarnation did you two fools end up in the pond?"

Jocelyn stopped splashing and looked up to see Hank Talbot standing at the edge of the water. "Your grandson threw me in."

"Not on purpose," Mack said, sliding up to the bank next to her. "I slipped."

"Well, you two need to get out of there and get your-selves cleaned up. Loretta just called from the hospital and said you need to get over there right away."

Chapter Six

J OCELYN ASKED HANK WHAT THE matter was, but he didn't have any details. Dread settled in the pit of her stomach as she and Mack sloshed toward the house. Their wet shoes squished out water and gathered dirt with every step as they hurried across the driveway.

"I can't go like this," Jocelyn said, wringing out her t-shirt as she strode. "I need two minutes to put on some dry clothes."

"Me too," Mack said, veering toward the caretaker cottage. "I'll meet you at the truck in five minutes."

"Make it four," she called as she raced up the stairs and into the house. It only took her three to change into dry clothes and pull her hair into a ponytail. She took an extra few seconds to swipe the mascara from under her eyes, then slipped her feet into a pair of sandals, grabbed her purse, and ran for the truck. Yoga pants and a hoodie probably weren't the nicest attire, but they were the best she could do.

Mack was already in the truck when she wrenched open the door. He wore a dry pair of jeans and a clean t-shirt, and the cab of the pickup smelled like a mix of laundry detergent and pond water. He hadn't combed his hair, and it stood up in damp tufts. "I left Savage with my grandpa. Just in case we have to stay for awhile."

She sucked in her breath as she slid onto the seat and sent up a silent prayer for her grandmother's health as she snapped her seat belt into the buckle.

"I'm sure she's fine," Mack assured her, as he put the truck in gear and headed toward the hospital.

They found a parking spot and hurried inside. Jocelyn took another deep breath as they headed down the hallway to her grandmother's room. Mack slipped his hand into hers and gave it a reassuring squeeze.

Preparing herself for the worst, she knocked, then pushed open the door.

She blew out a relieved sigh at the sight of her grandmother sitting up in bed, reading a paperback novel and looking no worse off than she had the day before.

She slammed the book shut and planted a hand on her bony hip. "It's about time you two got here."

"What's happened? Are you okay?" Jocelyn dropped Mack's hand and rushed to her grandmother's bedside.

"I'm fine. I keep telling the doctor that I don't need to be here. My leg can heal just as fast at home as it does here."

"Is that why you called us over here?" Mack asked, leaning back against the wall. "To break you out of this place?"

She shook her head. "No, but that's not a bad idea."

"We're *not* breaking you out," Jocelyn said. "And

you only have to stay here for one more night. It can't be that bad."

"It isn't that good," her grandmother said, pushing her bottom lip out in a pout. "I know I'll sleep a lot better in my own bed without fifteen nurses coming in at all hours of the night poking at me and checking to make sure I'm still alive."

Mack arched an eyebrow. "This is the Harmony Creek Hospital. I'd be surprised if they even have fifteen nurses on their whole staff."

"Well, it feels like fifteen." She wrinkled her nose and sniffed at Jocelyn's hair. "Why do you stink like pond water?"

"We fell in," Mack said at the same time Jocelyn spoke. "Mack tossed me into the pond."

He shrugged at the glare the older woman shot his way. "It was an accident."

"The only accident was that he didn't mean to fall in with me," Jocelyn said wryly, but her words didn't hold any malice. "And why are we even talking about our ill-fated fall into the pond? What's the big emergency that we had to race down here for?"

"Oh yeah. It's about the festival."

"Don't worry about the festival. Mack and I have it under control."

"You might think you do, but I just got a call from Agnes Bates, over in Woodland Hills," her grandmother said, referring to the next town up the mountain. "We play bridge together twice a month. You remember her grandson is the one who supposedly got bit in the leg by a rattlesnake and still managed to hike two hours out of the mountains."

"What does that have to do with the festival?"

"Nothing. I just thought that was real interesting. Don't you think that's interesting, Mack?"

"Yeah," he said. "Although I heard that he hiked for *three* hours. Which would be close to ten miles. And that sure seems unlikely with a rattlesnake bite *and* a full backpack. That story always sounded a little fishy to me."

"People," Jocelyn said. "Can we stay on track here?"

Her grandmother sniffed. "No need to get snippy."

"Sorry. You were telling us what Agnes called you about..."

"Oh yeah. She called to tell me their big chili cook-off they had scheduled a few weeks ago got snowed out, and they rescheduled it for *this* weekend."

"So?"

Mack groaned. "So that means all the people from Woodland Hills we were expecting to show up at the festival will now be going to the cook-off."

Jocelyn heaved a frustrated sigh. "Oh. That is bad."

"It's terrible. Woodland Hills is our next closest town, and we usually get several hundred attendees from there."

Jocelyn slumped into the chair. "Why don't we just invite more of the people from the next town up the pass, then?"

"I'm sure most of them will be going to the cook-off too," her grandmother countered. "Woodland Hills takes their chili very seriously."

"We'll just have to put our heads together and come up with an idea that will make them choose our event over theirs," Mack said.

Jocelyn sat up. "But what if they didn't have to choose? Why don't we invite Woodland Hills to have their chili cook-off at Harmony Ranch? We could schedule it between the tug-of-war and the dance."

"That sounds like a fine idea, except for the fact you'd have to convince them to switch the event to our town instead of theirs. Which I can't imagine they would ever do."

"Why not?"

Her grandmother sighed. "Because Emmet Scott, the patriarch of the family that puts on the cook-off every year, and I have a bit of a history."

"What kind of history?" How had she never heard of this before?

Her grandmother's gaze dropped to the blanket in front of her, and she picked at a loose thread. "We may have been high school sweethearts. And there is a possibility that I broke his heart when I left for college and then came back the next summer engaged to your grandfather."

Jocelyn huffed. "You never told me about this."

"I don't tell you *everything*." She flicked a quick look at Mack then stared pointedly back at Jocelyn. "We don't always share the secret desires of our hearts."

Hmmph. That was not a conversation she wanted to start right now. Especially not in front of the man who might be possibly her heart's most secret desire. Best to get the focus back on her grandmother. "But that was such a long time ago."

A small expression of sadness crossed Gram's face. "It doesn't matter how many years have passed. The heart remembers."

Jocelyn snuck a glance at Mack, who still leaned against the wall. He held her gaze just long enough for her stomach to flip and her hands to start to sweat.

She wiped them on her yoga pants. "Well, desperate times call for desperate measures. Sounds like we need to pay a visit to this Emmet guy."

Her grandmother wrinkled her nose. "You might consider a shower first. And I think you may have a piece of algae in your hair."

❧❧❧❧

Two hours later, Mack was back in the truck as he sat in front of Molly's house and waited for Jocelyn. They'd hashed it out with Molly and come up with a plan to persuade Emmet to join forces, but had agreed they both needed a shower and a fresh set of clothes.

He tried not to think about what would happen if the festival failed and they all lost their livelihoods. Well, not Jocelyn. She would just head back to the city and carry on with her life. He huffed out a breath.

He couldn't believe they were all hinging their futures on the help of the one person who had already proved she didn't care about Harmony Ranch. She'd deserted it—and him—once before, and he couldn't let himself trust she wouldn't do it again.

The front door opened and Jocelyn appeared, no longer dressed in workout pants and flip flops, but in jeans, black flats, and another one of her fancy tops. Her hair was loose and curled around her shoulders.

She was so pretty it made his chest hurt. She carried herself with a different kind of confidence and looked every inch the successful, fashionable woman from the city. And yet, since she'd been here, he'd also caught glimpses of the sassy, fun teenage girl he'd grown up with. And fallen in love with.

He cleared his throat, and cleared the memories of

that girl from his mind, as she jogged down the stairs and clambered into the truck with him. The scent of her shampoo and her perfume and her soap—the scent of *her*—filled the cab, and he fought not to bury his face in her neck and inhale the clean, sweet, slightly floral scent. "You look nice," he told her, his voice faltering on the last word. Ugh. He wanted to slam his palm into his forehead. Had his voice really just cracked? And why were his palms suddenly sweaty? He gripped the steering wheel tighter.

On the ranch he felt confident. He knew his job, and he did it well. But two minutes in the company of Jocelyn, and he felt like that dorky teenage boy who'd been in the math club and would have done anything to impress her.

"Thanks. You look nice too." She reached to smooth down a tuft of his still-damp hair, and he held back the shiver that threatened to run through him. "You clean up real good." Her eyes sparked with mischief as she teased him. "And you don't smell like fishy lake water at all."

A grin tugged at his lips as he put the truck in gear and headed toward the highway. He'd better not still smell like lake water. Not after that extra squirt of aftershave he'd impulsively hit his neck with after his shower.

The town of Woodland Hills was only six miles up the highway, and the two communities often attended each other's events. If only they hadn't had that crazy spring snow a few weeks back, then both events would have been well-attended.

"Do you know this Emmet guy?" Jocelyn asked, as

they pulled up in front of a small farmhouse fifteen minutes later.

Mack nodded. "I've met him a couple times. Not sure he'd remember me. But these small towns are so close to each other, we know just about everyone. And the Scotts are a big family around these parts. We went to school with several of the grandkids." His mouth twisted into a grimace. "And one of them brought me a picnic lunch earlier today."

Jocelyn eyes widened as she gasped. "Sophie is this guy's granddaughter?"

He nodded.

"Does he know that she works for his nemesis?"

Mack shrugged. "I have no idea. That's her business, not mine."

A sly grin stole across her face. "The plot thickens," she said, rubbing her hands together before opening the truck door. "You know how I love a challenge."

He laughed as he shook his head. "Yes, I know." A border collie ran to the truck, and Mack held out his hand for the dog to sniff as he got out. "Good dog," he said. It circled Jocelyn's legs as she came around to stand with him.

A man about Molly's age, wearing faded coveralls and a straw cowboy hat, came around the corner of the house and eyed them warily. "You look too old to be selling Girl Scout cookies, which is about the only thing I'm willing to buy from strangers that show up at my door these days."

"We're not selling anything, Mr. Scott," Mack told him, extending his hand. "You might remember me. I'm Mack Talbot, went to school with a few of your grandkids. And this is Jocelyn." He hesitated to bring up Molly's name just yet.

Emmet squinted at Jocelyn. "You look familiar. It's the eyes, I think."

She stepped forward and thrust out her hand. "I'm Jocelyn Stone. Molly is my grandmother."

His slight frown deepened. "That's it. I heard she got into a car accident. She okay?"

"She is. She broke her leg and has a slight concussion, so they've been keeping her in the hospital, but she should be coming home tomorrow."

"Just in time for the spring festival at Harmony Ranch," Mack said. "Which is what we came to talk to you about."

"Oh yeah? Is that this weekend?" A sly grin pulled at the corner of his mouth, leading Mack to believe he knew exactly when the festival was.

"It is," Jocelyn told him. "And we know you all had to postpone your annual chili cook-off until this weekend, and we were hoping to convince you to combine your event with ours."

Leave it to Joss to dive right in. Mack would have tried for at least a little small talk first.

"Why would I want to do that?" Emmet asked.

"For one thing, it would be the neighborly thing to do," Jocelyn told him.

The older man grunted. "That's something I've never been accused of."

"Okay, how about it's the more profitable choice. If we hold our events separately, we'll each only get half the attendance. But if we combine forces, we can have more people at both events, and we'll *both* make a higher profit."

He shrugged. "That makes sense. And I'd be inclined to do it, if Molly Stone weren't the one asking me."

"Actually, she's *not* asking you—I am. But what would it matter if it *were* my grandmother?"

"I'm not doing anything to make that woman's life easier."

"Why not?"

"Because she broke my heart." He stared off into the distance as if he were actually looking into a window of the past. "Made me fall in love with her, then left me behind."

His words hit Mack like a punch to the gut.

But Jocelyn just barreled forward, as if she weren't even making the correlation to their own story. "But that was a long time ago."

Emmet's shoulders lifted in a shrug. "Feels like yesterday to me."

"But how can you move forward if you're still clinging to the hurts of the past?"

He returned his gaze to meet her eye. "That's the age-old question, isn't it?"

"Look Mr. Scott, I understand all too well the pain of a broken heart," Mack said, trying not to look at Jocelyn. "But holding on to a grudge really only hurts the person holding on. Isn't there anything we can do to get you to change your mind and consider going in with us?"

Emmet pushed his hat back on his forehead as he lifted his chin. "Not a chance."

Chapter Seven

M ACK LET OUT A SIGH ten minutes later as they drove back down the pass to Harmony Creek. "That was a bust."

Jocelyn leaned forward, seemingly undeterred by their recent failure with Emmet Scott. "I guess now we move on to Plan B and B."

"What exactly is Plan B and B?"

She wiggled her eyebrows. "Bigger and better."

"Great plan. But just how do you propose we accomplish it?"

"I'm not sure. I'm still thinking." She drummed her fingers on the side of the seat. "In my world, when we want to go bigger, we either have to make the tech better or get more people to buy into the idea."

"So the first part of that is out, because we don't have any 'tech.'"

"But what if we did? What if we added a photo booth for selfies with period props? Or some interactive screens that teach visitors how to do something, like churn butter?"

"No. And no way in heck. You're totally missing the

point. There were no selfies at the ranch, and we don't do 'props'. The idea behind the living history ranch is to show them what history was *actually* like. It's not a play or dress-up, it's supposed to depict the realities and hardships of life."

"I get that. But…"

"No buts. I know your world revolves around tech and innovation, but technology wasn't exactly a big part of farm life in the early 1900s. Harmony Ranch barely had electricity. Sure, there were new advancements happening in science and new inventions, but most of the rural communities were focused on feeding their families and surviving the winter. And we, the interpreters, the docents, the staff, *we* are the ones who make the experience 'interactive.' So instead of visitors watching how butter is made on a screen, we show them in person. We let them *see* the cow, *smell* the fresh cream, *feel* the rough timber of the wooden handle used to churn the butter. Then we let them taste it after we spread it on fresh warm bread that was baked from scratch."

Jocelyn pressed a hand to her stomach. "Now you're just making me hungry."

"Well, why don't you pull a picture of a cheeseburger up on your screen and dig in?"

She leveled him with a glare.

He laughed. "Hey, didn't you just imply that seeing it with the 'tech' is just as good?"

She held up her hands in surrender. "Okay, okay. I get your point." She gestured to the one fast food joint in Harmony Creek. "I'll ease up on the techie stuff if you drive through that restaurant so we can get actual cheeseburgers."

"Deal," he said, turning on his blinker. "We just have to save a bite for Savage."

"Done." She pulled her wallet from her bag. "And I'm paying."

He shook his head. "Not a chance."

"Come on. You drove. Let me at least buy us supper."

"Maybe next time."

"Fine." She slumped against the seat, but perked up after he handed her a bag of food. She pulled out a fry and popped it in her mouth as Mack pulled back onto the highway. "I can't stop thinking about how we can get more people involved. What can we post to get more people to our event than theirs?"

She passed him his carton of fries, and he chewed one thoughtfully. "I swear I'm trying to think of something. And I'm committed to coming up with an idea that will put that video screen suggestion of yours to shame."

"Great. This is one instance where I would love for you to actually beat me at something."

"That's it." He snapped his fingers as an idea clicked. "That's the idea."

"I don't get it."

"It's what we just did. You know how you and I like to make everything into a competition?"

She tilted her head. "You mean how I like to *beat you* at everything?"

He chuckled and considered arguing, but she was already making his point. "I'm going to let that one slide—for now. But everybody likes a little healthy competition. So, instead of just *inviting* Woodland Hills to bring their annual chili cook-off to us, we need to *challenge* them to a cook-off of our own. Harmony Creek against Woodland Hills—who makes the better chili?"

"That's brilliant! I love it. But there isn't much time to round up some stellar Harmony Creek chili makers before Saturday night."

He shrugged, his lips twitching as he held back an elated smile and tried not to puff out his chest at her calling him brilliant. "Leave that to me. Harmony Creek normally does its own chili competition in the fall, and there are some regulars who compete every year. I'm sure I can get them to enter once they hear they have a chance to take down Woodland Hills."

"Perfect. What can I do to help?"

"Use your social media magic to promote the heck out of the competition and then prepare for your mouth to catch on fire. I can already think of a few people from both communities who would be willing to judge. But I know how you used to love a good spicy chili, so I am selecting you to be one of the judges for the contest as well."

"You're on. But you have to judge too." She rubbed her hands together. "So now we have some leads for the judges, and you think we can get the contestants— but will Emmet take the bait?"

"You bet he will." He pulled into the ranch and up in front of Molly's house.

Jocelyn passed him his hamburger, then took the bag as she climbed out of the truck. "I'm going to get to work on this right away. My mind is already racing with ideas of how to promote the competition. You want to come in to eat?"

"Nah. I don't want to mess up your mojo." He liked

seeing this side of her—motivated and excited to dig into an idea. "Besides, I have an errand I need to run. But I'll touch base with you later."

"Sounds good."

He watched her run up the porch steps, then turned the truck around and headed back to the highway and down the pass to Colorado Springs.

Jocelyn fell into bed hours later, exhausted but exhilarated. She'd come up with some great teasers for the event and scheduled posts to go out to all the social media channels at regular intervals over the next few days. She'd also emailed all the vendors and double-checked the times they were showing up, confirmed they had her and Mack's cell numbers, and answered questions. Her grandmother had given her the emails for all the staff and volunteers, and Jocelyn had sent out a newsletter of sorts sharing all the latest information for the Harmony Creek Hoopla, including updates on her grandmother's health and some of her and Mack's new ideas.

And if all that hadn't been enough, she'd successfully switched gears and spent an hour on a Zoom call with the marketing team from her firm brainstorming ideas for a new campaign they were working on. She felt like she'd used every brain cell she had, but she was also proud of the work she'd done and the fresh ideas she'd contributed to her team.

She was tired, but couldn't seem to get her brain to shut off. Thoughts of the promotion and how it could change her place in the company flitted through her mind, and she imagined how she would have led the Zoom meeting if she were in charge.

She'd just fluffed her pillow and lain back down, again, when her cell phone dinged from the side table next to her bed. She picked it up and was surprised, and pleased, to see a message from Mack.

Chili cook-off is a go. I made some calls and have confirmed at least ten entrants, his message read.

Great. Now we just have to inform Emmet, she typed back.

Already did. Called him and taunted him into taking the bait. Woodland Hills is in. He followed his message with a winky face emoji.

Awesome. I'll get a post written up on our page and continue the taunts. She added the emoji of the sly grinning devil face.

Perfect. He added a smiley face emoji.

By the way, I am both impressed and surprised by your proficient use of emojis.

Glad to know that I can still surprise AND impress you. Smiley face emoji wearing sunglasses.

He had no idea, she thought. She typed back, *I meant I was impressed that your phone could do emojis.*

He replied back with a string of random emojis. First a dinosaur, then a bowling ball, followed by a piece of cheese, then a mailbox, and finally a hamburger.

Jocelyn laughed out loud as she typed two laughing emojis with tears. Then, not to be bested by a "who could post the most random emoji' competition, she fired back with a cactus, a taco, an umbrella, an owl, and a woman dancing the cha-cha.

A grin spread across her face in anticipation as she watched the three dots indicating he was typing. She busted out in laughter as his emojis appeared. A shark, some bacon, a helicopter, a weight lifter and a crystal ball.

Before she could find suitable material to fire back, another message appeared from him.

Good night. The sleeping emoji.

She slumped back against her pillow, the smile still spread across her face. *Good night Mack.*

I'm glad you're home.

Me too.

The next morning, Jocelyn was still smiling as she grabbed her coffee and opened the front door to survey the farm in the soft light of dawn. A cool breeze caressed her cheeks as she inhaled the sweet mountain air. No smog, no sound of traffic or jackhammers or any of the construction noises that filled the sidewalks in the city.

It was no wonder her grandmother loved it here so much. It was perfect. She heard the low mournful bawl of Punkin, the Jersey cow she'd made the unfortunate decision to try to ride years ago, and an occasional whinny from one of the draft horses. Gazing out over the grassy meadow, she caught her breath as a mother deer and two tiny fawns made their way across the field, then stooped to eat the petals off one of the wild roses just starting to bloom next to Gram's gate.

A movement caught her eye, and she turned toward the caretaker's cottage. Savage dawdled his way around the house and up the porch steps to collapse over her feet, as if the journey across the yard had taken all he had.

"Good boy," she said, stooping to scratch his chin.

He looked up at her with big brown adoring eyes, and his long pink tongue snuck out to lick her hand.

"I saw him leave this time," Mack's voice said as he appeared around the corner.

Jocelyn's heart did a little tumble in her chest. Mack was wearing boots, taupe cotton trousers held up with brown suspenders, and a simple ivory button-up shirt. Her memories spun back to summers spent watching him on the ranch when he'd worn a similar outfit of period clothing. He was older now and had a beard, but he was so handsome he still made her pulse race—no matter the time period.

"Mornin', Mack," she said, raising her cup. "You want coffee?"

"I wouldn't turn it down," he said, following her into the house. He held a bundle of folded clothing in one arm.

Savage padded behind her, staying close to her heels as she poured Mack coffee and passed him a mug.

He set the stack of clothes on the counter to take the mug. "Sorry to do this to you, but we need your help. One of our usual volunteers called in sick, and we were hoping you could take her place."

"Me?"

"Yep. I know it's last minute, but it's festival week-end and we're slammed, so every available volunteer is already here. We've got back-to-back tours sched-uled for this morning, so we could really use the extra hand. Plus you know the place. You used to lead tours in the summer."

"That was years ago. I don't remember half the facts or details." Although there were things about the ranch she'd shared with visitors so many times, she could probably recite them in her sleep.

"Sure you do. And I'll give you something easy—like the Whitaker house."

The Whitaker house had always been her favorite. But she'd rarely led tours there. She'd usually helped her grandmother with the animals or done sewing or quilting demonstrations with Gram. She didn't know much about architecture, but she could hold her own in a quilting circle.

She chewed her bottom lip. She couldn't let Mac see her discomfort or act like she couldn't do it. If Sophie could do it, so could she.

Eek—where had that thought come from? She'd grown up competing with Mack, but she'd never competed *for* him. Not that she was doing that now. She was really just helping out her grandmother.

Uh huh, keep telling yourself that, sister. "Sure. Why not?"

He pushed the clothes toward her. "I did my best picking this stuff out. I tried to remember what you used to like to wear, but you can always grab something different if these don't work. There is a whole period clothing library in an unrestored room of one of the historic homes."

Jocelyn held up the long navy skirt and the pale pink blouse with a high collar adorned with fragile navy lace. "These are beautiful. I'll try them on, but they should work great." She peered inside the high-topped lace-up leather granny boots. "And you even got my size in boots. These are perfect."

"We have a whole bunch of them. When one of the ice skating rinks in Colorado Springs closed, they donated a bunch of their old skates to us. We took the blades off, and they made perfect boots."

"Nice."

"Don't forget—no makeup or jewelry. Your grandmother is a stickler for details and keeping the experience authentic for visitors."

"I remember." She smiled as she rolled her eyes. "I can just hear her saying she didn't want her volunteers looking like they worked in a saloon." She gathered the clothes and the boots in her arms. "What time do you need me?"

"First tour starts at nine, so you have a little bit of time." He glanced up at the wall clock. "I'm meeting the other volunteers at the Whitaker house at about twenty till for a quick orientation. I've got a couple of other newbies too."

She bristled at the term "newbie," but she had no right to. She hadn't been home in years, and that was her own fault. "Great. I'll see you then."

The clothes Mack had picked fit her fairly well, and she'd spent a few extra minutes pinning her hair up into a chignon at the back of her head. She felt a little naked with no makeup and had been tempted to sneak just the smallest swipe of mascara on her lashes, but had fought the temptation to keep the integrity of the period intact.

The boots fit snugly but weren't uncomfortable

as she made her way along the trail to the Whitaker House. Mack was just starting his introductions as she slipped in alongside the other volunteers. A tiny shiver of pleasure ran down her spine at the grin that overtook his face when he spotted her.

"Each tour of the house should only take about fifteen to twenty minutes, so the visitors will move through the house quickly," Mack explained. "Whoever is stationed at the door needs to make sure that visitors don the surgical booties over their shoes before entering. No exceptions, and no bare feet. Visitors will progress through the main floor, up the stairs to peek in the bedrooms and bath, then come down the back stairs to finish up in the kitchen where they will get a quick presentation and a small sample of blueberry cobbler. Please encourage everyone to visit our general store."

A few hands went up, and Mack answered questions and supplied encouragement, then dispersed the volunteers to their various stations. Jocelyn waited for him to tell her where he wanted her.

A young boy of about ten stood next to his mom's full skirts, and he waved Mack over. He looked adorable in an outfit similar to what Mack wore. "This is my first time," he explained. "And I'm a little nervous."

"That's understandable," Mack said, squatting down to get eye level with the boy. "Your name's Will, right?"

The boy nodded.

"Nice to meet you, Will. I'm Mack, and I started volunteering here when I was about your age too."

Will glanced up at his mom. "I'm homeschooled,

and my mom thought me volunteering would be a good assignment for our social studies spring project."

"That's a neat idea. And I get how you would be a little nervous. I heard that you were new, so I put you in the guest bedroom, which is one of the easier rooms. Usually folks just poke their heads in, you give them a couple of facts, and they move on."

Jocelyn hoped Mack had another "easy" room he could give her.

"That doesn't sound too bad. I've just never done anything like this before."

"I hear you. And it might seem a little weird at first, but it gets easier the more you do it. And I'll tell you a little trick."

The boy leaned in closer, and so did Jocelyn. She could use a trick, too. She was just as nervous as Will.

"If you start to get nervous, just pretend you are someone else, maybe someone you saw on television or read about in a book. And try to act like you think they would in that situation. Then if you feel dorky or silly or nervous, it's not really you feeling that way, it's the character you're portraying. Make sense?"

Will shrugged. "Kinda."

Mack patted his shoulder. "You've got this. Give it a try, and I'll check in on you in a bit."

The boy nodded and pushed his shoulders back, a determined look on his face as he followed his mother upstairs.

"I hope you've got a good pep talk like that for me," Jocelyn told Mack.

"You're plenty peppy. And you already know all this stuff." He gestured for her to follow him into the kitchen. "I figured I'd put you in here."

"I thought you said the person in the kitchen was doing a quick presentation."

"I did. But you just have to show them around the kitchen and tell a couple of stories about food or what cooking was like in the early 1900s."

"I don't *have* any funny stories about food or what cooking was like."

"You'll do fine," he said, heading for the back door. "I'll come back and check on you in a bit. Besides, after those pancakes you made me the other day, I already know you're a great cook."

"I made those with a mix. All I did was pour in some water," she called after him, but he was already gone.

A murmur rose as the first guests poured into the living room. She peered anxiously around the kitchen, but she didn't even have time to Google what some of these tools did. Apparently, she was just going to have to wing it.

Chapter Eight

A N HOUR AND A HALF later, Mack snuck up the back stairs of the Whitaker House, not wanting to interrupt Jocelyn's presentation. There had been more questions than usual at the end of his blacksmith demonstration, and it had taken him longer than he'd planned to return. He hoped the house tours had been going well.

He stopped just outside the door as he heard Jocelyn's voice. She had her back to him, and a group of five fascinated tourists was listening to her spiel. She waved her hands with a flourish as she pointed out the stove, the icebox, and the sink with the manual pump on its side.

She tossed out a few facts, then smiled sweetly as she asked if there were any questions.

One woman held up her hand. "Those look like some unique kitchen tools," she said, pointing to the gadgets sticking out of the crockery on the counter behind Jocelyn. "Can you tell us what some of those do?"

"Sure. You bet I can," Jocelyn said, turning to survey the tools in the crock. She chewed on her lip as she stared at her choices then finally pulled out a wooden spoon. "This is a tool that women often used to stir things."

Mack covered his mouth with his hand to keep from laughing.

"But what about that funny looking thing with the squiggles on the end."

"Great question." Jocelyn pulled the tool from the crock and held it up. "What do *you* think this is used for?"

One of the women shrugged while another one jumped in with an answer. "Oh, I know that one. It's a potato masher. My grandmother still uses one."

"Very good," Jocelyn said. "You're practically teaching this part of the tour for me."

"What about that crazy thing on the wall." One of the women pointed to the tool hanging by its handle on the wall by the door. Thick wire came out of the handle for about a foot and then was bent into a swirled pattern at the end.

Jocelyn picked it up and studied the pattern before waving it in the air. "Let's try to guess what this could have been used for. Was it some type of early racket used to hit a ball? Or maybe an early version of the fly swatter?" She turned it upside down. "Or could it have been used to stir up some biscuit batter? Any guesses? Anyone?"

The women shook their heads. "You'll have to tell us this one," the woman who had spoken earlier said. Apparently her grandmother hadn't had one of these.

Mack couldn't help himself. As much as he wanted to see what kind of crazy answer Jocelyn would come up with, he had to jump in before she had these women believing their ancestors were mixing up batches of biscuits with a carpet beater. "Good morning, ladies," he said, stepping into the kitchen and waving to the women. "Sorry to interrupt. Looks like you were just about to get a neat demonstration of an antique rug beater."

Jocelyn quickly flipped the carpet beater back around and held it aloft. "Yes, I was just about to expound upon all my wisdom about rug beating."

"It's unfortunate we'll miss that," Mack said. "I'm sure it was quite an extensive bit of knowledge, but we're a little pressed for time so we need to finish up for today."

The women shared their enthusiastic thanks as he passed them each a small sample of cobbler, then closed the door behind them.

"Sorry to step in on your presentation," Mack said, turning back to her. "I have a feeling it was just about to get good."

Jocelyn sagged against the counter. "Thank goodness you came in when you did. I had no idea what this was."

"And neither did the woman who fed you the answer for the potato masher."

"How long were you listening?"

"Long enough for you to artfully explain how to use a spoon."

She playfully swatted him with the carpet beater. "You could've saved me earlier."

"I was having too much fun watching you come up with creative answers."

She picked up a torturous silver tool that had several long sharp tines extending off one side of the long handle. "I'm just glad no one asked me what this was. It looks like a cross between a fork and a musical instrument, and the only thing I could think to do with it was either comb my hair or use it to brush a dog. But both things seemed painful."

His eyes crinkled with amusement as he took the tool from her. "It's actually used to cut cake. It's called a cake breaker, and this one is sterling silver. It's quite valuable."

"Glad I didn't try to comb my hair with it, then."

He laughed. "Yes, good thing. How did the rest of the tours go?"

"Better than that one. Most people just like to look around. And since I was at the end they were usually ready to peer around the kitchen, get their cobbler sample, and move on." She pointed up the stairs. "Although that kid Will has been cutting up the crowds all morning. I've heard them laughing up there, and most of them are still cracking up as they come down the stairs."

"Oh yeah?"

"Yeah. Apparently he took your advice to heart and channeled his favorite fictional character. Except his favorite book is Harry Potter, so he's been sharing the facts of the house in an adorable British accent."

<hr />

The muskrats frolicking in the pond caught Jocelyn's attention as she and Mack walked back across the field after polishing off the last of Mrs. Crandle's macaroni and cheese for lunch. She pulled her phone from her pocket to snap a photo.

"What are you doing?" Mack asked, turning his

body as if trying to block her from view. "You can't use your smartphone while you're in period dress."

"Oh shoot, I forgot," she said and stuffed it back into the pocket of her skirt.

"Your grandmother would give you what for if she caught you carrying that thing around."

"I know. I'm sorry." Warmth flooded her cheeks. She'd broken one of Gram's cardinal rules.

Mack shook his head. "Is it really *that* hard for you *not* to use your phone for a few hours?"

"It's a requirement of my job to use it. My livelihood depends on it," she said rather testily.

"I get that. Or I understand it, at least. I don't quite *get* why anyone would want to spend so much time in a virtual world when there are so many great things about the actual world to experience and enjoy." He cocked an eyebrow at her. "I'll make you a deal. If you agree to spend the afternoon in my world, *this* world, just for today, then I'll spend some time learning about your world tonight, after supper when the ranch is quiet. That means you have to turn your phone *off*. No sneaking peeks at it, no quick checks. In fact, give it to me, and I'll put it back in the house."

Panic gripped her chest at the thought of not having her phone...which was a bad sign that she just might be a little too addicted to it. "What if Gram calls? She's coming home from the hospital later this afternoon."

"My grandma is bringing her home, and she'll let us know when Molly arrives. I'm not asking you to get rid of the thing forever, just put it away for the next several hours and try to actually experience nature and history and people—without having to snap a photo of them or compose a tweet or post or whatever about what they're doing."

She pulled her phone from her pocket, then hesitated. It sounded easy. Just hand him her phone. So why was her stomach twisting into knots at the thought of not having the silly little piece of technology on her?

"What's the worst that could happen? You miss an email or a phone call? No biggie—you can call them back. You miss someone's post of what they had for lunch? You can catch up on all of it tonight." He held out his hand farther, then dealt the final blow. "I'll bet you can't give your phone up for the next six hours."

"Six *hours*?"

"Okay, five. I *dare* you to turn off your phone and give it up for the next five hours."

She scrunched her nose and glared at him. "You know I can't refuse a dare. Fine." She turned the phone off and slapped it into his hand. "Five hours."

"Five hours." He pushed her phone into his pocket. "Now go enjoy some life. Whitaker House is open for tours for another hour and a half. I'll check back with you later."

Three hours later, Jocelyn found she hadn't really missed her phone that much. She'd also been crazy busy finishing out the tours, getting the house shut back up, then helping another volunteer set up some quilting displays in the front room of another one of the historic homes.

She'd run into several people she'd known as a kid—volunteers who'd been around forever—and had spent a little time catching up. One had asked her to help organize the pieces needed for the yard games for the festival, and another had asked her to run an extra box of candy sticks over to the general store.

Everywhere she went, she heard people laughing and exclaiming over the sights and fun experiences at Harmony Ranch. There seemed to be something for everyone. A mom and two toddlers were laughing at the ducks in the pond, three teenagers were cracking up as they tried to master using the stilts in the grass, and an elderly couple was sitting on a bench listening to one of the volunteers who was picking a banjo.

Her grandmother had created a wonderful place that brought joy to so many people. She couldn't let her lose it. Jocelyn spotted Mack over in the lawn area, where he and another man were pushing numbered markers into the grass. She set her jaw as she marched toward him, her determination stronger with every step. She wouldn't let her grandmother down.

"How are we looking for tomorrow?" she asked Mack as she strode up to him. "What can I do to help?"

Without missing a beat, he handed her a ball of string. "Help me tie off these squares. They need to be about eight feet by eight feet. We've already set the posts, so just tie the string to one, then twist it around the next and keep moving to make squares."

"Okay." She peered around the funny setup as she tied a length of string to the first post. "What are we making eight foot squares for? Is this some kind of giant chessboard or something?"

"No. But that's a fun idea. And it tells me you've got the picture of what we want this to look like. It's actually the picnic area for the Boxed Lunch Social Auction."

"The what?"

"Didn't you see it on the list of events? It's one of our best fundraisers. Each of these squares is a picnic spot and participants create a covered box lunch. They can decorate their spot and the lunch however they want, but the actual meal is a surprise. And so is the participant. Folks get to peruse the lunch spots, then bid on them in a silent auction. The winners all get to eat the lunch with the participants in these spots at noon."

"How fun. But how do they know who they will end up eating with?"

"They don't. That's part of the fun. And why we put it all out here together. So everyone feels safe and this makes it feel more like a community thing instead of a romantic thing. Although plenty of guys have tried to impress women by bidding on the lunch boxes they were sure they'd made. One year, Kenny Jenkins spent a cool hundred dollars bidding on a lunch spot he was sure had been created by a gal he was sweet on at the time. Turns out it wasn't hers—it was his grandmother's. Which was good for the fundraiser, but has now turned into a yearly tradition for Kenny and his grandma and also earned him a wife out of the deal."

"A wife?"

"Yep. The girl whose lunch he'd thought he was bidding on heard the story and asked him out to the movies. They got married a year later, and now Kenny's grandma has an annual lunch date *and* three great granddaughters."

"Oh gosh."

"It's all in good fun. We've been doing it for years now and everyone seems to really love it. Some of the participants get really creative. Last year, someone set up a whole tea party thing, and another time there was a beach theme, and somebody did something once with teddy bears."

"Sounds great. Can I still sign up?"

"You?"

She planted a hand on her hip. "Yes, me. Why not?"

"Didn't you just explain to me this morning that you can't cook anything beyond adding water to a pancake mix?"

"You heard that, huh?"

He chuckled. "Yeah, I heard that."

"It doesn't matter. I can certainly come up with some kind of picnic lunch idea. And I want to do whatever I can to help raise money for the festival." She gazed toward the pond where a mother and father goose were leading their goslings into the water. "I really do love this place. So does my grandmother. And so many others. We can't lose it."

Mack put a firm hand on her shoulder and squeezed. "We won't. And you can absolutely enter the Boxed Social event. I'll add another square right now." He tilted his head, his reassuring expression turning mischievous. "And I look forward to trying to guess which one is yours tomorrow. I may have to put in a bid for it."

He turned away before he saw the smile spreading across her face.

Loretta and Hank Talbot brought Jocelyn's grandmother home from the hospital just before supper. Jocelyn and Mack had changed out of their period clothing and met them at the car when they pulled up in front of the house. Mack lifted Gram from the back seat, and carried her inside. He gingerly set her in her recliner and eased up the footrest. Jocelyn carefully raised her booted leg and piled a stack of pillows under it.

"What's this?" Jocelyn asked as Hank carried in a funny wheeled contraption.

"That's Midge," Gram told her. "She's a knee scooter."

Only Molly Stone would name her medical apparatus.

"Our friend, Shirley, from our bridge group loaned her to me," she continued. "She used her when she had bunion surgery last year and said she made all the difference. She dropped it off at the hospital this morning, and I've already been scooting around on it. It works like a charm. I just rest my leg on the seat and go."

"Is it safe?" Jocelyn studied what looked like a designer bag affixed to the front of the scooter.

"Oh yeah. This is the KneeTraveler Supreme—it's like the Cadillac of knee scooters. Shirley's loaded, and she buys only the best. This gadget has all-terrain wheels and even has a cup holder."

"I'm impressed."

"Lucky for us, Shirley's also a sweetheart and is generous with her friends," Loretta said as she set Gram's purse and the tote bag of things she'd had at the hospital on the table. "I think you're all set, girls. Unless you want me to whip you up some supper."

"Oh no. We've got plenty to eat," Jocelyn told her. "And you all have done more than enough."

Loretta huffed. "Nonsense. It's nothing when it's for

your friends. Your grandma did as much if not more for me a few years ago when I had knee surgery."

"I'm glad she has you," Jocelyn said, walking the Talbots to the door, then leaning down to give Loretta a hug. "I'm glad we both do."

"I'll call you later," her grandmother hollered from her recliner throne. "Thanks again."

"Glad to do it," Hank said. "We're here if you need us, honey. All you have to do is call." He gave Jocelyn a hug as well.

"Thanks." Hank smelled of Old Spice and pipe smoke. He'd been her grandfather's best friend, and hugging him somehow felt like she was getting a hug from her grandpa too.

She stepped back to find Mack next in line as the Talbots filed out the door. She opened her arms then closed them, then opened them again. How awkward could this get? Should she just hug him? Was it too late to transition to a handshake?

He seemed just as uncomfortable and ended up giving her a quick one-armed hug with a sound pat on the back before slipping out the door. He came back a second later with her phone in his hand. "Almost forgot to give you this back. I'm proud of you. I didn't think you could make it all afternoon."

She lifted one shoulder in a casual shrug, although his compliment was warming her insides like a cup of hot cocoa. "It was no big deal."

He offered her a grin that had her pulse racing as he waved, then took off after his grandparents.

She swore her emotions ran the gamut around that man. One minute feeling as comfortable as putting on an old sweater, the next feeling awkward and shy. Not to mention the moments of anger and hurt tossed in with bursts of happy memories and flashes of desire. It was like trying to hug a teddy bear who turned into a porcupine, then a hunky muscled blacksmith.

Pushing Mack from her mind, she shut the door, then directed her focus toward her grandmother. "Are you hungry?"

Gram shrugged. "I could eat."

"A couple of people dropped off meals today. You feel like lasagna or tuna tetrazzini?"

Gram made a face. "I've never felt like tuna tetrazzini in my life."

"Lasagna it is, then."

"Tell me how the setup for the festival is going," her grandmother said a few minutes later, as Jocelyn handed her a napkin and a plate of pasta.

Jocelyn sank into the chair next to her and filled her in on all the plans and preparations as they ate.

Gram cackled at the way they'd executed their strategy to get Emmet to host his chili cook-off at the ranch. "Very smart. And I hope the Harmony Creek contestants whip those Woodland Hills's high-falutin' fannies."

"Me, too." Jocelyn took their plates to the kitchen and came back with a warm mug of tea. She set it on the end table next to her grandmother's chair. "Are you really okay? Can I get anything else for you?"

"I'm fine, honey. Don't worry about me." Her face took on a wistful expression, and she reached out to touch Jocelyn's cheek. "You look so much like your mother did at your age. And she was just like you, so full of dreams and ambition."

"I'm *not* like her, though. I never turned my back on

you or this place." A chunk of guilt settled in her stomach, like one of her skipped stones had dropped to the bottom of the lake. "I'm sorry I haven't been back to see you more often." How could she explain that the reasons she'd avoided the ranch had mostly to do with Mack? Judging from the way Gram was looking at her—her gaze filled with love and understanding—she probably already knew. "I've let some not-so-great memories keep me away, but the past few days have reminded me of a lot of good memories, too."

"I'm glad. I want you to remember why you love it here. It seems like your mother has wiped this place from her mind completely. That was always something you and Mack had in common—neither of your mothers wanted to stay here. At least when your mom had you, she started out with a husband to help her. Mack's dad left when Mack was still a baby." Jocelyn felt a pang of sympathy. That was another thing she and Mack had in common: fathers who'd walked away. "His mother was left alone, and she was still very young—but with big fancy adult dreams."

Jocelyn's spine straightened. "I don't care how big and fancy her dreams were. It was wrong of her to abandon her son."

"Was it? It seems growing up with Loretta and Hank was probably the best thing that could have happened to him. Most likely saved him in a lot of ways. I mean, don't get me wrong, I know that his mom leaving tore that kid up. He was only, what, nine or ten years old?"

"Ten." They'd both been ten that first summer. She remembered how shy he'd been, the pain and haunted look that had clouded his eyes for most of the first month she'd known him. "I remember I used to challenge him to everything—who could run faster, jump higher, spit watermelon seeds farther. It was stupid, but at that age, it was the only thing I knew to do to try to get him out of his shell." Then when he'd opened up, when he'd laughed and started to tease and joke around with her, it had been like she'd won first prize at the county fair.

Jocelyn stared at her hands. "I tried to convince Mom to let me live with you and finish school here."

"Oh honey, I know." Molly covered her hand with hers. "But I truly believe everything happens for a reason. So there had to be a reason your mother took you away that last year of school and kept you from me and from Harmony Ranch. Or at least she thought she had her reasons. You know, she'd fallen for a local boy and gotten married too young, and she always wanted more for you—wanted you to have the chances at a career and a life in the city that she never had."

"It's hard not to wonder what would have happened if I had stayed for my senior year instead of moving to New York."

"I know."

"But I'd planned to come back as soon as I graduated—to move here—to be with you and..." her voice trailed off. She couldn't even say his name. Not in that respect. "I was already packed and ready to leave when Mom told me he'd gotten married. She said they'd done it at the courthouse, and I was too late."

Her grandmother squeezed her hand. "We can't change the past. All we can do is try to learn from it."

The past had been creeping up on her, surrounding her with memories and emotions that she'd thought she'd buried. She couldn't change the fact that Mack had moved on without her, that he'd married someone else—that he'd seemingly forgotten all about her and acted like they had never happened. Or that he had broken her heart.

What she *could* change was the subject.

She stuffed the hurts back into their drawers and pushed them closed. Lifting her chin, she forced a smile onto her face. "Speaking of the past, did you hear I worked in Whitaker House today? I did presentations in the kitchen, then handed out the cobbler. It was fun."

Her grandmother nodded. "I heard from several people what a great help you were today. They said you really pitched in."

"I know how much this place means to you. And I'm determined to do whatever it takes to keep you from losing it. I even signed up to do the Boxed Lunch Social auction. Although I'm not sure what I was thinking when I volunteered. I have zero ideas for a fun picnic idea, and pretty much the only things I know how to make are sandwiches."

"Nothing wrong with a sandwich."

"But I need something more—something to make people want to bid on it. But then not be disappointed if they win."

"All they have to win is something to eat for lunch. And you only need *one* person to bid."

Her grandmother made an excellent point.

Jocelyn's cell phone vibrated. She was surprised to see a text from Mack when she pulled it from her pocket.

You have a minute? his message read.

Sure, what's up? she typed back.

I want to show you something. Get your opinion.

I'm always open to sharing my immense font of wisdom. Laughing emoji.

Good, he responded. *Bring it with you. Meet me by the pond in ten.*

She typed in a thumbs up, pushed the phone back into her pocket, and looked up.

Her grandmother arched a knowing eyebrow. "Good text?"

Jocelyn hadn't even realized she was grinning. She tried for a casual shrug. "No biggie. Just Mack. He wants to get my input on something. I'm meeting him out by the pond."

Her nonchalance wasn't fooling her grandmother. "Sure. No biggie. But you might want to put on a different shirt. That one has lasagna on it."

Chapter Nine

TEN MINUTES LATER, WEARING A clean shirt, jeans, sandals, and a quick swipe of lip gloss, Jocelyn crossed the driveway and walked down the path leading to the pond. It was that special time of night just after dusk but not totally dark—a time when it feels like anything could happen. A full moon was already out, turning the steps of the path silver, and she paused to watch a baby bunny hop across the grass to hide under the lilac bushes.

What could Mack need her help with? Their relationship was so tender now, like a bruise she knew was there, but that only hurt when she pressed it.

She came around the corner, then froze in her steps and gasped at the gorgeous sight in front of her.

Mack's truck was backed up to the pond, and he sat on the edge of the dropped tailgate swinging his legs. The faint sound of country music filled the air, the tempo almost in time with the flickering flames of the mason jar luminaries circling the pond. Their lights reflected off the water, creating the illusion that the candles were glowing under it.

It felt like she'd stepped into a painting—it was breathtaking and magical at the same time.

"What do you think?" Mack asked as she approached the truck.

"It's beautiful. Did you do this?"

"Yeah. I got the idea this afternoon but wanted your opinion." He pushed off the tailgate and picked up one of the jars. "I forged these little hooks with candleholders at the end of them. One end hangs off the side of a jar while the candleholder part sits inside it. I made a bunch of them for a wedding last summer—some of them hold tapered candles and some of them hold those little tea light things. I thought we could set them out for the dance tomorrow night and also sell them."

"What a great idea. I'll give you twenty dollars for one right now."

"Sold."

"Your presentation is brilliant. I think we should set it up exactly like this again, and when people see this tomorrow night, they won't be able to buy them fast enough. And the music is the perfect touch." She peered into the bed of the truck. "Although I think I hear the Eighties calling. They want their boom box back."

"Hey, don't knock my boom box. I've had that thing since I was a teenager, and it still sounds great."

She squinted at it, transported back to a time when she'd sat on Mack's bed as he played a new CD. "I actually remember it. You got it for your sixteenth birthday. And now that I think about it, I'm pretty sure you still have my Garth Brooks CD."

He laughed. "If I do, I'm sure it sounds awesome on this thing."

"Oh yeah, much better than one of those newfangled Bluetooth speakers."

"I *have* actually taken a giant technological leap into your world. So before you make too much fun of me, check out what I bought last night." He pulled a new iPhone from his pocket and held it up.

"Wow. I'm impressed. But what happened to the flip phone? Did your grandma decide she wanted it back?"

"No, actually, it didn't survive our fall into the pond yesterday."

She cringed. "Oh, no. I'm sorry."

"Don't be. It wasn't your fault we fell in, and I've been thinking it was probably about time I got one anyway. And since you're the expert on all things techy, I was hoping you could teach me how to use a couple of things."

"Sure." Wow. After all the time he'd spent explaining stuff to her about the ranch the past few days, it felt good for him to want to learn something from her *and* for her to get a chance to be able to share a little of her expertise. She hitched herself onto the tailgate and held out her hand.

He placed the phone in it, then leaned against the truck next to her. "I've got the basics, like how to make a call and how to answer the dang thing. And I'm figuring out it's a heck of a lot easier to text on."

"Ah. Now I know how you were typing all those fun emojis last night."

He grinned. "It's like a whole new world has opened up to me, full of small images of cacti and multiple facial expressions."

She laughed as she nudged his shoulder. "I told you technology was cool."

"I'm not going to go so far as to admit you *may* have been right, but I think the email and the maps feature will come in pretty handy."

"Oh yeah, I use the maps all the time."

"I figured since the ranch has a Facebook page and using it could actually drive revenue and visitors, I should probably figure out how to post something to it."

"Yeah, sure." She crooked her finger and imitated her best wicked witch voice. "Come into my social media lair. Let me show you around."

He narrowed his eyes. "Now you're just scaring me."

She laughed as she patted the tailgate next to her. "Okay, fine. No wicked witch voice."

"Thank you." He settled in next to her. "I already downloaded the app and created an account."

"Nice work. Did you already stalk me?"

He pulled his head back. "*Stalk* you? Like follow you around? No, I wouldn't do that."

A corner of her lip tugged up in a grin. *This guy.* He was so darn cute. "I meant Facebook-stalk me. Like, you know, did you look me up and poke around in my photos to see what I've been doing the last several years."

"Um, maybe, a little," he stammered. "I guess."

Her heart gave a little leap. "Good. I'd be disappointed if I wasn't one of your first forays into Facebook stalking."

"You're weird."

"I know." She laughed as she opened his Facebook app. "Did you at least friend me?"

"No. I wasn't sure if..." his voice trailed off.

She typed her name in the search bar and friended herself. "Done. I'm your first friend."

"That's apropos since you actually *were* my first friend."

His comment hit her straight in the heart. He'd been one of her first real friends as well. Which was why his betrayal had hurt even more.

His body language changed—his shoulders seemed to stiffen as he scratched at a piece of mud on the tailgate. "I've been mad at you for a lot of years," he said. "For not coming back, for not even reaching out years later...but hanging out with you the last few days has made me realize how much I miss that friendship. You're one of only a handful of people that I can be my true self with, and I've missed that. I'd like for us to try to be friends again."

She'd been focused on building the settings in his app, but she'd heard what he said. She'd been mad too. And hurt. But bringing up blame and all their history felt like too much of a serious and complicated conversation. And she didn't want to do serious or complicated right now.

This night was too beautiful and they were having too much fun, laughing and teasing each other, to dredge up the old hurts. She wanted to enjoy the moment, enjoy the time they were sharing now. She liked having him back in her life and didn't want to ruin what they had now by fighting about what they'd lost then. It might have been cowardly, but they'd have time to hash things out later, when the moon wasn't shining in the twinkling reflections on the pond and the air wasn't full of night sounds and possibilities.

"I'd like that too," she said, determined to keep

things light. She pulled out her phone and accepted his friend request. "Done. We're friends again."

"If it's on Facebook, it must be true."

"See, now you're getting the hang of it." She pulled up a picture she'd taken earlier of the blacksmith shop and showed him how to post it to the ranch's page. She typed in a caption about a "must have" secret item the blacksmith was creating that would be available to purchase tomorrow night, which visitors to the festival would go crazy for. "There. See how we've created excitement and consumer interest by letting them in on a *secret* item that everyone is going to want to buy?"

"I don't know that a candle in a jar is worth all that hype."

"It might not be if we'd just posted a picture of it, but now visitors will be eager to see what the *secret* item is. And when they see them lit up and glowing around the pond like this, they will snap them up. Trust me. This is my job."

"That didn't seem too hard. But just so you know, I only plan to post stuff about the ranch. I'm not planning to *ever* share *anything* about my personal life. It's nobody's business what I ate for breakfast or where I'm spending my time or who I'm spending it with."

"Because you don't want people to know how much time you actually spend with your dog?" she teased.

He chuckled. "The dog probably cares about that more than I do. But I'm just saying, you will *never, ever* see me post anything personal. Even if I were on fire, and it was the only way to call the fire department. It's still not gonna happen. I'd rather burn."

"Okay. Okay. I think you've made your point." She

nodded at his phone. "Anything else I can show you on your newfangled contraption?"

He tapped the screen to get the apps to light back up. "Yeah, actually. I haven't quite figured out the camera. Can you show me how to take a picture of something and then fix it up?"

"Sure." She opened the camera app and showed him how to snap a picture, then held his phone up. "And this is how you take a selfie. Just in case you want to snap a pic of you and Savage." She laughed as she pulled a silly face and snapped a few selfies, then wrapped her arm around Mack's shoulder and pulled him into the screen's view. She leaned her head into his and snapped another pic, then nudged him in the side until she finally got him to smile for one.

She was glad to be laughing and teasing with him again as she showed him more features of the camera, explaining the aspects of each as she thumbed through the different options. "This is how you record a video." She pressed the button and did a quick video of herself waving into the screen. "Hi, Mack." Passing him the phone, she said, "Now you try."

He took the phone and was playing around with the options when a new song came on the radio. Both of them stilled.

Jocelyn swallowed at the sudden emotion in her throat. The notes of "their song" drifted into the air and settled around their shoulders like a warm blanket on a cool evening. "It's crazy to hear Chase Dalton on the radio. Remember when we heard him singing this song at the county fair? He was only a few years older than us and just starting out, and now he's a huge country music star."

Mack studied her face, as if trying to see if she remembered the significance of the song.

How could she forget? It was their first dance, on the night of their first kiss. The night everything changed for them.

"Yeah, I remember," he said. "I remember everything."

Her voice lowered to a whisper. "So do I."

He set his phone down, carefully resting it against the radio so it wouldn't fall, then held out his hand. "Wanna dance?"

Her heart tumbled in her chest. Without analyzing the moment or thinking it to death, she simply put her hand in his and let him lead her to the edge of the pond and pull her into his arms. He was taller now, but she still fit perfectly against him.

Stepping into his arms felt like coming home again.

She rested her head on his shoulder as they slowly swayed to the music. Remembering that he might belong to someone else now, she lifted her head and peered up at him. "Won't Sophie mind that you're dancing with me?"

"Why would she?"

"She brought you that romantic picnic. I assumed you two are like a couple."

His lips curved into a grin. "So you *were* jealous. Well, fancy plates and fried chicken for lunch doesn't strike me as romantic. I'm a simple guy. I'm just as happy with plain sandwiches, some chips, and a cold glass of iced tea." He pulled her closer. "I'm not a couple with anyone."

She smiled back, a little unnerved at how happy that made her.

The song, "My Heart Is Your Home," had been the start of Chase Dalton's career, the one that shot him to stardom. She swallowed as he sang about love and belonging, the lyrics still as powerful today as they had been that summer.

A soft breeze blew a strand of hair across her cheek, and Mack reached to brush it back and tuck it behind her ear. He gazed into her eyes, and she felt as if he were looking directly into her soul. "Just dance with me. Don't think about all that other stuff. Leave the past behind us and the future ahead of us, and just be in this moment. Here. Now. With me."

She let out a breath and relaxed in his arms. He drew her even closer and moved them around the grassy dance floor.

"You've gotten better at dancing," she said, as she stole a glance up at him.

His gaze held hers for a moment, then slowly dropped to her mouth. "I've gotten better at a lot of things."

Her heart fluttered like the soft ripples on the pond next to them. And she couldn't seem to tear her eyes away from his.

She couldn't breathe, couldn't think, as time seemed to stand still. Everything else fell away, everything except the two of them dancing in the moonlight, the candles flickering around them like tiny fireflies, and their song filling the night air.

Chapter Ten

A S HE GAZED INTO JOCELYN'S gorgeous eyes, Mack was catapulted back in time to another warm night, another dance floor. Chase Dalton, his voice already low for a seventeen-year-old kid, had been singing the same lyrics about love and stolen moments on hot summer days and offering that one special girl a place in his heart—a place to come home to. When he sang the line about taking a chance, about it being now or never, it was like he was singing right to Mack.

He'd been in love with Jocelyn Stone since he was ten years old, since he first understood what love was. Heck, Jocelyn was the one who'd taught him about love.

He'd wanted to kiss her that night at the fair, right there on the dance floor, but he'd been fifteen and too scared to do it in front of half the town of Harmony Creek. But later that night, with Chase Dalton's words in his ears, he'd dared to do it. Then he hadn't stopped kissing her for the rest of that summer and the next two years.

How fitting that those same words were playing in the background as he took another chance tonight—asking Jocelyn to dance. She smelled like spearmint and some kind of flowers, and holding her against him felt new and thrilling, yet also familiar and easy, and so perfectly *right*.

She leaned her head on his shoulder, and he pulled her close again. This wasn't a memory of a decade ago; this was now. Jocelyn was here, at Harmony Ranch, back in his arms...right where she was supposed to be.

But she's not really back. Not for good. She was only here to help with the festival. Then she'd leave again, just like she'd done before.

Pain tightened his chest—another familiar feeling—as the song ended and she stepped away.

She crossed her arms over her chest and then put them down at her sides as if she couldn't figure out what to do with them. And suddenly she couldn't quite look him in the eye. "I should probably be getting back," she said, lifting her thumb toward the house. "Check on my grandma."

"Yeah, sure." He couldn't seem to get his feet to move. It was like they were glued to the grass, and they'd lost their memory of how to take a step.

She raised her eyes, peering up at him from under her lashes, and a shy smile curved her lips. "Thanks for the dance."

He smiled back—couldn't help it.

Her smile broadened to the kind of impish grin a kid got after being handed an ice cream cone. "See you tomorrow," she said, then turned and scurried up the path toward the house.

He watched her until she disappeared around the

trees and out of sight, and then his feet finally remembered how they worked. And suddenly it seemed like he was walking on air as he sauntered back to the tailgate of his truck.

It wasn't until he picked up his phone to put it into his pocket that he noticed the camera was still open, with a little timer running at the top of the screen. *What the heck?* He touched the red dot under the word *video*, and the timer stopped at a little over three minutes. He'd been messing with the different options, and he must have accidentally started the video.

He tapped the photo in the corner and then touched the little diamond shape like Jocelyn had shown him how to do earlier. Sucking in a breath, he watched himself and Jocelyn walk hand in hand toward the grass then turn and step awkwardly into each other's arms.

Captivated by the scene, his eyes stay glued to the screen as they relaxed into each other as they swayed to the music. He could see their lips move and her head toss back as he made her laugh. Because the phone had been leaning against the speaker, Chase Dalton's deep voice singing about warm summer nights and taking a chance on love was the only soundtrack to the video.

He couldn't believe it. It seemed crazy that he'd set the phone down in just that spot to capture their dance. The scene wasn't framed perfectly, their bodies were off to one side, but with the candles glowing off the pond in the background, it made it seem almost perfect.

Transfixed, Mack brought the phone closer as

Chase eased into the chorus and Mack gazed into the eyes of the girl he'd loved for over half his life.

When it was over, he sagged against the tailgate of the truck, swallowing at the thickness in his throat. Then he tapped the screen and watched it again.

Jocelyn hurried up the porch steps and quietly let herself in the front door. She jumped as a voice spoke from inside.

"What's wrong?"

She pressed a hand to her chest as she turned to see her grandmother sitting at the kitchen table, elbow-deep in flour as she rolled out a circle of dough. "Holy cow, Gram. You scared me. And why do you think something's wrong?"

"I just saw you scurrying across the driveway like something was chasing you. Did you see a bear? They're starting to come out again. Although you know you shouldn't run when you see one. You should just back slowly away and give them their space."

"I didn't see a bear. And nothing was chasing me."

"All right. You just seem a little winded, and your cheeks are all flushed like you were running." A light dawned in her eyes. She pushed the rolling pin across the dough as she feigned innocence. "How was your visit with Mack? What did he need your help with?"

"It was good. He was good. I mean..." Jocelyn blew out a breath. "Mack is fine. He wanted to show me these cool luminaries he made and get my thoughts on selling them at the festival."

"Ahh. So that's the 'secret item' the blacksmith has

been working on? Like the ones he made for the wedding last summer?"

"Yep. And I'm super impressed you already read my Facebook post."

"Read it, liked it, and left a comment." She tapped the side of her head, leaving a smudge of white flour on her temple. "See, I listen when you tell me this stuff. I know comments and interactions drive more views."

Jocelyn smiled. "Exactly. I think you're more up on the social media scene than Mack is."

"I'm sure of it. I'm pretty dang hip, ya know. I've got a Twitter account and everything."

"I know you do. I saw that tweet you posted last week about iced coffee being your love language. That was a good one. It cracked me up."

"I am quite hilarious."

"Yes, I know." She crossed the room to peer down at the table. "What in the world are you doing?"

"Making a pie. What does it look like?"

"It does indeed look like you are making a pie. But why? You've been home from the hospital for like four minutes."

Her grandmother waved her concern away with a flour-dusted hand. "I'm fine. And I'm making this for the pie auction tomorrow. I make one every year. I usually make *several* a year, but this dang car accident messed everything up, and I ran out of time. I figured I could at least manage to crank out one, and my Old Fashioned Apple is the best seller."

"Why didn't you tell me? I would've made it."

"Do you know *how* to make my Old Fashioned Apple pie?"

"No. I don't know how to make any kind of pie," Jocelyn admitted. "But I could've at least helped."

"You can help me now. Grab one of those pie plates from the cupboard over there."

Jocelyn pulled open the cupboard and took the top one from a tall stack of pie tins. "You have at least ten more tins in here. If you show me how, I could put together some more and get them baked tonight."

"Are you sure? They take a while to bake. And I've probably only got about another hour in me."

"I'm sure. I don't mind staying up. Especially if I'm doing something that can bring in more revenue for the ranch. How much do your pies usually go for?"

Her grandmother shrugged. "It varies. They normally start the bidding around fifteen or twenty dollars, but I've had one go as high as fifty one year. But that was just because your grandpa was trying to drive the bidding up, then the other bidder let him have it. He got stuck shelling out fifty dollars for a pie I would have made him for free."

"I love that guy." Jocelyn's heart filled at the memory of her grandfather. "I'll bet I can make ten more pies tonight, and if we can get twenty dollars apiece for them, we can make at least two hundred dollars. How many other cans of pie filling do you have?"

"Cans?" Gram wrinkled her nose as if she smelled something bad. "Who do you think you're talking to? I teach a class on canning for the ranch, and I can jars of homemade pie filling from the apples we pick in the fall from the orchard outside. And not just apple. I've got jars of peach, blueberry, strawberry, and cherry pie filling."

"Of course you do. Sorry, Gram. Don't know what I

was thinking." Jocelyn crossed to the sink to wash her hands. "Sounds like we're in business. Now you just need to teach me how to make the crust."

"I think my time would be better spent showing you how to make the pies." She pointed to the bag hanging off the front of the knee scooter next to her. "Grab me my cell phone out of that bag. Loretta can knock out ten crusts in less than an hour. I'll see if she's still up and willing to make them, then we'll get Hank to bring them over."

"Sounds like a plan," Jocelyn said, passing her the phone.

An hour later, Jocelyn was covered in flour and sticky from pie filling and the secret caramel mixture her grandmother made to pour over her lattice crust. But they had two pies in the oven and had assembled three more.

"Five down, five to go. I got this," she said as she herded her grandmother down the hallway. "Now go to bed."

"I'm not *that* tired." Her grandmother punctuated her statement with a yawn as she pushed herself along on the scooter.

"You sound like a little kid. Like I used to, when you made me go to bed." She wrapped an arm around her grandmother's waist and helped her into bed, then lifted her booted leg and placed it on a pillow. "I'm setting your phone here on the nightstand." She plugged it into the charger. "And I've put a glass of water, a great book, your reading glasses and two extra ibuprofens next to it." She pointed to the prescription bottle of Percocet. "You sure you don't want one of those painkillers? They gave them to you to use."

"Nah. I used them in the hospital, and they just made my head fuzzy. Besides, painkillers are for sissies."

Jocelyn shook her head. "That is not even the least bit true. But I'm not going to force you to take them. Call me if you need me, and I'll come back and check on you in a bit." She leaned down and kissed her grandmother's cheek. "Good night, Gram. Go to sleep. We've got a big day ahead of us tomorrow."

"Good night, honey." Gram patted her hand as she closed her eyes. "I'm awfully glad you're here."

"Me, too."

Her grandmother was already snoring by the time Jocelyn made it to the bedroom door and slipped from the room. Jocelyn still had several hours of work ahead of her. She was walking back to the kitchen, wiping flour from her cheek and contemplating making a pot of coffee, when she heard a knock on the front door.

Perfect timing. That had to be Hank with the next round of pie crusts.

She opened the door then took a step back at the sight of the bearded blacksmith who stood on her doorstep holding a cardboard box. The memory of their earlier dance had heat rising to her cheeks.

"What are you doing here?" she asked, her voice breathier than she'd intended.

"Delivering pie crusts. I got a call from my grandma with orders to drive to her house to pick them up and bring them over here. She said you needed them ASAP." He walked past her and set the box on the table, then raised his head as he sniffed the air. "It smells amazing in here—like caramel apples and peach cobbler. What's going on? Why do you need what feels like a dozen pie crusts at nine o'clock at night? You having a pie-baking marathon?"

"Yes. Actually, I am."

He raised an eyebrow then pushed up his sleeves. "Okay. A pie-making marathon it is. What can I do to help?"

"Really?"

"Yeah. Of course." He pointed to the door she was starting to close. "But don't shut that just yet. My assistant is still on his way."

Jocelyn looked down to see Savage slip through the partially open door and trundle into the kitchen. She laughed as he flopped onto the floor as if he'd traveled a great distance and finally completed his epic journey. "That dog cracks me up."

"He's a good boy. But he's also strategically placed himself in the middle of the action in hopes of some stray pie crust falling his way." He rubbed his hands together. "So, pass me an apron and tell me what to do."

"An apron?"

"Yeah, a lot of famous chefs wear aprons. Besides, I don't want to mess up these jeans."

"The same jeans you typically use as a napkin?" she teased him, as she rifled through her grandmother's impressive collection of aprons. Finding the perfect choice, she handed him a frilly light pink apron covered in hot pink cupcakes, with bright red cherries atop each one. The bodice read, "Calories Don't Count on the Weekend" in glittery gold letters.

He peered at the apron with an amused smile. "Nice

try, but you think I'm threatened by a little glitter and some hot pink cupcakes?"

She lifted one shoulder in a teasing shrug.

"I forge hot iron for a living. I think I've got a pretty firm grip on my man card." He laughed as he pulled the apron over his head and tied the frilly strings behind his waist.

Jocelyn held back a sigh as her gaze raked over his broad shoulders and strong arms, and then she laughed with him. "That glitter goes perfect with your eyes."

"Quit trying to butter me up and pass me a pie crust," he said as he washed his hands. "How many more do we need to make, and what's your game plan?"

"I've got five made, two almost finished baking and three ready to go in. I am trying to have ten pies ready for the auction tomorrow, so I only need to make five more."

"Easy."

"Easy? It was easy with Gram telling me everything to do, but it's going to be harder now since I have exactly one hour of baking experience."

"Good thing you have me then. I'm pretty skilled with pies." He dumped a crust into an empty pie plate and crimped the edges. "Remember, I was raised by Loretta Talbot, who fancies herself a Master Chef, and she always had me assisting her in the kitchen."

"I always thought that was sweet of you, the way you helped her."

He shrugged. "I think she was the one helping me. We had a lot of great talks in the kitchen. I'd get home from school, and she'd put me to work chopping vegetables or kneading bread dough. I think it was easier to talk about my day and what was going on with me when my hands were busy. Not that we always talked. Sometimes we just listened to the radio or she told me stories about her and my grandpa or growing up in Harmony Creek. It was good. Plus I learned how to cook."

"You're lucky. All I ever learned about cooking from my mom was how to order takeout and how long to heat a frozen meal in the microwave."

"She taught you other things, I'm sure."

"That's true. But once we moved to the city, she was pretty busy with her career. And I took a part-time job after school. We were so busy we hardly ever saw each other. And when we did, sometimes we fought."

"What about?" He started a second pie crust as she mixed a batch of pie filling.

"Mostly about her moving us to New York. I was constantly trying to convince her to let me come back to live with Gram and finish out my senior year here."

"I didn't know that."

"No, you wouldn't."

He raised an eyebrow. "There was a little snark in that comment. What's that about?"

"Nothing, really." She kept her gaze trained on the pie filling, lifting the spoon and mixing the granular brown sugar and vanilla into the sliced apples. "I just thought after I left—after we'd made all those plans— that we would keep in touch."

His hands stilled on the edge of the crust he was shaping. "What are you talking about?"

"I figured you didn't remember."

"Remember what?"

"There was a day that last summer where we were poking around in a bunch of stuff in the attic that had been donated to the museum, and we found a stack of these letters. They were love letters, and we spent most of the afternoon curled up on that lumpy sofa reading bits of them out loud to each other." The attic had been hot and stuffy, and Jocelyn could still remember the scent of mothballs and the body spray Mack had used back then. Reading the letters out loud had been funny and weird, but also wildly romantic. "And that afternoon, we made this silly promise to only write letters to each other after I moved away until we could be together again the next summer." She shrugged and turned the mixture again, catching a stray piece of apple with her spoon and pushing it to the center of the bowl. "I figured you must have forgot about it or thought we were just joking around."

Mack reached out his hand to lift her chin so she had to look at him. He stared at her, his eyes hard as they narrowed in intensity. "I didn't forget, Jocelyn. I wrote you every week for the first four months you were gone, sometimes twice a week. But you were the one who never wrote me back. Not even a Christmas card."

Chapter Eleven

J OCELYN GRIPPED THE SIDE OF the counter as her knees threatened to buckle. "You wrote me letters?"

"Tons of them. *And* sent you cards."

A hard knot formed in her stomach. "That can't be true. I never got a single letter from you. And I *did* write to you. I found this stationery in a card shop that looked like old parchment, and I wrote you a letter on it at least once a week."

"I never got them. In fact, I never heard anything from you that whole school year. So, I figured you must have met someone new or forgot about me and moved on."

"No, I never forgot about you. About us." Her voice dropped to a whisper. "And I've tried, but I still haven't figured out how to move on."

His hand moved to cup her cheek. "I haven't either."

Spellbound, her body frozen, her eyes rapt in his gaze, she tried to make sense of what he'd just said. "But you *did* move on. You didn't even wait for me to come home that next summer."

"I didn't know you were coming back. I told you, I figured you found someone else and forgot all about me."

"How could you think that?"

"Why would I think any differently? I hadn't heard from you all year. And why would I think you'd come back to some stupid skinny hick kid when you'd probably met tons of cool kids in New York?"

Pain ripped through her chest. "How can you say that? I loved you."

His hand dropped from her cheek. "I don't have a real great track record when it comes to people coming back for me. My mom said she loved me and that she'd be back too. And look how that went."

"It wasn't like that. I was *trying* to come back. I told my mom I didn't care what she said, I was buying a ticket and taking a bus to Harmony Creek. She tried to tell me you'd already forgotten about me, that you'd moved on to some other girl, but I didn't believe her. Not until I called my grandma, and she told me it was true."

Mack shook his head. "I hadn't moved on. You broke my heart. And I didn't know how to handle it. I went from depressed to angry and back again. When Ashley started coming around, I tried to tell her I wasn't interested, but she kept at me. I was a teenager, and she was a distraction."

"A distraction?" she sputtered. "You *married* her. That doesn't sound like just a distraction to me."

He sighed and scrubbed a hand across his jaw. "Come on, Jocelyn. You were already gone."

"And Ashley loved you," she said.

Mack shrugged. "I don't know if she loved me as

much as she loved the idea of being married. And I think she saw me as her ticket out of here. She wanted to move to California. But then my grandpa got sick, and I told her I was staying. I wanted to start a family here. Eventually, she told me she'd decided to go to California without me and that she wanted a divorce. You know, we just did a simple Justice of the Peace wedding, but it was easier to get divorced than it had been to get married. Signed some papers, filed them at the courthouse, she packed up her stuff, and I moved back in with my grandparents. Thank goodness Grandma Lo hadn't already turned my bedroom into a sewing room."

"I had no idea."

He pulled his arm out from under hers. "Why would you? You weren't around. And you never asked."

"I thought you'd moved on. I swear I never got your letters."

"I never got yours either."

She gave a frustrated shake of her head, trying to make sense of all he'd told her. "I know time feels different here, but it's not like you were actually *living* in the 1900s. Why didn't you try to call me?"

He flinched at her words, a pained expression in his eyes as he swallowed. "Because I'd written you umpteen letters professing my teenage love. And I *never* heard back from you. I was angry and embarrassed and felt like an idiot. And I don't know if you're aware of this fact, but teenage boys don't always make the greatest decisions."

"Apparently neither do teenage girls." She slumped against the counter. "How could *none* of our letters have made it to each other?"

"I don't know. Unless someone was purposely intercepting them. But why would anyone do that? My grandparents love you, and they knew how much I was hurting."

A lump filled her throat. "It was my mom. It had to be her. She was the only one with a key to the mailbox." She thought back to that first time she'd written him. "I remember holding that first letter—it was in a pink envelope—and asking her for a stamp. I can recall her telling me how stupid it was to write you, but then her expression changed and she said it was kind of sweet and to give it to her and she'd drop it in the mail room at her work. From then on, I just left the letters on the kitchen counter, and she took them to mail them." She shook her head. "Or, I guess now it seems like she just took them. I never imagined she wasn't mailing them."

"Why would she do that?"

"I don't know. Who knows why she does anything? She's been in an argument with her own mother for over a decade now. But Gram was just telling me tonight that the main reason my mom moved us to New York was because she didn't want me to get stuck in this town like she'd been. She wanted me to go to college and have a chance at the kind of career that was only obtainable in a big city."

"And you have that. There aren't a lot of social media marketing-managing-whatever-your-title-is in a town the size of Harmony Creek. Our local paper only goes out once a week, and our main method of communication is still the bulletin board inside the door of the Price Rite."

"But I didn't want that at the expense of losing

you." She fought back the tears that filled her eyes. They had wasted all that time. All that anger. And hurt. "I've missed you."

"Me too."

"So what do we do now?"

As if in answer to her question, Savage stood up and bumped his short squat dog head into the back of her legs, driving her forward so that she stumbled into Mack's cupcake-aproned chest. His hands instinctively raised to steady her and fell around her waist.

She looked up at him, sure that the question in her heart was conveyed in her eyes. She couldn't speak, didn't want to break the moment with words. Instead, she hoped their connection, that way they had communicated all those years ago, with nods and smiles and knowing looks, still held.

They had known each other so well. Even though they had only spent a few months together each year, those first summers were everything. Months would pass without seeing each other, but as soon as they were together again, they would fall into the same easy rhythm of talking and laughing—the true bond of friendship when one is so comfortable in knowing that the other person already loves them and accepts them, with all their ugliness, and beautifulness, and weirdness, that they can just relax immediately into their true selves without having to play that game of getting someone new to like them.

Jocelyn peered up at Mack, her question changing to a message as she tried to express that emotion of caring, of acceptance, of love. They'd broken each other's hearts—not intentionally, but it had hurt all the same. This one moment felt like a chance to heal some of that pain...to start anew.

Mack must have felt her message, because he slid his arms around her back and pulled her into a hug. His touch was tender, and he smelled like cinnamon and sugar and apple pie, and everything she'd been missing the last ten years they'd been apart.

His arms wrapped tighter around her, and she melted into him, sighing as her body recognized his and settled into the familiar, yet still new and exciting, feel of being held in his arms again.

***

Despite their late night of pie-making, Mack was still up the next morning with the sunrise. He had hours of work ahead of him before the festival started—setting up, guiding volunteers, plus doing the numerous daily chores he normally did of feeding and caring for the animals and the grounds.

Which meant he needed to get his mind off a certain blonde pie-baking city girl and back onto the tasks at hand. Except the image of her in the kitchen the night before with flour dusting her flushed cheeks kept sneaking into his overworked brain. It was so good to be laughing and joking around with her again. *Too* good.

It was something he could get used to. If he let himself. But he couldn't let himself.

Because Jocelyn might be back for now, but she wasn't back for good. This time they were spending together was going to come to a screeching halt when the festival ended and Molly got back on her feet. Then he was going to be back in the same place he was all those years ago, still here, on the ranch, missing her and trying to pretend his heart hadn't been broken. Again.

Focus on today.

He'd told her to quit worrying about the past or the future and focus on the time they had together *today.* Which is what he needed to do as well.

He could laugh and have fun with her today, maybe even indulge in another hug, as long as he kept his heart in check and kept things between them light. They'd both said they wanted to be friends again. Being friends seemed safe. He could do that. At least for now.

Savage lumbered along behind him as he tossed hay into the corral for the horses and into the pen holding the sheep and Punkin, the Jersey cow whom Jocelyn had tried to ride when they were kids. Even though she hadn't been here for years, Jocelyn was still everywhere on this ranch. Everywhere he turned, a memory of her edged its way into his mind—the general store where they'd purchased handfuls of candy sticks, the trails around the property they'd spent hours exploring, the spot behind the barn where they'd stolen hugs and kisses.

He'd worked so hard to push all those memories out of his brain, but with her here, catching glimpses of her coming out of the general store or searching the pond for the muskrat, they all came rushing back. But it wasn't just the memories, it was also the tightness in his chest, the reminder of the pain of losing her, of hoping she'd come back and waking up every morning to another day without her.

Savage let out a whine and his tail started thumping. Mack looked up to see Jocelyn walking toward him, her arm upstretched in a wave. Her cornflower blue dress matched her eyes. Her hair was curled and tied at her neck with a ribbon, and she wore a hat with a wide blue fabric sash and a spray of flowers affixed to its side.

His heart dropped all the way to his feet. He could tell himself to keep his heart in check until the cows came home, but it was too late. He was already gone.

Jocelyn smiled at him, then crouched down to pet Savage, whose tail was wagging hard enough to power a wind farm. "Good morning. You ready for this crazy day?"

"Ready as I'm ever gonna be."

She stood and peered out over the ranch. "It looks good. The tents and the booths are ready, and I've already been letting a few of the vendors and crafters in to get set up."

"We've got about half an hour before the volunteers arrive. Most of them have done this event for years and they know what to do. And I think we've done a great job of preparing the others."

Jocelyn rubbed her hands together. "Now we just have to wait for the visitors and the money to start rolling in."

"From your lips to God's ears." He followed her line of sight. "The ranch does look great." The white tents gleamed against the backdrop of perfect blue sky, and bits of green could be seen everywhere, from the new growth of grass underfoot to the fresh leaves and tiny buds sprouting from the trees. The majesty of the mountain range rose up behind Molly's house, a dusting of snow capping its peaks.

"I miss the mountains." Jocelyn inhaled a deep breath. "The air just smells different here."

"Like the absence of smog and fuel emissions."

She nudged his arm. "Yes. But also like ponderosa pines and the algae from the pond and the smell of the horses and the dust in the corrals and the sweet scent of the chokecherry trees blossoming behind Whitaker House."

"That's a lot of smells." He was teasing her, but he knew what she meant. It smelled like spring.

She shrugged. "It smells like home."

A funny knot twisted in his gut. Because this wasn't her home. Her home smelled like asphalt and the scent of too many cars and too many people and the warm aroma of grilled meat emanating from carts lining the sidewalk. "Hopefully it smells like cash soon. And lots of it. Speaking of which, I'd better get back to work." He reached into the tool pouch he'd been carrying around that morning and handed her the item he'd spent an hour revamping before he'd gone to bed the night before. "Here. I made this for you."

Her eyes widened as she took what appeared to be an antique camera in a case. "Thank you. Does it work?"

"No. It's been busted for years. But I knew you were going to want to take a million pictures today so I hollowed out the guts of the camera and built a little shelf inside the case. You should be able to set your iPhone in there, and it should align so you can hold it up and take pictures. To everyone else, it will look like you're using an antique camera, but you'll actually be able to take pictures with your phone."

She stared down at the camera as she turned it

over in her hands then gazed back up at him. "Wow. Thank you. I can't believe you did this. It's amazing." Her voice had that hushed tone of awe, and tears pooled in her eyes.

Oh crud. "Come on now. Don't cry. It's not that big of a deal."

"Yes. It is." She blinked back the tears as she pulled the camera strap over her hat and let it hang around her neck. Then she threw her arms around him, pressing her cheek to his chest. "This is just so sweet. I love it."

I love you.

He swallowed back the words, thankful he hadn't spoken them out loud as he returned the hug. He *had* loved her. At one time and with all he had. But that was a long time ago.

How could he even think he loved her now? They barely knew each other. They were different people now. They'd been kids, teenagers, when they'd known each other before. Now they were adults who led very different lives. *In very different states and halfway across the nation from each other*, he reminded himself.

She felt so good against him. He wanted to bury his face in the soft length of her neck and inhale the scent of her skin. She smelled like vanilla and cookies and something floral, and the heady mixture of it was making him dizzy with need and want. Which were feelings he couldn't afford.

The price of that desire was too high. He'd paid it before and promised himself he'd never owe it again.

He pulled away, clearing his throat as he tried to return to business mode. "I need to get going. But I'm glad you like it. I hope you get some good pictures to-day."

"I can't wait to try it out. Thanks again, Mack."

"Like I said, it's no big deal. And it was really more for the ranch, so we can keep promoting the event to-day and try to draw a bigger crowd."

The shining smile on her face faltered. "Oh yeah, sure, of course. I'll be sure to get some good action shots early on and get them posted on Facebook and Insta with some great copy about the festival going all day, and there still being time to make it down to the event."

"Sounds good." He tapped his pocket. "I've got my phone on me today, so call or text me if you need me. Otherwise, man your battle stations and pray we have a huge crowd."

Jocelyn peered down at her picnic setup. She had about five minutes before the gates officially opened, and she was the only one left in the roped-off Boxed Lunch Social arena.

She'd thought she was being cute and clever with the rusty pail, the cute fabric, and the old blanket that she and Mack had used to haul out to the meadow to eat lunch on. But looking at the other setups sur-rounding her blanket, her picnic site looked dismal in comparison. There was one blanket set up with teddy bears having a tea party, one with a black and white cow theme, and another with a French countryside-inspired premise. Some were funny, but most were gorgeously decorated with flowers or fancy tableware.

She was much better at putting ideas and thoughts

together on a screen. She should have stayed in her lane—she knew what she was doing in the world of marketing. Why had she thought participating in the Boxed Lunch Social thing would be a good idea?

And what kind of crazy twist of fate had put Sophie's picnic setup in the site directly next to hers? She recognized the picnic basket and the silver vase holding a spray of tulips from the spread the other woman had set out for Mack a few days before. Sophie's tablecloth blanket was bright blue-and-white-checked and had even been *ironed*. Two glossy white porcelain plates were perfectly placed across from each other with complete silver place settings and napkins formed into the shape of roses.

Seriously? How could she compete with that? She'd added flowers to her picnic too, but they were just a handful of lilacs she'd cut this morning and stuck in a mason jar—another sign for her intended bidder. She'd left several, including the blanket and the lilacs.

Her grandmother had told her she only needed one bidder, and she'd set her sights on who that bidder would be. But Mack might not figure out the most obvious clue: the forged iron heart covered in dried flowers and tied to a length of jute circling the top of the pail. If he didn't bid on her picnic, she'd be eating lunch alone. No one else would waste their money.

Her only saving grace was that the sites were anonymous. So if no one bid on hers, she would just not show up either, and then inconspicuously clean up the evidence of her dumb idea later. *Way* later. After the festival was over. She'd starve before she sat out there eating that grim lunch on her own.

Jocelyn and Mack had prayed for people to show up, and their prayers were answered—in droves. Within the first few hours, hundreds of people had spilled through the gates. The steady sound of the tractor hauling hay-rack riders through the fields and the occasional shriek of children laughing was music to Jocelyn's ears.

She and Mack had been racing from one end of the ranch to the other, answering questions, running change to the gatekeepers, and dealing with every issue from a vendor's electrical problem to a request for a bandage for a skinned knee. She only wished she'd been wearing her Fitbit, because she knew she was logging tons of steps.

Despite the crazy rush of activity, the festival was going great. Every event attracted crowds, and there were constant lines at the food vendors. Visitors carried around bags of kettle corn and drank cups of the ranch's signature lemonade. Everyone seemed to be enjoying themselves. With luck, all that fun was converting to cash.

The festival had always been such a good time, and she hated to keep thinking about it in terms of dollars, but this year was an exception and they needed the income. Or there wouldn't be another festival next year.

Jocelyn sagged against the side of the general store, taking a moment to catch her breath. She almost choked at the sight of her grandmother waving as she pushed toward her on Midge, the wonder knee scooter.

"Gram, what are you doing out here? You're supposed to be resting."

Her grandmother waved away her concerns. "I'll rest when I'm dead."

"How did you even get out here?"

"Hank helped me."

"Of course he did."

"I had to wait until Loretta left to run the pie auction booth, then I made my escape."

Jocelyn peered behind her. "So what happened to Hank?"

Her grandmother shrugged. "He's probably hiding from Lo. She's gonna read him the riot act when she finds out he aided and abetted my escape plan."

"I'll bet she will. I'm a little ready to, myself."

"Oh, please. My leg is sore, but other than that, I'm feeling fine. And there's no way anyone is keeping me cooped up in the house on festival day. I need to be out here, in the action, helping if I can. Plus, I could smell the kettle corn all the way in the living room."

Jocelyn knew her grandmother well enough to know this was a battle she wasn't going to win. "Fine. But let's find you a place to sit, at least."

"I'm only sitting if it's somewhere in the middle of things. My legs might not be able to run, but my mouth sure can."

Jocelyn pressed her lips together to hold the laugh in. "You said it, not me."

A large tent had been set up at the main entrance where volunteers sold event tickets, set up tours, scheduled hayrides, and peddled yearly memberships to the living history museum. That seemed the best place to park her grandmother. Jocelyn was sure the other volunteers would do their best to keep an eye on Gram and not let her do too much.

It took them twenty minutes just to get to the tent because her grandmother had to stop to talk to everyone they passed. That woman seemed to know the entire population of Harmony Creek. And not just them, but their spouses and their kids and their neighbors' spouses and kids too.

By the time she got her grandmother set up with a chair, a bag of kettle corn, and a promise to stay put for the next few hours, it was almost noon.

Jocelyn's nerves tensed as she tried to casually walk by the sign-up board for the Boxed Lunch Social. A large grid had been drawn on butcher paper in the same setup as the picnic sites, and each site had a lined sheet of paper for the public to mark their bids on. Some pages were full of names and bids, while others only had a few. Jocelyn could see from several feet away that Sophie's page was crowded with bids.

She only needed *one* bid, and Jocelyn could see something scrawled on the first line. *Thank goodness.* Mack had figured out her clues and bid on her box lunch.

She held her breath as she got closer and zeroed in on her page. She couldn't believe it. Someone had made a *fifty dollar* bid for her lunch. But her heart sank as she read the name next to the bid.

It wasn't Mack's.

Chapter Twelve

J OCELYN READ THE NAME NEXT to the exorbitant bid again. *Clyde Barrow.*

The name had a familiar ring to it, but she couldn't place it. He must have been a local, or maybe a friend of her grandma's.

The sign-up was across from the general store, and she nonchalantly wandered over and climbed the steps of the store's porch while still keeping an eye on the board. There were only a few minutes left before the auction closed, so if Mack was going to outbid this Clyde person, he'd have to hurry.

The minutes ticked by and a few bidders raced to the board to get in a last-minute bid, but Mack was nowhere to be seen as a volunteer walked up and tacked an "Auction Closed" sign at the top of the board.

Jocelyn tried to conceal her disappointment as she made her way to her picnic site. Although really, Clyde was the one who was about to be disappointed. He'd shelled out fifty dollars for a simple lunch of sandwiches and the pleasure of her mediocre company.

She'd been sure Mack would get her clues.

At least I won't be eating alone, she thought, as she approached her picnic blanket. And whoever this Clyde guy was, he'd made a good donation to help the festival and her grandmother. Maybe he *was* a friend of Gram's and had just put his name and his money on the only page that didn't have any bids. That would make sense.

Due to the heat, the participants had been given the option to pack their lunches in coolers and store them in a small covered area next to the Boxed Social grid. Jocelyn pasted on a smile and waded into the frenzy of excited picnic creators who were laughing and chatting happily about all the bids their sites had received. She grabbed her cooler and made her escape as quickly as she could.

Her mystery donor must still be paying for the lunch, because her site was empty. Or so she'd thought. When she sat down, she found a thin white box, tied with a pink ribbon, tucked in between the jar of lilacs and the pail.

As she lifted the box into her lap, she peered around her. Who had left it?

She opened the lid—and let out a gasp. Then she smiled, admiring the gorgeous iron-forged long-stemmed rose inside. Taped to the stem was a note that read, "For Bonnie, my favorite partner in crime."

Clyde Barrow. The name came back to her now. Her grandfather had always teased her and Mack when they were younger, calling them Bonnie and Clyde when they got caught after causing trouble or cooking up some crazy new scheme.

A shadow fell across the blanket. She beamed up at the talented blacksmith who'd crafted her this beautiful rose. He dropped onto the blanket next to her, and she playfully swatted his leg. "Very clever. You really had me going."

"What? I thought you'd figure it out easy."

She shook her head. "I totally should have. My brain must be on overdrive. I thought Clyde was one of Gram's friends who felt sorry for me." She narrowed her eyes. "So why the fake name? Were you worried people would know you bid on my lunch and think something was going on with us?"

He cocked an eyebrow. "I'm sitting here with you, out in the open for everyone to see, aren't I?"

She tentatively nodded. "Ye-es."

He leaned forward to speak into her ear, his voice deep and roguish. "And unless I just imagined that moment in the kitchen last night, it feels to me like there *is* something going on between us."

His breath tickled her cheek, and his words sent a shot of heat down her spine. He smelled like aftershave, cinnamon gum, and the faint scent of woodsmoke present in the blacksmith shop. She nodded, trying to keep the smile from completely taking over her face. "Yeah, it feels that way to me, too."

He held her gaze for another moment, long enough to convey an unspoken message—a promise of something more to come. Then he knocked the side of the cooler with his knuckles. "I'm starving. I can't wait to see what you brought. What kind of amazing lunch did I buy with my fifty dollars?"

A laugh bubbled out of her. "You may have overshot your gastronomical expectations. I never expected anyone to spend fifty bucks." She reached into the cooler and spread out her offering of peanut butter and jelly sandwiches, individual-sized bags of kettle chips, and a small clear tub of oatmeal cookies. "You did say last night that you appreciated a simple lunch of sandwiches and chips." She handed him a large mason jar filled with iced tea and lemon slices, the sides of the glass slick with condensation from the ice she'd packed the jar with. "And I didn't forget the cold glass of iced tea."

"Looks perfect." He picked up the container of cookies. "Are these oatmeal scotchies?"

"Absolutely."

"I haven't had one in years. These used to be my favorite cookies."

"I remember. I got up early this morning and made a batch just for you."

Peeling back the lid, he pulled out a cookie and took a bite. He groaned as he closed his eyes. "Mmmm. These are amazing." He opened his eyes and pushed the container toward her. "You want one?"

She shook her head. "I'm good. Between the bites of dough and the half-dozen warm cookies I had for breakfast, I think I'm good for a while. But I love how you dig right into the dessert before you've even unwrapped your sandwich."

"I paid fifty bucks for this meal, I'll eat it in whatever order I please." He grinned and stuffed the rest of the cookie in his mouth. "Sometimes life calls for you to grab the good stuff first, before you miss your chance."

Yeah, sometimes it did.

They heard another satisfied groan next to them and looked over to see Hank sitting on Sophie's blanket. His eyes were closed in bliss as he tore off another bite of Sophie's famous fried chicken.

"Grandpa?" Mack glanced from Hank to Sophie, then back to Hank again. "What are you doing?"

Hank's eyes popped open, and he licked a crumb from the corner of his mouth. "Enjoying a piece of the best fried chicken in the county." He ducked as if something might fly through the air toward him. "Don't tell your grandmother I said so."

"Your secret's safe with us," Jocelyn said, sneaking a glance at Sophie to see if she appeared to be seething in jealousy that Mack had picked someone else's lunch offering. But the other woman was smiling at Hank, her face beaming with pride at the compliment to her chicken.

Sophie waved a hand at Mack's grandfather. "Oh Hank Talbot, you old so-and-so, you already won the lunch, you don't have to flatter me." She offered Jocelyn a genuine smile. "It looks like we both lucked out in getting to share our lunch with the Talbot men—two of the handsomest men on the ranch."

Jocelyn smiled back, not quite sure what to make of Sophie Scott. She seemed so nice and sincere, but she'd also just winked at Mack after she'd called him and Hank handsome. Was that a friendly "just teasing" wink? Or a flirty wink?

Mack had told her they weren't a couple, but that didn't mean Sophie wasn't still interested in him.

She glanced at Mack, who was happily digging into a peanut butter sandwich. Maybe it wasn't with quite the same enthusiasm Hank had for Sophie's chicken, but he still seemed to be enjoying it, and he *had* chosen her picnic. Jocelyn touched the cool metal of the iron rose and did feel lucky indeed.

Mack's afternoon flew by. He would've loved to spend another hour hanging out with Jocelyn, but the festival was in full swing, and he had classes to demonstrate and the chili cook-off to get set up. And sitting on a blanket surrounded by half the town of Harmony Creek wasn't the most private of settings.

Not that they'd needed privacy. Sitting there with just the two of them, talking and laughing like they used to, made it feel like they were in their own little bubble. He didn't think either of them even noticed the other people around them.

Although if it had been just the two of them, he might have given her a thank-you kiss to go along with the quick hug of appreciation for the lunch. The hug alone would no doubt start a few tongues wagging, but he'd never cared about town gossip before, and he wasn't about to start now.

He liked being with her, liked to make her laugh. But their time of laughter was going to come to a quick halt when she went back to New York. That thought sobered him as he yanked long rods of steel from his workshop wall in preparation for his next demonstration. It wasn't for an hour yet, but he liked to have everything in place when the audience started shuffling in.

The door to his shop opened, and the object of his musings burst through, her cheeks flush with color.

"Hey, I'm glad I found you," she said, her voice a little breathless.

"What's wrong?"

"Nothing's wrong. I just needed you. A group from Woodland Hills challenged a group from Harmony Creek to an obstacle course, and I need a partner. Hank is discreetly passing around a hat taking bets, and we want that cash, so I'm looking for a guy who can pull his weight in a three-legged race and a gunny sack hop."

He chuckled. "I'm your guy. I'm also pretty proficient at running with an egg balanced on the end of a spoon."

"Perfect. You're hired." She laughed as she waved him forward. "Let's go. We're starting in ten minutes."

Mack couldn't help but laugh as he hurried after her. This was why her grandfather had given them the Bonnie and Clyde nicknames. The two of them were always ending up in some kind of wacky scheme, whether it was starting their own newspaper or setting up a lemonade and zucchini stand. And Jocelyn was typically the one leading the charge. As usually happened, just like today, Mack jumped on the crazy train with her and went along for the ride.

The last few days had been like a wild trip on a roller coaster with his emotions zooming up and crashing down. He normally considered himself a pretty even-keeled guy, but having Jocelyn pop back into his life had thrown him completely catawampus.

This morning, he'd tried to back off, to step back from the feelings coursing through him. But he couldn't stay away or keep his thoughts from her. He found himself concocting the Bonnie and Clyde plan to bid on her picnic, just because he thought she'd get a kick out of it. And because he enjoyed teasing her a little, then earning the reward of her laughter.

She was laughing now as she dragged him toward the starting line where the other teams were already strapping their legs together in preparation for the first leg of the race. "I'm counting on you, Talbot. The first section is the three-legged race, then we have to hop around the hay bales in gunny sacks. At the end of that leg, we have to carry two eggs on spoons while walking over a balance beam. We have to get at least one over the line, then one of us has to walk on stilts for the last section."

He shook his head. "Geez-o-pete. Who came up with this nutty obstacle course? This is crazier than anything they have on *Survivor*. Can I just request to be voted off the island now, and you can do this thing without me?"

Jocelyn planted a fist on her hip. "Oh, is this race too challenging for you?" She peered around at the audience gathering behind him. "Should I try to find another partner who might be a little more athletic? More up for the task?"

"That's a low blow—questioning my commitment to a challenge." He grinned as he grabbed a swath of fabric from the table. "I'm in. And not just in—we're gonna *win* this thing. Now get your leg over here and let me strap it to mine."

She pumped her fist in the air. "Yes, there's the Mack I know. Let's do it." She grabbed the folds of her dress, hiking it up as she pressed her ankle to his.

He tied the fabric around their calves, trying not to be distracted by the smooth skin of her bare leg.

"Hurry up. They're getting ready to start."

He stood, and they stumble-walked to the starting line along with the other contestants.

"This dang dress is so cumbersome," Jocelyn grumbled, struggling with the extra yards of cloth. "You'll have to put your arm around me and anchor us while I try to keep a hold of my dress."

"I can do that." He slipped his arm around her back and took a firm grasp of her waist. "Are we starting on our right or our left foot?"

"Are you kidding?" She pointed to where her left foot was strapped to his right. "Did you forget how this works?"

He shook his head. She'd distracted him by asking him to anchor her. "I can't think straight with you this close to me," he muttered. "Plus you smell so dang good, I'm having a hard time focusing on anything other than when I'm finally going to get a chance to kiss you."

Her eyes widened as she stared up at him.

"Shoot. Did I say all that out loud?"

A coy smile curved her lips, and she beamed up at him. "You sure did."

"Get ready!" a volunteer yelled from the starting line, breaking the moment.

"Focus, Talbot." Her mouth drew together in a tight line, then she tapped their tied legs. "Remember how we used to do this? This leg was one, our outside legs were two."

"Got it." He tightened his grip on her waist and leaned forward.

"Get set!"

She held up her dress with one hand and wrapped the other around his back, her fingers securely clasping his belt loop. Leaning sideways, she whispered, "We can circle back to that kissing idea *after* we win."

He choked and almost stumbled forward, but she held him up even as her body shook with laughter.

"Go!"

She stopped laughing as her jaw set in concentration. "One!" she commanded, drawing their joined legs forward. "Two!" They found their rhythm as other couples around them yelled similar instructions.

"Right! Left!"

"Your other left!"

"Just move your leg!" The couple next to them tripped and pitched forward. A few went to their knees or dragged their partner next to them.

Mack focused on Jocelyn's count, and they pulled ahead of the pack. Ted Wilkerson, a Woodland Hills native who ran the Big R Mercantile, and his ten-year old son Ned were right on their heels. Ted's face set in concentration as he lifted the boy off the ground and practically broke into a run.

"One, two. One, two." Jocelyn's count grew more feverish as they neared the finish line. "Don't worry about them. There's plenty of race left."

She always knew what he was thinking. "We made it," he said as they crossed the line, and he immediately bent to untie their legs.

Jocelyn grabbed two gunny sacks and tossed one to him, then stepped into the other one. "Help me stuff this dress in here," she told him, as she shoved piles of material into the sack.

He grabbed one side. "Here, I'll hold the bag. You shove in the dress." Together they got her in the bag, and she took off hopping as he yanked his gunny sack up to his waist. "Go! Go! I'm right behind you."

They'd lost a little ground with the extra time they took with the dress, but she was making up for it now as she leapt around the hay bale course. He tried to focus on his hopping, but she was cracking him up as her hat bounced on her head with every hop. He couldn't believe it hadn't fallen off already.

Ted and his son were just ahead of them as Jocelyn made it across the new finish line and started wriggling out of her gunny sack. Mack doubled his efforts, hopping harder, then dropping the bag and stumbling out of it.

Jocelyn already had two eggs, and she handed him a spoon. "We only have to get one of these across." There were four balance beams set up, and if a contestant fell off in the middle, they had to get in line again. She sprinted to the far beam where there was only one person in front of her.

He ran to the line next to hers, figuring they could try to get to the other side at the same time. Who was he kidding? He totally wanted to beat her. "Hurry up, kid," he told Ned, who had just stepped onto the beam ahead of him. *Dang.* Little weasel raced across like it was nothing. Now the Wilkersons would have the lead.

He stabilized his egg on the spoon before stepping on to the beam. *Steady. Steady. You can do it.* He made it halfway across—then his foot slipped and hit the ground. He lunged his hand out and caught the egg before it fell. Circling back, he got in line behind Janice Newberry, a woman who ran the coffee shop in town and occasionally volunteered at the ranch. He shifted his weight from one foot to the other as he waited his turn.

Jocelyn's straw hat had slipped forward, and some of her hair had come loose, but her feet were steady as she focused on her spoon and stepped solidly across the beam. "Come on, Mack," she encouraged from the other side. "You got this."

Three more steps, and he had it. He jumped to the ground on the other side, and his egg went tumbling off the spoon and hit the grass with a splat.

"Dang it," he shouted, staring at the yellow yolk leaking from the mess of egg shell fragments.

"Don't worry. We still have one," she said, her enthusiasm undeterred.

"Easy for you to say. You still have your egg."

Laughter bubbled from her as she grabbed his sleeve and pulled him toward the final leg of the race. "Don't pout. We're still in this." She nodded to Ted Wilkerson, who was already taking his first tentative steps on the stilts. "I know I can take him."

Mack picked up a stilt. "In that dress? No way. I got this part."

"You're terrible on stilts. I can win this for us."

"You haven't seen me use these in years. I'm better now."

"Seriously? Have you been practicing?"

"Occasionally. And I'm sure I've been on stilts more often than you have in the past decade. Unless you often take a stroll through Central Park on a pair of them."

"Quit bickering, you two," Molly yelled at them from the side lines. "Woodland Hills is taking the race, and I've got a twenty bet on this."

They froze and jerked their heads toward the race area. Ted was halfway across. Mack pushed the stilt toward Jocelyn. "Molly's right. We've got to get out there. You do it."

She looked from him to Ted, chewing her lip, then thrust the stilt back at him. "No. You're right. This dress will probably trip me up. You do it."

"You sure?"

"Somebody get on the dang stilts!" Molly shouted.

"Go," Jocelyn ordered.

He stepped onto the small platforms, then took off across the raceway. This was his chance to redeem himself after dropping his dumb egg. Taking large solid strides, he passed two people. Ted still had a good lead on him, though. He picked up the pace.

"Come on, Mack!" Jocelyn yelled her encouragement. She and Ned had run around the side of the track and were now standing on the other side cheering him and Ted on.

"Go faster, Dad," Ted's son screamed. "Squash that guy like a bug."

Geez. Ned seemed to have inherited his competitive streak from his dad. But Mack had a competitive streak of his own, and he was going to win this thing. He and Ted were now the clear frontrunners, and Mack was gaining on the other man.

Ted looked back, his eyes going wide as he saw how close Mack was. That panic was the other man's fatal mistake, as he fumbled the next step and fell to the ground.

Now was his chance. Mack took four giant steps and crossed the finish line.

"You did it! We won!" Jocelyn shouted, racing toward him and throwing her arms around his neck.

He dropped the stilts and lifted her in the air, spinning her around. Caught up in the moment, he apparently forgot they were surrounded by half the town of Harmony Creek, as he set her down and went in for that kiss.

Chapter Thirteen

WELL, *DANG.* JOCELYN REALIZED WHAT was happening a second too late. She'd thought Mack was coming in for a hug and had just turned her face toward his shoulder when his lips collided with the side of her cheek. She turned back, hoping it wasn't too late—or too awkward to try again. But the moment was gone.

"I wasn't sure you were going to take that thing," Hank's voice came from behind her. "Those Wilkersons almost beat you."

Jocelyn stepped back, but still gripped Mack's forearms, holding onto him to steady herself. Her brain was dizzy from the spin and the barely missed kiss. Mainly the kiss.

"Oh, leave them alone," Gram said, scooting up next to them. "Let them enjoy their victory." She patted Jocelyn's arm. "Great race, you two."

Jocelyn turned to her grandmother as she dropped her hands to her sides. "Thanks, Gram. It was fun. I was a little worried in that last bit, but Mack pulled it out."

"I had a good partner," he said, dropping his arm around her shoulder. "Even if she is a little bossy."

"I'm not bossy. I'm confident." She playfully nudged his belly with her elbow. "Confident that I ran that race better than you."

"*Better* than me? We were on the same team."

She laughed, her grin mischievous as she tried not to be sidetracked by the warm pressure of his arm resting casually around her shoulder. "I know. I'm just saying, not that it matters now, but I'm not the one who dropped my egg."

He smiled. "*Touché*."

"You both did great," her grandmother told them. "You seem like the perfect team to me."

Jocelyn wiggled her finger in Gram's direction. "Don't think I don't know what you're doing."

"What?" Gram said, with feigned innocence. "I'm just making an observation that you two seem like a great couple, er, I mean, team." She grinned, then her eyes widened as she spotted something behind Jocelyn. "There's Loretta. I gotta go before she catches me and makes me go back to the house to take a nap."

"You *should* go back to the house to take a nap," Jocelyn called after her. But it was too late. Gram had already scooted her way into the crowd of people heading toward the food vendors.

"I should go too," Mack said. "I've got a blacksmithing demonstration I need to finish setting up for."

"Anything I can do to help?"

"Nah, I got it. But I'll catch up with you at the chili cook-off afterwards." He started to lean forward like he wanted to try to kiss her again, then must have changed his mind because he just squeezed her shoulder, then dropped his arm. "I'll see you later."

"Thanks for helping me win the race."

"Thanks for not dropping your egg." He shot her a wink as he walked away.

Jocelyn had plenty to do to keep busy, but she still somehow happened to find herself outside the blacksmith shop an hour later. She should probably check on the volunteers at the gates to make sure they had enough change, but she was drawn to the door of the shop and the deep voice coming from inside. She could just pop in and listen for a minute.

She slipped inside the door and stood at the back of the room. No one noticed her. They were all too busy watching the man at the hearth as he worked, pounding and molding the hot iron to his will. He looked so strong and handsome, his big hands working the iron.

He wore khaki trousers and a lightweight cotton shirt, and had a leather apron wrapped around his waist. Jocelyn imagined he looked much like blacksmiths had in the early 1900s—the tools and trappings of the craft having stayed much the same.

"This bit I'm raking up is called the coke." Mack was pulling a small forked tool through a pile of burnt coals on the hearth. "It's coal that's already been baked from a previous fire."

"Why don't you wear gloves?" a young boy at the front of the audience asked. "Doesn't that hot metal burn your hands?" Jocelyn had been wondering the same thing.

"I try not to touch the hot part," Mack said, grinning at the boy. His smile did funny things to Jocelyn's stomach. "This is the way I was taught when I apprenticed with the Master Blacksmith. Gloves are kind of bulky, and the best tongs are my hands," he explained. "And the iron isn't hot on this end." He waved the boy forward. "Would you like to come up here, and you can tell everyone how it feels?"

The boy's head bobbed as he eagerly vaulted from his chair. Mack showed him how to touch the cool end of the piece, then handed the boy the hammer and let him bang the hot iron. Jocelyn remembered Hank letting them do the same thing when they were kids and hanging around the blacksmith shop.

She saw a lot of Hank in Mack—in the confident way he worked not just the iron, but the audience as well. He kept up a lively conversation, teaching them, but also tossing in a few corny jokes and making them laugh.

A man in the audience nudged his wife as he whispered, "See, babe? I told ya dis would be cool. Dat ain't sumpin' you nah-mally see in Central Pahk."

Jocelyn turned her head as she caught the thick East Coast accent. She expected to feel deeper pangs of homesickness for New York, but instead she realized how much she was enjoying being back in Colorado and the slower pace of life on the ranch.

Her chest tightened as she suddenly felt unsure of where she belonged. There were so many things she loved about New York: strolling through the museums, catching a Broadway show, and nobody did a Maple Bacon Melt and tots like the Meltshop. But a piece of her also felt at home in Harmony Creek. No one in New

York made an Old Fashioned Apple pie like her grand-mother, or mac and cheese like Mrs. Crandle.

And there was no Mack Talbot in New York.

Her eyes were drawn to him as he laughed and forged two fiery pieces of metal into one intricate shape, and her heart both filled and hurt at watching him.

Mack had found his place here. This ranch, this job as blacksmith and caretaker, it suited him. He had followed in his grandfather's footsteps, but he'd also made it his own. And he'd settled into it like a comfort-able chair.

This was where he belonged. She'd always thought she belonged here with him. But if she had come back, she would have missed out on so many of the amazing experiences she'd had in New York. And she wouldn't have the job that she currently held and loved. Or a chance at the promotion she was fighting for.

Being here, on the ranch, with Mack, it was easy to slip into their old patterns, teasing each other, compet-ing over who was better at using stilts, even sneaking hugs that had her toes curling in her old-fashioned boots.

But this was *his* life, not hers. *Wasn't it?*

Everything about her life was forward-thinking and technology-driven, while everything in his was focused on the simplicity of the past.

But could they find a way to meld their lives togeth-er, the way Mack was forging the two pieces of steel into one complete design?

The audience clapped as the boy took a bow, then returned to his seat. Mack tipped his head, giving the boy the acclaim. His gaze traveled over the rest of the group, then lit on Jocelyn standing by the door. His lips curved up in a smile meant just for her.

And all thoughts of their differences, their two separate lives, disappeared as she fell into that grin. Her heart tumbled, hammering in her chest, and all she could do was hold on. And smile back.

The chili cook-off had been set up in one of the outbuildings. It wasn't part of the original homestead, but had been built in the Eighties, and it housed a small kitchen and a large meeting room. They often used it for cooking or quilting demonstrations or if they needed a bigger area for more people.

Since it had originally been a Woodland Hills event, the visitors had offered to set everything up, but had coordinated it with Hank. Mack's grandfather had long been held in high regard as a chili aficionado and often served as a judge for both communities' cook-offs. Long tables ran one length of the room and folded placards sat in front of various crockpots, stating the contestant number and the category in which the chili was entered.

Jocelyn inhaled the sweet and spicy scents of tomato sauce, onions, and chili powder as she stepped into the room. Since the contestants had to pay a fee to enter, she was thrilled to see so many crockpots lining the wall.

Hank stood in the center of the room and waved her toward the judges' table at the front. "Thanks for volunteering to do this, Joss," he said as he met her at the table. "You're in for a real treat."

"I'm excited. But also a little nervous."

"Don't be. I assigned you to the Sweet and Sassy category, so you won't have to judge the real hot stuff."

"My mouth *and* my stomach thank you."

He pointed to the chairs lined up behind the table, where a few other judges were already taking their seats. "You'll be Judge #5. I put you next to Janice Newberry. She's an old hat at this thing, and she can show you the ropes."

"Perfect." Janice had been around forever, and Jocelyn had known her since she was a girl. She took her place next to the other woman. "Hey Janice. Good to see you."

The other woman gave her a hug. "Good to see you too, honey. I wanted to give you a squeeze earlier, but we were on the obstacle course and in the throes of competition."

"That was fun. I'm glad we're on the same side in this contest, though. Hank told me I'll be judging the Sweet and Sassy category."

"That's probably good." Janice wiggled her eyebrows and gave her a mischievous grin. "Because judging by the smoldering looks I saw Mack Talbot giving you earlier, I don't think there's a chili here that's spicy enough to compare to that heat."

Warmth flooded Jocelyn's cheeks. *Speaking of heat,* she thought. "I'm sure I have no idea what you mean."

The other woman smiled knowingly. "I'm just teasing you. It's good to have you home."

Home. Harmony Ranch had always felt like home to her. But her life, her job, and her dinky share of an overpriced apartment were in New York. Not to mention the promotion she'd just spent the last several months of her life working for.

Except she was starting to wonder if the most important part was here—her heart.

Mack made it to the chili cook-off just as they were announcing the winners. The room was packed, which was good because after the winners were announced, spectators would be able to buy bowls of chili and sample the various entries. He hoped they all brought their appetites *and* their wallets.

He craned his neck to see the judges' table. Spotting Jocelyn sitting next to Janice, stacks of paper bowls littered across the table in front of them, he made his way forward, then dropped into the vacant chair beside her. "Sorry I'm late," he leaned in and whispered. "How did it go?"

"Great. It was fun," she whispered back. "And hard. There were so many good ones. I'm glad your grandpa gave me the sweeter ones to judge, though. The ones in the spicy category were apparently pretty fiery this year."

"Oh yeah?"

"Yeah. Buster Kegan was on the judging panel for those, and he was bragging about how there wasn't a chili hot enough for him, so he was taking huge bites of each sample. But I guess one of the contestants used a ghost pepper in their "Burn Down the Barn Chili" entry, and he took several bites before it really kicked in. Sweat was pouring off his face, and he was swearing and hollering for somebody to get him some milk. He was fine a couple of minutes later. But it was awful and hilarious at the same time."

Mack chuckled. "I'm sorry I missed that."

"You also missed the Molly Stone "Dodge and Duck Show" as Gram tried to watch the cook-off while evading Loretta. Every time I looked up, the two of them had changed places in the room as your grandma chased mine around trying to catch her—no doubt to try to convince her to rest."

"I can imagine they'll both need a lie-down after that game."

Mack's grandpa stepped out of the back room and held up his hand for attention. He tapped the top of the microphone he was holding and patted the air with his hand in an effort to quiet the room.

"The results are in. It's been a whopper of a contest, and you all are in for a culinary adventure with this array of chili masterpieces."

"Wow. Grandpa's laying it on a little thick," Mack whispered to Jocelyn. "But the audience seems to be *eating* it up."

She arched an eyebrow. "Seems he's not the only Talbot with a skill for corny jokes."

Mack shrugged with modesty. "We're a pretty talented bunch."

To much applause and some lighthearted booing, his grandfather announced the winners of each individual category, then gave a dramatic drum roll as he motioned for Loretta to hold up the cook-off grand prize "trophies," which were mounted wooden spoons that had been dipped in gold glitter. "And now the moment you've all been waiting for—the grand prize winners. In third place, for a trophy and a gift card for a free haircut at the Harmony Creek House of Hair, the award goes to Frank Ferguson's 'Four Alarm Firehouse Chili' from Woodland Hills."

Mack's grandmother passed Frank his prize as Hank announced the next winner. "In second place, for a trophy and a fifty-dollar gift card to the Hole-In-the-Wall Café, the award goes to 'Lonnie's Legal Lip Remover' from Harmony Creek."

The audience went wild, clapping and cheering as Lonnie Schultz sprang from her seat, shrieking and whooping like she'd won the lottery.

"That makes one winner from Harmony Creek and one from Woodland Hills." Mack leaned toward Jocelyn to be heard over the chaos in the room. "Cross your fingers we get the next one. Otherwise, we'll never hear the end of it."

His grandfather held up his hands to calm the room again. "And the grand prize, for a trophy, a hundred dollars cash, and bragging rights until the next cook-off, the winner of this year's Harmony Creek Hoopla Chili Cook-off is...." He paused for dramatic effect. "'Chili, Chili, Bang, Bang' by Daryl Pitts from Woodland Hills."

Mack dropped his chin to his chest. *Dang it.* He shook his head at Jocelyn, who looked as disappointed as he felt. He leaned closer to whisper, "I'm real glad we're making a bunch of cash on this cook-off, but my competitive streak was still hoping Harmony Creek would win."

"Mine too," Jocelyn whispered back.

Meanwhile, Daryl was going crazy as he ran to the front of the room and snatched his trophy from Loretta. He hooted in victory as he held the glittery spoon over his head.

"Wait!" a woman called as she came running out of the kitchen, several tin cans clutched in her hands. "I think Daryl should be disqualified! I found these in a trash bag in the bed of his truck. Six cans of Hormel Angus Beef Sweet and Spicy Chili. And nothing else. So it sure looks to me like he just poured cans of pre-made chili into his crockpot. So, who's the real winner, Daryl or Hormel?" She punctuated the air with a jab of one of the cans.

"Who's that?" Jocelyn asked.

"Glenda Summers," Mack told her. "She thinks the contest should be more natural and canned goods shouldn't even be allowed as an ingredient."

Several people in the front of the room booed and called for Daryl's disqualification. Mack's grandfather motioned for them to hush. "Now Daryl, these are some mighty big allegations Glenda is accusing you of," he said. "What do you have to say for yourself? Does your entry have *any* other ingredients besides cans of prepared Hormel?"

Daryl raised his chin and puffed out his chest. "Yeah. Of course it does. It has four other ingredients."

Glenda slammed the cans down on the table. "Salt and pepper don't count. I demand Daryl and his bogus chili recipe be disqualified and eliminated from the contest."

Daryl squinted his eyes, scanning the room as if judging how much support he was going to get from the crowd. Guessing from the number of boos and taunts, it didn't sound like much. "Fine. Whatever. I withdraw my entry. This contest is stupid, anyway." He stomped out of the building.

Glenda crossed her arms and stared triumphantly after him. "There's no place for that kind of attitude in this contest," she called after him.

"All right, Glenda. Simmer down. You've had your say," Mack's grandfather told her as he picked up the spoon trophy. He dusted it off and held it up. "I guess now that Daryl is out, 'Lonnie's Legal Lip Remover' will take the grand prize, 'Frank's Four Alarm Firehouse Chili' will take second place, and Troy Deever's 'Big Troy's Toe-Curling Chili' will move into third. Congratulations to all the winners. Now if you all want to form an orderly line against the south wall, Loretta can take your money, and we'll start serving you up some of this delicious chili."

Jocelyn's eyes sparkled, and she held up her hand as she turned back to Mack. "Yes. Harmony Creek won. Another victory for the Hoopla."

Mack slapped her hand in a high five. "Now let's just hope we sell every bite of the stuff."

Chapter Fourteen

JOCELYN STEPPED OUT ONTO THE porch as Mack approached the house an hour later, and his heart practically stopped in his chest. She was so beautiful.

More beautiful than ever. Older, a little curvier than she'd been as a teenager, with the same gorgeous smile, the same hair color, the same spark of mischief in her eyes.

Another thing which hadn't changed was the way she made him feel. Just looking at her still had his heart racing and his palms sweating. She might have the curves and grace of a woman, but he still felt like a gawky teenager who had a crush on the pretty girl next door.

Was that what he was feeling now? Those old sparks from his teenage crush?

He only wished that were the case. A crush he could get over. What he felt for Jocelyn Stone was so much more. She was the first girl he'd ever fallen in love with, the first girl he'd truly given his heart to. And it still belonged to her. Even after all these years.

For just a second, he remembered how she'd looked a couple of days ago, standing by the railing, gazing out over the ranch, a pensive expression on her face, as if so many decisions rested on her shoulders. He wondered what she was thinking now. What thoughts lay behind that wistful look? The health of her grandmother? Her job in the city? Him?

He hoped it was him. Then he wouldn't be the only one whose brain was stuck in overdrive thinking about the two of them being together again.

She was probably thinking more about how much money the festival was generating and if they had a chance to save her grandmother's beloved ranch. Those thoughts had been on his mind today, too.

What would he do if the bank took the ranch? Would someone else buy it and let him stay on as caretaker? Or would someone just want the land and get rid of the living history museum altogether?

He shook his head. He couldn't go there. Not tonight. Tonight was for the festival, and he just wanted to focus on walking this gorgeous woman to the dance.

There had been a bit of a lull between the time when the chili cook-off ended and the dance began, so Jocelyn had convinced Molly to go back to the house with her to freshen up and change. Or at least that was the excuse she'd used. It probably had more to do with getting Molly to rest for a few minutes.

He and Jocelyn had said they'd meet later at the dance, but somehow he found himself outside her house, hoping he'd catch her so they could walk over to the barn together.

He raised a hand in greeting. "Hey there."

"Hey yourself," she said, offering him a smile. She'd

changed into a different period dress, this one a deep cranberry color with a high waist and a bit of an open neckline. A dark velvet ribbon strung with a cameo brooch was tied around her neck. She no longer wore the hat, but had instead pulled most of her hair up into some kind of knot at the back of her head.

Stopping at the bottom step of the porch, he leaned his arm on the railing as he gazed up at her. "You look really pretty."

She ducked her head, and he loved the way the slight tinge of pink colored her cheeks. "Thanks," she said as she walked down the steps. "You look pretty good yourself. But not as handsome as this guy." Oblivious to the dust settling on the hem of her dress, she crouched down to ruffle the floppy skin around Savage's neck.

Mack peered down at the mutt. "I hadn't realized he followed me from the cottage. And now I'm thinking I should have told him to stay there if I'd known he was gonna upstage me in the handsome department. Thanks, pal."

The dog tilted his head, looking up at him with sad eyes as if to say he was sorry. Except that's what his eyes always looked like, even if he was overcome with happiness, so Mack wasn't falling for it.

Something caught the dog's attention, and Savage jerked his head to the side to watch Pepper, one of the ranch's cats, walk across Molly's porch and perch on the top step. She peered down at Savage with disdain as she slowly licked her paw.

"Uh oh," Mack said. "You'd better stand back. These two have a history. You're about to see just why Savage earned his name."

Jocelyn's eyes widened, but before she had a chance to reply, the cat sauntered down the stairs, flicked her tail at the dog, then took off across the yard.

Savage gave chase, loping after the cat, his big jowls rising and lowering with each step. His giant ears flopped, intermittently whacking him across the eyes and flying out to the side like he was about to ascend in flight. He let out a low *woof* as his short legs carried him across the grass—for about twelve feet. Then he stopped and flopped down on his stomach, his legs splayed out as if he'd just run a marathon and couldn't make it another step.

The cat meandered back toward the dog, circling around him once, then settling next to his head and bending to lick his ears.

"Poor Savage," Jocelyn said, laughing, as they watched the dog roll over to his back and stretch out his neck to let the cat rub her head against it. "That's quite a name to try to live up to."

"You can see he's a lover, not a fighter."

"Not much of a runner, either."

Mack shrugged. "Really, why run, when you can lie down instead?"

She let out another laugh. The sound filled an empty spot in his chest—a spot that had been waiting for her for the last decade.

He said, "I think I'll let him stay here while we head to the dance. If you're ready."

"Sounds like a plan. I'm good to go."

"Did you ever convince Molly to take a nap?"

"No. But I talked her into lying down and then heard her snoring when I checked on her a few minutes later. I left her a note to tell her I was heading to the dance and delicately suggested she take it easy and stay in tonight."

He grinned. "I've got five dollars that says she shows up anyway."

Jocelyn shook her head. "That's too easy a bet. How about that she shows up within thirty minutes of the band starting to play?"

"I'll bet fifteen."

"You're on."

"Bonus five if she gets out on the dance floor with the knee scooter."

Jocelyn laughed. "I'm taking that bet because I can't refuse a wager with you. But I have a feeling I should just hand over my twenty dollars now."

They laughed as they walked toward the barn. Mack was conscious of every time the backs of their hands brushed. They stopped to let a mother duck and her four ducklings waddle across the path in front of them on their way to the pond.

"They're so sweet," Jocelyn said, her shoulder touching his as they waited. He twisted his pinkie around hers...and then she interlocked her fingers with his.

He couldn't believe they were holding hands as they walked to the dance together. If there had been a longer route to the barn, he would've suggested taking it. Instead, they too quickly arrived at the dance, and within seconds their hands dropped as they were swallowed into the excitement of the crowd and carried into the barn.

"I'll find you later," Jocelyn called as one of the volunteers pounced on her with a problem with one of the credit card machines.

"Mack, I'm glad you're here," his grandfather said as he clapped a hand on his shoulder. "I need you to give me a hand with the amplifier."

Jocelyn had to laugh when she spotted her grandmother roll through the barn doors within minutes of the band's starting up. She knew she shouldn't have taken that bet. But she'd never been able to resist a wager with Mack. Heck, she'd never been able to resist Mack, period. And it seemed she still couldn't.

She searched the crowded room and spotted him across the dance floor. He was caught in a conversation between Lonnie Schultz and Frank Ferguson, probably still bickering about the chili cook-off.

As if he could feel the pull of her stare, he glanced up and caught her eye. His lips curved into a roguish grin, a grin meant just for her, and her heart practically fell out of her chest.

Then Sophie scurried up to him, and he bent for her to speak closer to his ear. The room *was* noisy, but the intimate ease they had with each other still sent a sharp pain through Jocelyn's heart.

Jocelyn had to turn away as the two of them hurried off together, toward whatever crisis had made Sophie hasten to him in the first place. She fought against the hard pangs of jealousy ricocheting through her chest. She had no claim to Mack and no right to be jealous. Sophie had been here for years. She'd worked with Mack on a weekly basis. And even though Mack had said he wasn't interested in her, that could change at any time. He'd fallen for a hometown girl before. It was obvious to anyone how suited those two were for each other.

This thing, whatever she and Mack were doing, was temporary. Yes, it was great to be spending time with him again, to sneak in a few hugs and revel in the feel of being in his arms again. It had felt so easy, so right, to slip her hand into his as they'd walked over here.

Although he'd dropped her hand pretty quickly when they'd gotten inside the barn. Was that because there were so many people around and he was trying to protect her from town gossip? Or was he protecting himself? Was he embarrassed for people to see them together again after she'd broken his heart before? Her heart had been broken, too. And he was the one who'd taken up with someone else.

She'd dreamt so many times about having a second chance with Mack Talbot. But that's all this was—a dream. A fantasy. Because if she were being honest with herself, she would have to admit that she knew this was all temporary, a short break from her actual life. She was only here for a few more days, another week at best. Then what would happen? The same thing as before? They'd lose touch and he'd find someone else?

She wasn't sure she could go through that again. Not after finally being with him again. But *she* was the one who was leaving. And Sophie was staying. Sweet, kind, pretty Sophie. Mack could do a lot worse. And Hank and Loretta already loved her. Plus Hank loved her fried chicken, so that was something, too.

"What's wrong, honey?" Her grandmother's voice broke into her thoughts. "You look a million miles away." Gram wheeled up to her, the crowd of people parting for the knee scooter to pass like the waves of the Red Sea.

Jocelyn forced a smile. "Nothing's wrong. I was just wool-gathering," she said, using one of Gram's favorite sayings.

"Well, come back to the present, because I need your help."

"What's wrong? Does your leg hurt? Do you want to go back to the house and lie down?"

"No, I'm not in pain. Well, at least not from my leg. But it's killing me to not be able to dance. I think I could manage it if the dance floor weren't so crowded." She wheeled the knee scooter back and forth as she gave her hips a little wiggle. "I think Midge is up for it."

"No way. You are sittin' this one out. And be thankful the dance floor is so crowded. Just imagine all those dancers as dollar signs. The more people boogie-ing, the more money is going into the bank."

"Good point. And it's probably a blessing that I can't dance tonight anyway."

"Why's that?"

"Because Emmet Scott has already asked me twice if I thought I could manage it. The man is a complete paradox—last week he acted like we're enemies, tonight he's asking me to dance. He changed his tone with me after I complimented his shirt this afternoon at the chili cook-off, as if I was flirting with him. All I said was that it was a good color for him, and he's acting like that was somehow a pickup line."

"As if."

"Right? I mean, give me some credit. We were at a chili cook-off, for goodness' sakes. The opportunities were endless, if that's what I'd been trying to do." She planted a hand on her hip and affected a coy tone. "The chili around here isn't all that's hot. Although your chili must be spicy, because you're making my heart burn.'"

Jocelyn giggled, then got in on the game. "I may not be chili, but I'll bet I can spice up your life."

Gram bent forward, holding her stomach as she burst into laughter. "I think you might be my missing ingredient."

The two of them doubled over in giggles. Jocelyn put her arms around her grandmother and gave her a hug. "I've missed you, Gram."

"I've missed you too, honey," she said, squeezing her back. "All this talk of spicy chili has got me thirsty. Will you help me get some punch?"

"Sure." Jocelyn stepped forward to make a wide berth for her grandmother to turn around. The band started up a new song, and Mack came back through the door on the other side of the room. Sophie came in behind him holding a stapler and a roll of receipt tape in her hand. They must have gone for supplies.

The crowd parted again as Gram made her way back across the room. Jocelyn wasn't sure why she even needed her. As they approached the punch table, Jocelyn spotted Loretta holding out her hand to her grandson. It made Jocelyn's heart do another one of those funny tumbles as she watched Mack smile down at his grandmother as he led her out to the dance floor. They were so dang cute.

Gram had already poured herself a glass of punch by the time Jocelyn caught up to her. "It looks like you and Midge managed just fine. What did you need me for?"

Her grandmother's brow furrowed. "Oh shoot. You're right." She plunked the cup down, then wheeled the knee scooter forward, edging Jocelyn into the dancers. "Really, I just needed your help to…" She peered over Jocelyn's shoulder. "Oh look, there's Loretta." She waved as she called to her friend. "Hey Lo, would you mind helping me with this punch?"

Jocelyn turned to see Loretta and Mack had circled around the floor and were right behind her.

Loretta smiled sweetly at Jocelyn. "Oh honey, I'd better help your grandmother. Would you mind taking over for me here?" She grabbed Jocelyn's hand and put it into Mack's as she scooted around to her other side, then gave the couple a little nudge. "You two look adorable together. Enjoy your dance."

Jocelyn looked up at Mack as she fell into step with him. "Hi."

"Hi," he said, wearing an amused smile as he shook his head. "Could those two be any *more* obvious?"

"I don't think so."

He pulled her a little closer as he led her around the floor. "Just so you know, I *was* going to ask you to dance with me. All on my own."

She bent her forehead to his. "Just so *you* know, *I* was going to ask *you* to dance with me. All on my own."

He let out a soft laugh. "Will you ever stop competing with me?"

She shook her head. "Probably not. Although I do owe you ten dollars. Gram walked in within seconds of the band starting, and she started right off complaining about how she couldn't get Midge to cooperate when she tried to dance."

"That was an easy bet. You practically *let* me win that one."

She teased him with a flirty smile. "If you want to place a bet on whether I'll let you kiss me after the dance, I'll let you win that one too."

Apparently, her grandmother wasn't the only one with mad skills when it came to cheesy pickup lines.

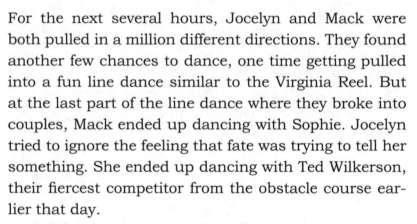

For the next several hours, Jocelyn and Mack were both pulled in a million different directions. They found another few chances to dance, one time getting pulled into a fun line dance similar to the Virginia Reel. But at the last part of the line dance where they broke into couples, Mack ended up dancing with Sophie. Jocelyn tried to ignore the feeling that fate was trying to tell her something. She ended up dancing with Ted Wilkerson, their fiercest competitor from the obstacle course earlier that day.

As the dance was winding down, Jocelyn escaped out the side door. She lifted her hair off her neck to let the night air cool it. The soft strains of the music carried through the open upper windows of the barn, and she could hear the chirp of a cricket and the occasional soft splash of the muskrats playing in the pond beside her.

It was a perfect spring night. She could already feel the hint of summer in the air.

She heard footsteps and turned to see Mack had followed her out. He came up behind her and put his arms around her waist. She leaned her back against his chest and breathed a contented sigh.

"You having fun?" he asked. She shivered as his deep voice tickled her ear.

"Yes." She rested her hands on his arms. "This whole day has been perfect."

"Wow. A perfect day. That's a rare find."

So was Mack Talbot.

Staying in the circle of his arms, she turned around and laid her head on his shoulder. "Being here is like stepping back into the past. And it's wonderful. But I have to keep reminding myself that this isn't my future. My life is in New York. And your life is here."

He lifted his hand to touch her cheek as he peered down at her. "So forget about the past and the future, and just be in the present." His gaze softened as he pulled her still closer. "You're here now, and we're together. That's enough."

She let out a soft contented sigh as she snuggled into his chest. He was right. It was enough. It was more than enough. For now.

"This night, and this day, have been amazing. I've had the best time," Jocelyn told Mack an hour later when the dance finally finished. She, Mack, Molly, Hank, and Loretta sat at a table in the back as the band packed their gear and volunteers began to fold up the tables and chairs.

"But now we're at the moment of truth," Mack said, although the truest moment of the night had been when they'd been outside, and he'd held her and hummed in her ear as they swayed on their own private dance floor to the music drifting through the windows of the barn. "Now that all the people are gone and we've sold the last luminary and the final bag of kettle corn, it's time to count up the money and see if we really saved the ranch."

She sighed as a heavy feeling settled in her stomach. "Do we have to? Can't we wait until the morning? Right now, this has been the perfect day. I want it to end on this note of success. I want to forget about the fact that we have to have made twenty-four thousand dollars or we'll lose the ranch. I heard so much laughter and saw so many families enjoying the day. I just want to focus on that. Just for tonight."

"Sure. We can do that. We probably need to wait for the vendor sales, anyway." In truth, he was fine putting it off...not just because losing the ranch would upend his world, but because they'd had such a great night and he didn't want it to end it with Jocelyn's being upset. He'd seen the gate sales and after doing this festival for so many years, he had an idea of about where their revenue would land. And he was sure they'd be short.

Heck, he'd been sure of that before they'd even started. They'd never made that much at a festival, even with adding in all the new things they'd tried this year. But he didn't want to be the one to destroy Jocelyn's spirits.

"That's fine with me," Molly said, stifling a yawn. "I'm too pooped to make any sense of the numbers tonight anyway. Let's all get a good night's sleep, and we'll meet at my house in the morning to find out together."

"Sounds like a plan," Loretta said. "We'll be there. And we'll bring cinnamon rolls and prayers."

"Good," Molly told them. "I'll think we'll need plenty of both."

Chapter Fifteen

THE NEXT MORNING, LORETTA AND Hank arrived at Gram's early, a box of freshly baked cinnamon rolls from the Harmony Creek Bakery in their hands. Jocelyn had just brewed a pot of coffee, and poured a cup for each of them as they exchanged greetings and settled at the table next to her grandmother, who had her foot propped up on a pillow on the chair.

"Smells delicious in here," Mack said when he appeared a few minutes later, the box with the festival's profits in his hands and Savage trotting at his heels. He set the box on the table and picked up a roll. "Thanks," he told Jocelyn, as she set a cup of coffee in front of him.

The tension was evident in the room as Loretta wrung her hands, Mack paced from the living room to the kitchen and back, Hank's leg wouldn't stop shaking against his chair, and Jocelyn raced around trying to make sure everyone had food and that her grandmother was comfortable. Like Jocelyn, they were all eager to find out how the festival had done, but also worried about what would happen if they hadn't made enough.

Gram smacked the table in front of her, making them all jump. "Well, no use putting off the inevitable. Let's get to it." She pointed to the box. "Sort out the sections, Mack, and give us all something to count." They each took a separate portion of the festival proceeds to add up.

Forty minutes later, they stared grimly at each other over the piles of cash and receipts, finally at the moment of truth.

"Before we add up the final numbers," Gram said, putting her hand over the calculator. "I just want to tell you all how much this whole thing means to me. I wouldn't be here without your love, friendship and support, and that means more to me than any piece of property. No matter the results, I know each one of you worked so hard, and we gave it our all."

"We love you too, Gram," Jocelyn told her.

"Okay." Her grandmother inhaled a deep breath and pulled her hand back. She gripped her fingers together, kneading them in her lap as she nodded at Jocelyn. "Let's do it. Add 'em up."

They all passed her the slips of paper with their totals on them. Jocelyn took each one and punched the numbers into the calculator.

A hard knot of disappointment settled in her stomach as she stared down at the total. "With the entrance fees, the dance, the pie auction, the sale of the luminaries and hearts, the vendors, the chili cook-off, *and* the kettle corn sales..." She paused to take a breath. "We made just over twelve thousand dollars."

"Twelve thousand dollars?" Her grandmother stared

at her in shock, her mouth agape. She clapped it shut as she shook her head. "I can't believe it."

"I'm so sorry, Gram."

"Don't be. There's nothing to be sorry for. That's incredible. I didn't think we'd even break ten. Twelve thousand dollars is amazing. That's the most we've *ever* made in one festival weekend. I'm thrilled."

"You might be thrilled," Mack said. "But it's not nearly enough to pay back the bank. We're still shy twelve thousand bucks. And the festival was our best hope to make a bunch of cash. We've only got a week left. We'll never make enough to save the ranch."

Gram lifted her shoulders in a shrug. She put on a brave face, but Jocelyn heard the small quiver in her voice. "Well, we gave it a good go, and I've had a great run here. Maybe it's time I moved into town, anyway. If the bank takes the ranch, I just hope they try to sell it to another investor. It will break my heart if they tear it down and turn it into a shopping mall."

"A shopping mall?" a voice shrieked from behind them.

They all turned to see Mrs. Crandle standing inside the front door. "I was planning to bake some lemon bars and needed my pan back," she said, bustling over and dropping into an empty seat at the table. "What's all this nonsense about losing the ranch?"

"It's not nonsense, I'm afraid," Gram told her. "I owe the bank a lot of money, and it's due next week."

"Yes, I heard. Twelve thousand dollars."

Dang. How long had she been standing there?

She took a cinnamon roll from the box and tore off a bite. "So, what are you going to do next to try to raise it?"

Jocelyn smiled. She loved this woman. She might be a bit of a crabby-pants, but she was all business and didn't waste time on useless words. "We have no idea," Jocelyn told her. "We were hoping the festival would make enough, but we fell way short."

"I understand that. But it sounds like you have a week left. What else can you do to try to make money?"

She liked this woman's attitude. Their time wasn't up yet. They still had options. Jocelyn pushed her shoulders back and lifted her chin. "I was thinking I could visit the bank tomorrow to try to take out a loan."

Mack nodded. "I was thinking the same thing. I can give you a ride."

"Don't you dare," Gram said, leveling a hard stare at both of them. "I will let you work as hard as you want the next week to try to earn the money, but I refuse to let you go into debt personally for me or the ranch. I don't care if you *can* get loans. I won't accept a dime from either one of you if it means you would now owe the bank instead of me." She pointed a thin finger at one then the other. "You hear me? I'm not joking about this. I'll call the bank manager myself if I need to, and tell them not to loan to you."

Jocelyn held up her hands in surrender. "Okay. Okay. We hear you. Although if you really have that kind of clout with the bank manager, why don't you just get him to give you more time on the loan?"

"Believe me, I've tried," Gram muttered.

"We'll table the loan idea," Mack said. "For now. But that brings us back to trying to come up with an idea for another great moneymaker we could pull off this week."

Jocelyn chewed her bottom lip as she stared at the pile of receipts. "What was the most successful part of the festival? And by successful, I mean what made the most money?"

Mack scanned the stack of papers and receipts. "The dance was probably our most profitable. And that's not including the food, drinks, and luminaries and hearts we sold. But we had a pretty cheap band."

An inkling of an idea sparked in Jocelyn's mind. "Soooo...what if we did *another* dance slash concert thing? But made this one bigger and better?"

"Another Plan B and B?" Mack asked.

She grinned. "Exactly."

"That sounds good, but how do you suggest we accomplish it?"

"I'm thinking," Jocelyn said. "I'm trying to imagine some other great events. What makes them so successful?"

"A ton of people combined with a fun activity," Gram said.

"Okay, so what if we did another concert, but had it outdoors, and made it an all-day event?"

"You mean like Woodstock?" Hank asked.

"Yeah. Sort of. That same kind of idea, but it would only be one day. Like all afternoon and into the night, so no camping. We could do it this Saturday and use that big field out behind the barn, so it wouldn't be *on* the ranch and wouldn't take away from the integrity of the living history museum."

Mack tilted his head. "I'm listening. But it seems like a lot of work to do in one week and not a lot of time to advertise to get a good crowd out here."

Jocelyn sat up a little straighter. "That's the power

of social media. We don't need a ton of *time*, just a ton of *people*. And it wouldn't take that much work. We could borrow a big flatbed trailer and pull it out in the field to use as a stage. And maybe some of the vendors would come back. I'll bet we could get some food trucks to come out too. We just need some kind of cool theme and a way to make it sound so fun that no one would dare miss it."

"That sounds perfect," Gram said. "What could we use for a theme?"

"What kind of music would it be?" Loretta asked.

"Probably country. Or maybe bluegrass. Something people could dance to."

"This could work," her grandmother said, leaning back in her chair to look at the ceiling. "Some good country music and a bunch of food. What if we called it Tunes and Takeout? Or maybe Music and Munchies?"

"Country Music and Country Cookin'?" Loretta suggested.

"Guitars and Gravy?" Hank tried.

Jocelyn tapped her finger against her lips. "How about Fiddles and Vittles?"

Mack nodded. "That's pretty good. I like it."

"I love it," Gram said. "You're really good at this stuff, Joss. I can see why you're up for that promotion."

Jocelyn smiled at the praise, but a hard lump settled in her stomach at the thought of going back to New York and leaving these people behind. Especially a certain handsome blacksmith.

"I've got an idea," Mrs. Crandle spoke up. "I think you need to make it a benefit concert. Why not let your neighbors and this community help you? Goodness knows you've helped all of them plenty of times. And they love this ranch as much as you do. Well, maybe not *as* much, but they do love it. And they love you. I know they'd want to help."

Gram folded her arms across her chest. "No. Absolutely not."

"Why not?"

"Because it's embarrassing."

"Oh, please. Wetting your pants is embarrassing. Using six cans of Hormel chili as your cook-off entry is embarrassing. This is nothing. We all understand money troubles. There isn't a one of us that hasn't found ourselves in a pinch at one time or another."

"This is more than a pinch. This is twelve thousand dollars."

"All the more reason to get the community involved," Jocelyn said. "I agree with Mrs. Crandle. Harmony Creek loves a good cause. And what could mean more to this town than rescuing Harmony Ranch?"

They spent the next several hours brainstorming ideas, hashing out the details, and coming up with a concrete plan. They talked through lunch and into the afternoon. In the end, Gram agreed to let the community help, and the Fiddles and Vittles Benefit Concert was born.

Over the next few days, Jocelyn worked tirelessly. She spent hours bent over her laptop or with her phone plastered to her ear, either working on projects due at her job or setting things up for the benefit concert. She'd created a Facebook page and scheduled numerous promotional posts and tweets using the hashtag #RescuingHarmonyRanch.

Mack had taken on the task of finding local talent, and he'd booked several bands to fill slots throughout the afternoon and evening. Most of them knew Gram or had grown up going to the ranch and were glad to help. A few of the bigger bands cut their normal rates in half and most of the smaller ones offered to play for free, figuring they could use the publicity and help Harmony Ranch at the same time.

The mason jar luminaries had been so popular that Jocelyn set up a preorder form and took orders for jars to be used at the concert, then taken home that night. She'd taken several pictures of them the night of the dance and had posted the gorgeous shots on social media. Mack spent hours in the smithy shop creating the candelabra hooks as he tried to keep up with the demand.

Jocelyn's heart was focused on helping her grandmother, but her head kept reminding her of the looming promotion. She was waking up early and staying up late trying to cover the bases of both.

On Wednesday afternoon, she glanced up at the clock and figured it was time for a break. Her hands were cramped from typing, and her eyes burned from staring at a screen. She'd spent the morning and early afternoon working, creating content, and taking virtual meetings. She needed some fresh air and to stretch her legs.

She tugged on her sneakers and stuck her phone in her pocket. "I'm going to get outside, take a walk," she told her grandmother and Loretta, who were playing cards at the kitchen table. "Anything I can get you all before I go?"

"No, we're good," Gram said. "Except maybe could you grab that tin of cookies and bring it over here?"

Jocelyn opened the tin and snuck a chocolate chip cookie before handing it to the women. Gram had her leg up on the chair next to her, and Jocelyn straightened the pillow under her foot. "Anything else?"

"Nope. Have fun on your walk."

Jocelyn started toward the door.

"Except maybe could you could bring the coffee over and give us a little warmer?"

Jocelyn smiled as she brought over the pot and filled the women's cups.

"Where are you headed?" Gram asked, after taking a sip of coffee.

"I don't know. I just thought I'd take a stroll. Explore a bit."

"I think I saw Mack heading to the barn. He said he was going to spend some time with the horses this afternoon," Loretta told her. "Do me a favor—see if you can track him down for me and tell him I'm..." She paused and her eyes shifted to the side as if she were trying to think of something to ask. "Tell him I'm making meatloaf for supper."

"You want me to 'track down' Mack just to give him an update on the dinner menu? That seems like quite the urgent message. I'll make sure to find him right away."

"Well, I, um, yeah." Loretta kept her gaze on the cards in her hand. "It is rather important, because earlier I think I told him we were having chicken."

"What are you now? The message police?" Gram

asked. "Just find Mack and tell him about the meat-loaf, would you?"

Jocelyn raised an eyebrow as she looked from Mack's grandmother to her own. They thought they were sneaky, but she saw right through these two. "Yes. Fine. I'll do it. Meatloaf—not chicken. Got it. I'll guard this imperative message with my life."

Her grandmother playfully swatted her leg as she walked by. "Go for your walk and quit being so sassy."

"I'll be back in a bit. Stay out of trouble while I'm gone."

"No promises."

She smiled as she shoved her arms into an old flannel shirt that was hanging by the door, then waved and made her escape. Wrapping the edges of the shirt around her, she walked down the porch steps and crossed her arms against the slight chill in the air. Springtime in the Rockies—one minute the sun could be shining and people would be walking around in tank tops, and the next minute, it would be cloudy and they'd be pulling on hoodies.

Jocelyn wandered her familiar route down the path to circle the pond. A turtle sunned itself on the edge of the bank, and she caught a glimpse of one of the muskrats darting through the water. She checked on the chickens, the sheep in the corral, and the new baby piglets in the sty before she finally made her way to the barn.

Time to deliver the critical message.

Truth be told, she didn't really mind having an excuse to track down Mack—even if it was a lame and completely obvious excuse.

She poked her head in the barn and spotted him

just inside. A large draft horse was tied to a support-
ing post, and Jocelyn could hear Mack softly humming
to the mare as he dragged a brush over her coat. Not
wanting to spook him or the horse, she called out to
him as she entered the barn. "Hey there."

"Hey," he answered, stopping for a second to greet
her, then turning back to the horse to continue his
brushing. "What are you up to?"

"Just taking a walk, stretching my legs. I've been
at the computer all morning and needed a break. *And*
your grandmother asked me to find you. She had a
message she wanted me to give you. It seemed pretty
important."

Mac paused and turned to face her. "Okay, I'm listening."

"I think you're going to want to find a paper and
pencil so you can jot down some notes. It's a big
change in plans."

His eyes lit with amusement as he grasped her
sarcasm. "I'll take my chances on remembering it. I'm
pretty sharp."

She took a deep exaggerated breath. "Okay, here it
is. Loretta will be making meatloaf instead of chicken
for dinner tonight." She blew out a breath. "Whew."

He shook his head. "Meatloaf, huh?" He patted his
chest where a pocket might be. "Now where did I put
that pen and paper? You're right—that does seem important. Imagine what would've happened if I'd spent
the whole day anticipating roast chicken and then got
blindsided with a meatloaf?"

"Right?"

"I'm surprised she didn't try to find me herself."

"Oh no. It seemed pretty imperative that *I* be the

one to find you and relay this critical info. She and Gram are pretty busy playing cards and drinking all that coffee."

He shook his head, amusement teasing the corners of his mouth. "I think our two grannies are playing at something more than cards."

"Ya think?"

He smiled. "Do *they* think we don't see what they're doing?"

She laughed and put a hand up to stroke the horse's neck. "I don't think they care. And I don't think I necessarily mind either." She fluttered her lashes at him. "Maybe I was glad to have an excuse to come out here to see you."

His eyes sparked with mischief as he gently took her hand in his. "Yeah?"

"Yeah." She pushed up on her toes and pressed her cheek to his. He wrapped his free arm around her, pulling her close, and she lost herself in the feel of him, shutting out the rest of the world.

A long low howl wrenched through the air, startling them *and* the horse.

The mare took a step back and let out a huff as Mack pulled away and put a calming hand on her back. "Whoa there, girl." He turned to Savage, who must have just wandered into the barn, because Jocelyn hadn't seen him before. The hound was sitting next to an empty stable in the far corner. "What are you howlin' about, Savage? Can't you see I'm in the middle of important business here?"

The dog let out another mournful howl and nosed the hay in front of him.

"All right, fine. I'm coming." He put down the brush

he was still holding and lifted his shoulders in an apologetic shrug. "Sorry. I'd better see what he's found. It's probably just a dead mouse, but he won't stop howling 'til I check it out."

"It's fine." She trailed behind him. "I'm curious too. He seems pretty upset."

Mack shook his head. "I'd keep your expectations low. I've seen him get that upset over a feather caught in a tree."

He crouched down. "All right, boy. What'd you find?" The dog trotted to him, and Mack rubbed his hand soothingly over the dog's head, scratching at the folds of his neck. But whatever Savage had found was obviously more significant than getting a neck rub, because the dog ran back to the stable and snuffled his nose into the hay.

They approached the stable together and peered into the shadowy space.

Jocelyn gasped and pressed a hand to her chest, her eyes widening at what Savage had found in the straw.

Chapter Sixteen

J OCELYN CROUCHED TO THE FLOOR of the barn. "Oh no. Poor babies." She reached her hand out to one of the two small scruffy dogs curled together in the hay. One was dark brown and the other more golden. "It's okay, baby," she told the lighter one, who was cautiously sniffing her hand.

Mack reached in and gently picked up the darker brown one. "Hey fella. It's okay." He cradled the animal to his neck, and the dog tipped his head and made a half-hearted attempt to lick his chin.

"I got you, sweetheart." Jocelyn picked up the other one and cuddled it to her. "How did they get here?"

Mack shook his head. "Who knows? Neither of them is wearing a collar."

"We need to get these two some water and find them some food."

"Here. Hold this guy a second." He passed her the dog and hurried back into the barn, where he grabbed a half-empty water bottle from the workbench. Hastening back to her, he crouched down and poured a little water into his cupped hand, then stretched it out to the dogs.

They both whined and wiggled in her arms to get closer to lap the fresh water from Mack's hand. With his other hand, he gave Savage a neck scratch. The basset hound had lain down in the hay, his legs splayed out, as if he were exhausted from the enormous effort it took to lead them to the abandoned dogs. "Good boy, Savage."

He gave the dogs a little more water then nodded toward the mare. "Let me put Delilah away, then we'll take these guys up to my house and get them cleaned up and fed." He led the mare back into her stable and put the lead rope and brush on the workbench. Then Jocelyn and the basset hound followed him back to his house.

It had been a long time since Jocelyn had been in the caretaker's cottage, and back then it had been Hank and Loretta's home. She wasn't sure what to expect, but was pleasantly surprised when Mack let her in the front door.

Loretta's quaint sofa and Hank's old recliner were gone—probably taken to the apartment they'd moved to in the assisted living community. Also gone were the kitschy decorations and rows of knick knacks that used to cover most every available space.

The small cottage had undergone some renovations, like having the wall between the kitchen and the living room knocked out to turn it into an open concept living space. The large stone fireplace was still the focal point of the room, but the old beige shag carpeting had been replaced with hardwood flooring and a plush brown rug in the living area. An intricately forged iron chandelier hung above the counter, forming a peninsula between the two rooms.

This was definitely a man's house, evidenced by the large overstuffed sofa and recliner, the sparse furnishings, and the lack of feminine touches like throw pillows or decorative floral arrangements.

A stack of books sat next to the recliner, and Jocelyn wished for the chance to paw through his reading material, curious what filled his mind when he was alone. Inside the door was a built-in set of oak shelves with a bench, where Jocelyn imagined Mack sat to remove his boots and shoes. A row of boots sat neatly lined up against the bench. Jackets and coats hung from black forged hooks on the wall above the bench.

She touched the side of the shelves. "Did you build these?"

"Yeah. I did a lot of the renovating when my grandparents moved out and I officially took over the house." He gestured around the living area. "If you look, you can see a lot of the iron work is mine. I get an idea for something, and it's pretty easy to build it in the shop."

"You do great work." She glanced around, noticing other touches that must have been his—the hinges on a sliding barn door that housed the pantry, and a heavy iron candelabra resting on the fireplace mantel.

What would happen to Mack's beautiful cottage if they lost the ranch? Her grandmother could move into the same community where Hank and Loretta lived, but Mack would lose everything—not just his livelihood, but his home, too.

They couldn't let that happen.

She started to ask him if he had a contingency

plan, but the dogs squirmed in her arms, and she realized they had more pressing matters to deal with.

Mack had already moved into the kitchen and was opening a can of wet dog food and scooping it onto two paper plates. "Let's get them fed, then we can give them a flea and tick bath and get them cleaned up."

"Good idea." The dogs must have smelled the food because they were wiggling like crazy in her arms, and the brown one was whining and arching his back toward the plates Mack set on the floor. She put the wriggling pups on the floor and they dug into the food.

"I just gave them each a little to start," Mack explained as he pulled items from the cupboard and beneath the sink and set them on the counter. "Let's see how they handle this, then we can give them more."

The dogs finished the food in seconds, licking every morsel from the plates. Mack picked them both up and nodded to the things he'd just set out. "Grab that stuff, would ya? We can give them a bath while we let that first bit of food settle."

Jocelyn picked up a jar of peanut butter, a spatula, and a bottle of flea and tick shampoo and followed Mack into the bathroom. "I don't get it. What's the peanut butter for?"

"You'll see," he said. "It's a trick I've learned with Savage. He used to hate baths, and now he loves them. And Bassets are known for their fragrant scent, so he needs washing up quite often."

Savage had followed them into the bathroom to check on what was going on. Jocelyn had noticed the dog did at times smell a little pungent, but she'd thought it would be rude to mention it.

Mack turned on the warm water, then gingerly set

the dogs in the tub. "Give me a scoop of that peanut butter, please."

"Oh-kay," she said, still confused. She scraped a portion of the peanut butter onto the spatula and passed it to him. She was even more confused when he spread a big chunk of it onto the side of the bathtub.

The method to his madness became clear a second later when both dogs started licking at it. "They'll be so focused on that peanut butter, they won't even care that we're giving them a bath."

"Ahh. Smart."

"But we don't have long, so roll up your sleeves and wash one of them, would ya?" He squirted a line of shampoo over each of their backs. "Just massage that shampoo into all her fur and really rub it in. Make sure you get her belly and her ears and in between the pads of her feet."

Jocelyn knelt beside Mack and set to giving the beige dog a thorough washing. The shampoo lathered in her hands, but she was still gentle.

Savage moaned and cried and planted his feet on the edge of the tub. "That's so cute how he wants to see these little dogs," Jocelyn said.

Mack scoffed. "He doesn't want to see the pups, he wants that peanut butter. That dog will eat anything at any time. I once dropped a twenty dollar bill out of my pocket, and Savage grabbed that thing and gulped it down before I even had a second to stop him."

"A twenty? That dog has expensive tastes."

"You're funny."

She grinned as she put her focus back on the dog, trying to ignore the heavy pressure of Savage leaning against her side as he continued to whine. The shower had a sprayer attachment, and Mack washed the shampoo from the coats of both dogs. As much as she was concentrating on the animals, Jocelyn was still hyper-aware of Mack's solid shoulder pressed into hers and the warm pressure of his hand every time it brushed hers.

"I think we got it," Mack said. "Can you grab one of those towels?" He nodded his head toward a gray towel hanging from the rack next to the tub.

Jocelyn reached for a towel and must have bent her body just enough to give Savage the break he'd been hoping for. He gave a loud bark as he scrambled over the side of the tub. Water splashed everywhere, dousing both Jocelyn and Mack as the dog's body hit the water in a less than graceful belly flop. He fell in front of the sprayer, redirecting the water directly toward Jocelyn.

She shrieked as she leaned back, slapping the water with her hands. Mack shot forward, jerking the faucets to turn the spray off.

The two dogs leapt out of the way as Savage tackled the side of the tub, licking his huge pink tongue over what was left of the peanut butter.

"Dang dog," Mack said, then turned to her. The concern on his face changed to amusement, and he pressed his lips together to keep from laughing.

"Don't you dare laugh," she said, lifting her sopping bangs from her face and flipping them back over her head. She'd taken the brunt of the water and was soaked to the skin. She pulled her wet shirt away from her body. "I think I'm going to need to borrow a shirt."

Having licked the bathtub wall clean, Savage plunked his bottom down and the smaller dogs clambered over his larger body. They each stopped to shake the water from their coats, sending more droplets through the air.

Jocelyn sputtered and held her hands up to defend herself from the fresh onslaught of spray. "Oh, come on," she said, then had to laugh at the hilarity of the situation.

Savage leaned his head toward her, offering her a sad-eyed apology. She scrubbed a hand over his wet head. "I know, boy. It's hard to resist when it comes to peanut butter."

An hour later, Mack and Jocelyn made their way back to Gram's house. Jocelyn's jeans were still damp, but she wore Mack's dry Harmony Creek High Football t-shirt. Her arms were full of two sleeping puppies.

They stopped on the front porch as they heard a raised voice coming through the screen door.

"I just don't know why all those cars think it's okay to park in front of my house," Mrs. Crandle's annoyed voice stated. "And someone dropped their trash in my yard last week."

Jocelyn pushed through the door, hoping to save her grandmother from having to reply to Mrs. Crandle's complaints. "We're back. And we brought some new friends." The little dogs woke up at the sound of voices and squirmed in her arms. She set them on the floor to explore.

"What's this?" Gram asked, leaning her hand down to beckon the dogs. "Where did these little guys come from?"

"We're not sure," Mack said, crossing to give his grandmother a hug. "We found them in the barn."

Mrs. Crandle sat on one corner of the sofa. She tried to hold her chin aloft, but snuck a glance at the dog batting at the shoelace of her orthopedic shoe.

"Come here, you little rascal," Jocelyn said, scooping the dog up and holding it in her lap as she dropped onto the other end of the sofa. "You leave Mrs. Crandle alone."

The dog ignored Jocelyn's reprimand and trotted across the cushion. He nosed Mrs. Crandle's arm up, then wiggled underneath it and into her lap.

"Oh goodness," she said, her expression softening as the dog curled up and rested his head on her other arm. He let out a contented sigh and closed his eyes.

"Looks like you've made a friend," Jocelyn told her.

"I hope he doesn't shed. I just washed these slacks," the other woman said. Her tone was cross, but the tender look on her face as she gently rested a hand on the dog's back told a different story.

The other dog was standing on Gram's lap, doing her best to lick every inch of the woman's neck. Her little tail spun in a happy circle, wagging a hundred miles an hour. "What are you going to do with them?"

Jocelyn shrugged. "We don't know. For now, we gave them some food and a bath." She glanced down at herself. "I got a bit of a bath in the process too. Which is why I had to borrow a shirt from Mack." She gestured to the dogs. "They're both really sweet and adorable. I'm sure they'd make great pets. We figured we'd take them over to the shelter and hope they get adopted."

Mrs. Crandle pursed her lips. "Or you could keep

them here until you find them a suitable home." She glanced down at the little dog sleeping contentedly in her lap. "They don't seem like much trouble. Maybe I could take this one. You know, just for a little while, just until you find a home for it."

"Oh would you? That would be great. But are you sure it won't be too much trouble?"

Mrs. Crandle sniffed as if she'd been insulted. "I think I can handle one little dog." She cradled the dog against her chest as she pushed up from the sofa. "I'll just take him over to the house now and get him settled in. I'll call you later to let you know how he's doing." She was out the door before Jocelyn could even think to argue.

"I think that dog just found a home," Jocelyn said, grinning at Mack and her grandma.

Mack chuckled. "I've never seen that woman move so fast in all the years I've known her."

Gram cuddled the other dog to her chest. "Now what are we going to do with this one?"

By Thursday, they felt like they had done all they could do ahead of time for the upcoming concert. Hank had mowed the field, and he and Mack had set up an extra parking area. They had food vendors scheduled and a local cider brewery had created a special cider for the event.

Gram and Loretta had made some calls to see if anyone had heard about two lost dogs, and they had put up some posters, but no one knew where they'd come from or who they'd belonged to.

The little dog at Gram's house seemed to have already decided she belonged there. She'd spent the day either trailing after Jocelyn or cuddling up in Gram's lap—which had the added benefit of making Gram stay put on the sofa.

Jocelyn peered down at the sleeping pup stretched out between her leg and the inside arm of the recliner. The little sneak had crawled up there some time ago and fallen asleep while Jocelyn worked. The dog's small scruffy head rested contentedly on Jocelyn's knee. She was so cute. It was easy to fall in love with her.

But Jocelyn couldn't let herself submit to that particular emotion. Not with the dog...or the handsome blacksmith who had been taking up too many of her thoughts today.

She wasn't staying. She couldn't. Could she? No matter how tempting her feelings for the endearing dog, and the hunky man, she had a life, a job, in New York. And not just a job, a career. A livelihood she'd spent years cultivating. Could she give that all up to pursue this *thing* with Mack?

She didn't even know what this thing was. Were they rekindling an old flame or just having fun together while she was home? Mack had hinted at their relationship, even shared a few of his feelings, but he was a man of few words and it wasn't always clear what he was thinking. And she wasn't sure she wanted to ask, since she didn't know what she wanted herself.

This felt like a big deal. It must be, if she was even considering giving up New York and all that she'd worked for to try to pursue something with him.

Back up, sister. Where had that thought come from? *Giving up New York?* Until the last few days, she wouldn't have even considered the notion. But now, things felt different.

Mack was the only man she'd ever loved. And he'd been the yardstick she'd held up to every other mand she'd tried to date. And she'd found them all lacking.

When she'd returned to Harmony Ranch, she hadn't planned on even seeing Mack, but she couldn't deny those feelings were still there. Didn't she owe it to herself? To him? To see if they had a chance at something?

Stop it. Talk about putting the cart before the horse.

She wasn't even sure that Mack was interested in getting back together with her. Sure, they'd danced, and hugged, and he'd held her hand. But that didn't mean he still had feelings for her or wanted a future together. Although there had been feeling in those hugs, in the way he held her in his arms.

Jocelyn sighed and closed her laptop. It was late and time to turn her brain off. She glanced at the clock and was surprised to see it was almost nine. Her grandmother had gone to bed awhile ago, but she'd been so engrossed in the latest thing she'd been working on for the coffee shop that she'd lost track of time. She'd turned in the final proposal earlier that afternoon, then tonight had thought of another cute idea. This was the part she loved, and she was really having fun with the new marketing concepts she'd come up with for them.

Hmmm. A job she loved doing, and a company she loved working for—that didn't feel like something she was considering giving up.

A knock sounded at the front door, and she gave a little jolt, startling the dog. Jocelyn pushed out of the chair and the dog stretched, then hopped down to follow at her heels. She rubbed her sore neck as she pulled open the door.

Mack was standing on her porch, and Savage was sitting by his feet. Speak of the gorgeous bearded devil. "Hey. What are you doing here?"

"Delivering this," he said, carrying a flat square box into the kitchen and setting it on the counter.

"What is it?" Her curiosity piqued, she tried to look over his shoulder as she followed behind him. The little dog ran around Savage's sturdy body, her tail furiously wagging with excitement.

"I don't know. It's probably dumb," he said, looking suddenly shy as he shoved his hands in his front pockets. "We just spent all that time working on those pies for the auction and never got to eat any. And you've been working so hard on the concert this week, I thought you deserved a treat."

Jocelyn's lips curved into a smile as she peered into the box. "You bought me a pie?"

"No. I *made* you a pie."

"You *made* this?" She stared at the round dessert, marveling at the perfectly piped whipped cream that formed a lattice pattern and the curls of chocolate shavings sprinkled over the top.

"I did. And it's not just *any* pie. It's peanut butter."

"You're kidding." She breathed in the heavenly scents of peanut butter and chocolate. "Like the kind Gram used to make us when we were kids?"

"Exactly the same kind. I used her recipe."

Her gaze bounced from him to the pie, then back to him again. "I can't believe you did this. For me. It's so nice." She swiped her finger through a dollop of whipped cream and pie filling then licked it off and let out a groan. "Oh my gosh. And it's so good."

She took another big swipe, then held her finger out to Mack. He started to lean forward, then she let out a laugh as she twisted her hand and smeared it across his mouth and chin.

He grinned as he licked it from his lips. "You're right. It is good. Makes me hope you'll invite me to stay and have a piece."

She grinned back as she teased him. "I don't know. It's pretty good pie. But I guess I could share one piece. Since you made it and all."

He swiped at the pie filling on his chin. "How do you feel about letting me eat this piece with a fork?"

"A fork? I suppose next you're going to want a plate, too?"

He shrugged. "I've been known to eat a piece of pie out of my hand."

She laughed as she dug through the drawer for a pie cutter. Setting it on the counter, she turned back to Mack and rested a hand on his forearm. "Thank you." Her tone softened as she gazed into his gorgeous blue eyes. "For the pie. For trying to help my grandmother. For everything."

He held her gaze, his voice dropping to a husky whisper. "I would do anything for you."

She sucked in a sharp inhale at the intensity of his words.

"And for this place," he said, dropping his gaze. "It means a lot to me."

"Me too," she whispered. But what she wanted to say was, *You mean a lot to me too,* but the words stuck in her throat.

The smaller dog had given chase to Savage, racing around Mack and Jocelyn's legs in an attempt to get the bigger dog to chase her. The basset hound lumbered forward then tripped on his long droopy ear, and he crashed into the side of their legs.

Mack took a step back, then crouched down to run a hand over Savage's back. "You all right, pal?" The basset issued him a sad look, but tipped his head up to lick the remnants of whipped cream drying on his chin. Mack smiled up at Jocelyn. "He seems to be fine."

She got plates and forks out and served them each a slice of pie. Carrying their plates to the table, Jocelyn moved the printouts of some of the artwork and graphics she'd been working on.

Mack slid into the chair next to her and picked up one of the pages. "What's this?"

"One of the graphics for the new marketing campaign for the coffee shop I told you about."

"This is good. I like how the froth in the cup creates two hearts. I don't think anyone down at Harmony Perk knows how to make something like this."

"Some of the baristas in the city take their froth art pretty seriously." She tilted her head to study the picture. "I feel like this is good, though—maybe the best work I've ever done. There's something about being here that's opened up my creativity. The inspiration for this whole ad came to me as I wandered around the ranch the other morning. The entire campaign is based on their coffee tasting like home in a cup."

"I like it."

"I hope they do too. This is the account that my promotion hinges on. I've been working on this stuff for a month now, picking colors and making graphics and really branding the whole thing together. I turned in the preliminary package today, and I'm nervous, but I think they're going to love it. And I hope it shows my boss that I'm the best choice for the new position."

"Your face lights up when you talk about this stuff."

"I love it."

"I see that. I guess I thought that with everything that's happened, you were considering..." His voice trailed off.

"Considering what?"

"Nothing. Never mind." He shook his head. "I guess I just didn't realize the promotion meant that much to you."

"It means everything to me."

His brow furrowed, and he pushed his chair away from the table and stood. "It's getting late. I should probably go."

"Go? But you haven't even finished your pie."

"I guess I'm not that hungry." He whistled for the dog, and Savage trotted out the door in front of him. "I'll talk to you tomorrow," he said, pulling the door shut behind him.

Jocelyn slumped back in her chair. *What the heck just happened?*

Did he want her to stay here?

Only one way to find out. She pushed away from the table and hurried after him.

Chapter Seventeen

J OCELYN CAUGHT UP TO MACK as he was stomping up the steps of his cottage. Was he mad at *her*? What was going on?

"Hey," she called out, stopping him in his tracks. "I feel like something just happened there, but I'm not sure what it was."

"I don't know what you're talking about."

"Yes, you do. One minute we're sharing peanut butter pie and joking around, and the next, you're running out the door like the house is on fire."

He turned as he reached the landing of the porch. Crossing his arms over his chest, he leaned against one of the posts as he regarded her. "That's a funny way to put it—joking around. I guess I just realized that's all this is to you."

She jerked back. *Joking around*? How could he think that? Their relationship—or whatever they were doing—was no laughing matter to her. "I certainly don't think of the time we've been spending together as a joke. But as far as what we're actually doing, I honestly don't know what to think. It's not like you're really good at sharing your feelings."

"What do you want me to say? You know I'm a man of few words. But my actions should have spoken volumes to you. I thought we really had something here."

He thought they had something? Her throat tightened, and she found it hard to speak. Her voice came out husky, raw. "We do. I mean, I think so too."

"Just not enough for you to consider sticking around to figure out what it is."

Come on. Now he was just trying to make her mad. She planted a hand on her hip. "I didn't even know you *wanted* me to stay."

He scrubbed a hand through his hair and let out a sigh. "Of course I want you to stay."

"You never said so."

"I shouldn't have to," he stated, his tone bordering between anger and frustration. "Couldn't you tell by the way I held you? By the way I hugged you as if I might not ever see you again?" His eyebrows were drawn together as he strode down the porch steps two at a time, then wrapped his arm around her waist. Pulling her to him, he pressed his lips to hers and kissed her hard. And thoroughly.

He pulled back, his breath ragged as he leaned his forehead against hers. "Now do you know how I feel?"

She knew how *she* felt—dazed, breathless, and suddenly very warm. His emotions had come through in the intensity of the kiss, but she still wanted to hear him say it. "Yes, but..."

"No. No buts. I care about you. I always have. You were the first—and the last—girl I ever fell in love with. I thought I'd buried all those old feelings, put my past with you away. But then you came back, with your fancy clothes and city-girl attitude, and you were more beautiful than I'd even remembered." He reached to brush his fingers over her cheek, his gaze intense as he studied her face. "You were different, and I was sure you'd changed. But then you smiled, and it was like the sun came out on a cloudy day. And then you started teasing me about my beard and you climbed in my truck and let my stupid mutt drool on your leg, and I knew you hadn't really changed."

She reached up and lightly touched the side of his face. "You do have a pretty great beard."

He put his hand over hers and held it to his cheek. "Joss, I thought I was over you. Then you came home and every day that I've spent with you has me falling back in love with you again."

She swallowed.

"Is that plain enough for you?" He repeated the words. "I'm falling in love with you again. And I want you to stay and give us a chance to see where this thing goes." He let go of her hand and raked his fingers through his hair. "But I saw your face tonight when you were talking about your job. You've worked hard and put a lot into getting this promotion. I can't ask you to give all that up."

Isn't that what she'd been wanting him to do? Ask her to stay with him and give "them" a chance? But now that he had, panic was constricting her chest.

Could she really give up everything? For the guy who had shattered her heart into a million pieces the last time she'd trusted him with it?

She ran her fingers along his jaw. "I'm falling in love with you again, too. This last week I've been happier than I have been in years. I didn't realize what I was missing until I was with you again. But this is a big decision. I need some time to think."

He pulled away, and she immediately missed the warmth of his arms. She crossed her arms around her middle to fight off the sudden chill. Is this what going back to New York would feel like? Like all the warmth had suddenly left her body?

"Take all the time you need," Mack said. "I'll be here. I know what I want, and I'm not going anywhere."

She watched him walk back up the steps and go inside the cottage before she turned and headed back to Gram's house. Still holding her stomach, she walked slowly, as if trying to hold up the enormous weight of this situation on her shoulders.

Could she really uproot that life and move to Colorado? Where would she even live? Would she move in with her grandmother? Sure, that seemed like a *great* idea—then her and Mack's relationship could be on display and under the microscope of their matchmaking grannies.

And would there even be a place to move in to? Mack claimed he wasn't going anywhere, but that choice might not be his. If they couldn't save the ranch, then they'd *all* be out of a place to live. What would happen then?

She went back inside and locked the door. There were so many factors in this equation. But the most important one was rescuing Harmony Ranch and keeping the livelihoods of Mack and her grandmother secure.

The little dog jumped off the sofa and circled her legs. Jocelyn reached down and scooped her up. The dog licked her cheek, then nuzzled into her neck. She was so sweet. But the dog was one more problem Jocelyn wasn't sure how to solve. She couldn't keep her, and she wasn't sure Gram could handle taking on a dog along with all the other stuff she was dealing with, like a fractured leg and dire financial problems.

Her phone's ringtone interrupted her thoughts, and she spied it on the table. She'd been in such a rush to follow Mack, she must have left it behind. She grabbed it and peered at the name on the screen. Why was her boss calling so late?

She answered it. "Hello."

"I'm so glad I caught you." Andrea's words came out in a breathy rush, as if she'd literally been running after her.

"What's wrong?"

"Nothing's wrong. Everything is wonderful. I took a call from Midtown Perk earlier, and they loved the campaign proposal. Like *loved* it. So much that they want to meet you. Tomorrow."

"*Tomorrow*?"

Jocelyn did the panicked calculations in her head. There was no way she could get a flight back to New York tonight.

"Yes. Tomorrow. Why? Did you have other urgent plans for the day?"

"No." Nope. No plans—just a huge benefit concert event and a plot to save her grandmother's legacy. Other than that, she was totally free. "But I'm not sure how fast I can make it back to New York."

"You don't have to. When I told them you were visiting family in Colorado, they said that was perfect. They're looking to expand into Denver, so they flew there today. They're scouting a couple of locations for new stores tomorrow. They want to set up a lunch meeting, and then have you go with them to tour the facilities. They want you to take some "before" photos to maybe use in the social media blitz you've prepared."

"Wait." Jocelyn's mind was swirling. "Does that mean I got the account?"

"Fingers crossed. But it's looking that way."

Jocelyn did a quick wiggly dance. The dog raced around her legs. Jocelyn bent down, ruffled the pup's neck, and tried to calm her pounding heart. Because she still had one more question to ask. "And the promotion?"

"If all goes well tomorrow and they agree to sign with us, the promotion is yours. As you know, it comes with a title, your own office, and a pay raise. Plus you'll get a fifteen thousand dollar signing bonus on the spot. Now remember, it's pretax money, so after Uncle Sam takes his cut, you'll probably only end up with ten or twelve thousand."

Ten or twelve thousand dollars?

Exactly the amount needed to save her grandmother's beloved ranch and living history museum. And Mack's job.

Mack.

Taking the job would mean staying in New York—not coming back to Colorado. To him. They still had the benefit concert, but...how likely was it that they would really clear ten thousand dollars?

Taking the promotion would mean she'd have the money to save her grandmother, no matter what happened with the concert.

"Joss? Hello? You still there?" her boss asked.

"Yes, I'm here. Sorry." She clutched the phone in her hand.

"Okay, so can you get yourself to Denver tomorrow to meet the clients?"

Jocelyn chewed the loose cuticle of her thumbnail as she considered her options. "I'm a few hours from Denver. I'd have to rent a car."

"That's fine. You can expense it. We want you to take the clients out for dinner and drinks—really wine and dine them. At the end of the night, I don't want them to be able to imagine *not* working with us. Got it?"

"Got it."

Even though she was standing in her grandmother's kitchen with the shadow of the mountains just visible through the window, she suddenly felt like she was back on New York time—talking fast, making deals, scheduling travel and discussing clients and proposals.

This was it, the real deal—her ticket to the future career she'd spent years trying to obtain. Pulling this off would take careful thought, planning and real effort. She couldn't just toss some salt and pepper into a few cans of Hormel chili and call it done. She had to show up with the real goods—beef, beans, and some sweet and sassy chili powder.

"I'll email you the contract and the schedule for tomorrow," Andrea said. "Print out the contract and get it signed and back to me."

"That will be a bit of a problem. I'm at my grandma's, and she doesn't have a printer. Well, not one that works. But she has a fax machine."

"A fax machine? Where are you? The Nineties?"

A nervous laugh bubbled out of Jocelyn. "I know. But it's the best I've got. I'll text you the number."

"Fine. Now go get ready for tomorrow."

"You can count on me," Jocelyn told her boss. "I've got this."

She hung up and did another dance in the kitchen. She'd done it. Well, she'd *almost* done it. The promotion was within her reach. And the signing bonus was the answer to their prayers.

Jocelyn could literally save the day. She wasn't doing this just for herself. She was doing it to rescue her grandmother as well. Of course, Gram would never accept the money from her outright, so she'd have to figure out a way to wire it directly to the bank loan. Or maybe she could make an anonymous donation. Gram would never have to know.

She couldn't believe the bonus was the exact amount they were lacking. There was no way this was a coincidence—it was meant to be.

Except she'd thought she and Mack were meant to be. What would this mean for them? Would Mack consent to a long-distance relationship? She groaned. They'd tried that before, and it had ended in disaster. Would her taking the job mean she'd have to give up Mack? Should she just break things off now before things went any further?

That felt like closing the barn door after the horse escaped. Not a half an hour before, they'd admitted that they were falling back in love with each other. Things had gone pretty dang far. But maybe this was a sign that they *weren't* meant to be.

She slumped into the chair, ignoring the dog's attempts to get her to throw a stuffed animal, as all the obstacles ahead of her surfaced. How was she going to tell her grandmother that she was leaving tomorrow? And that she would most likely miss the benefit concert?

She'd just have to make it clear that it was part of her job, and it couldn't be helped.

But how was she going to explain it to Mack?

The next morning, Jocelyn was up early. The little dog had slept in her bed, curled up next to her shoulder. Another part of her heart she was going to have to leave behind.

She'd gone to pack her things the night before and been shocked to find that the handle of her suitcase had been repaired. There was a new line of stitching, and a small iron loop had been forged to replace the clasp that had broken.

At the sight of it, her legs had almost given way, and she'd slumped onto the bed. Mack had done this. For her. And never said anything about it.

That was the kind of man he was, quietly taking care of things and never asking for any of the credit.

What was she doing? Was she making the right decision to leave?

She'd wanted to text him to thank him for fixing the handle. But if she did, he'd wonder why she was packing, and she hadn't been ready to tell him yet. She needed more time to think, to process, to come up with a way to make him understand.

By morning, she still hadn't quite figured out what she was going to say. But the clock was ticking and the rental car would be here within the hour, so there was no time to waste. She needed to talk to both Mack and Gram now.

When she'd packed her stuff, she'd left out her favorite power outfit—the one that made her feel confident and like she could tackle anything. Dressed in a slim black pencil skirt, a white designer blouse, and her high-heeled leather boots, she felt like she was ready to face her new client.

But no outfit would give her the courage to face her grandmother.

Gram was standing in the kitchen, her knee resting on the scooter, as she poured a cup of coffee. The little dog was sitting next to her, nose tipped up as if she were waiting for a crumb to fall.

Her grandmother's face broke into a grin as she caught sight of Jocelyn. "Mornin', honey." Her smile fell as she saw the suitcase. "What's going on? Are you leaving?"

The little dog ran over to her, and Jocelyn crouched to scratch her chin. In the short time since they'd found the dogs, Jocelyn had already fallen for this adorable little mutt. She was afraid if she picked her up, she'd be tempted to stick her in her tote bag and bring her along.

With a sinking heart, she stood back up. She couldn't take the dog. And she wouldn't be here to work on finding her a new home—another loose end she was leaving her grandmother with. "I'm so sorry. I got a call from my boss last night."

"About the promotion?"

Jocelyn nodded and filled her in.

Gram sagged against the counter. "Well, I'm happy for you, of course. But I can't say I'm not disappointed that you're leaving so soon. What about the concert? Do you think you can come back for it?"

"It'll depend on what happens with the clients. I'm going to try, but if they need me to start immediately, I may have to fly home from Denver."

"I understand."

"I'm really sorry, Gram. I feel like I'm deserting you." She wished she could tell her that the biggest reason she was taking the job right now was to get the bonus to save the ranch. But she knew her grandmother's pride wouldn't let her accept it outright. "Mack and I have done everything we can for the concert, except the final stages of setup, which he would be in charge of anyway."

Her grandmother grimaced. "Have you told Mack yet?"

A familiar man's voice spoke from the doorway behind Jocelyn, "Told me what?"

Chapter Eighteen

J OCELYN INHALED A DEEP BREATH, then pushed back her shoulders as she turned to face him. Dang these small towns and their policy of just walking into each other's houses. "I was on my way over to talk to you."

His eyebrows drew together as he glanced down at the suitcase then back up at her. "Looks to me like the time for talking has already passed."

"Now Mack, give her a chance to explain," Gram said as she scooted herself out of the kitchen and toward her granddaughter. She held out her arms and folded Jocelyn into a warm embrace. "I love you, sweetheart. I appreciate you flying back to help me. I'm always here for you." Her eyes were wet with tears as she pulled back and laid a weathered hand on Jocelyn's cheek. "You always have a home here. And you're welcome to come back. Anytime."

Home. Jocelyn wasn't even sure where that was for her anymore. Was it the closet she called a bedroom in her cramped New York apartment? Or was it in the arms of the blacksmith in the mountains of Colorado?

When she thought of it like that, the answer seemed easy. Except none of this was easy, because taking the job meant she'd be able to save the home of that black-smith *and* her grandmother.

Jocelyn leaned in and gave her grandmother another squeeze. "I know. Thanks Gram. I'll call you when I get there."

Gram nodded, then called the dog to follow her as she scooted down the hall and into her bedroom. She pushed the door shut behind her.

The sound of the wood hitting the frame felt like a door was also closing in Jocelyn's heart. She prayed she could explain this to Mack, to convince him to try another long-distance relationship, but she knew she had to put her grandmother first. Gram had always been there for Jocelyn. And now Jocelyn needed to be there for her, too.

She gripped the handle of her suitcase, more to have something to hold onto, to anchor her than anything else. "I'm sorry, Mack."

"That's an auspicious start. Sorry for what? For trying to sneak out of here without even telling me? Without even saying goodbye?" His tone was angry, but Jocelyn heard the hurt in it, like the water of a stream rushing just under a layer of winter ice.

"I told you I was coming over to talk to you."

"So you said." He crossed his arms over his chest, his body signaling to her that he was already closing off from her.

"Let me explain."

"I'm listening. Just like I was listening last night when you told me you wanted to make a go of this thing between us. I guess I didn't understand what you meant by the term 'go'." He gestured to his suitcase. "I get it now though."

"No. You don't. I meant everything I said last night."

"It sure doesn't look that way to me."

"Look, this all happened really fast. After we talked last night, I got a call from my boss. The clients—the ones with the coffee shop—they loved the campaign proposal I sent. They're expanding into Colorado so they flew into Denver yesterday, and they want to meet with me. My boss said the promotion was mine for the taking if this meeting goes well."

His expression stayed hard, his jaw set. "Sounds like you're getting everything you want."

Not everything.

"I want *you*, Mack."

"You got a funny way of showing it."

"I know. I'm sorry. This isn't how I wanted this to go. I wanted us to have more time to talk about it."

"Then why didn't you call me last night? If you were so excited, it seems like I'd be the person you wanted to share your good news with. But I didn't hear my phone ring, and I don't seem to have any missed calls."

"I couldn't call you last night. I was still process-ing everything—not just us, but the promotion and the clients. I'm meeting them in a few hours and needed to prepare."

He jerked back as if she'd slapped him. "So, pre-paring for the *clients* was more important than calling *me*?" His frustration radiated through his tone—he'd practically spat out the word *clients*.

"No, I didn't mean that. There's more to all this. They offered me the promotion *and* a signing bonus, and you know we need that money." She had to make him understand she was doing this not just for her, but for her grandmother and for him too.

But he wasn't listening. He was pacing back and forth in the living room, shaking his head as his fists opened and closed. He scrubbed a hand over his jaw. "I don't get it. Last night, you acted like you wanted to give us a chance—a real chance. You said you were falling... Never mind. It doesn't matter."

"It *does* matter. *You* matter."

"I don't believe you. Last night, you practically begged me to ask you to stay. Which I did, by the way. And if that's what you need, I'll ask you again. Stay. Give us a chance."

She swallowed as she looked from her suitcase to him. "I can't."

He yanked open the front door. "That's what I thought. This is just like before. We made plans for a future together, then you leave and I never hear from you again."

"No, Mack. I swear this isn't like before."

"Oh? Are you coming back this time?"

"I don't know."

"Well, at least you're not making a bunch of empty promises like you did before." He let out a shuddering breath. "I can't go through this again. Losing you the first time almost broke me. And had me making decisions that I still regret."

"This isn't like last time. I promise."

He blew out a harsh laugh.

"Okay, maybe you don't want to hear my promise." She wanted to tell him he'd broken promises too. But he was the one staying here, and she was the one leaving. "I have no idea what will happen. But I know I want to try. And I think we can make this work. I can fly back for weekends, and you can come to New York."

"And what? Stay with you in your closet apartment?"

"I haven't figured it all out yet. But I don't want to lose you again. Just because I'm taking the promotion doesn't mean I'm choosing my job over you."

"Doesn't it?" He glanced down at her bag. "It seems to me like you already made your choice. And long-distance relationships don't seem to end well for us."

"Please, Mack—"

He held up his hand to stop whatever she was about to say. "I can't. I've got to go." He pushed through the screen door and let it slam behind him.

She winced at the bang, then ran to the door. "I'll call you later, and we can talk some more. You're not even listening to what I'm telling you. There's more to this whole thing—more I need to explain."

"Don't bother," he called over his shoulder, not even turning around as he stomped away. "You've said everything I need to hear."

Mack made it around the corner and out of Jocelyn's sight before he stopped and bent forward, planting his hands on his knees. He felt nauseated, and he swallowed at the bile rising in his throat.

How could he have let her do this to him again?

She'd all but destroyed him when she'd left before.

But she'd finally come back. Jocelyn had been here on the ranch, in *their* place. She'd flirted with him and joked around and challenged him, just like she used to. They'd danced to their song, and she'd kissed him with such passion and desire. He let himself believe they had a chance again.

He'd kept his guard up, even after they'd hugged the first time, trying to keep things light with jokes and banter. But then they'd hugged again. And again. Each time breaking down another wall of his defenses.

Then last night, she'd taken a sledgehammer to that wall when she'd said she was falling in love with him again.

How had he forgotten that this is what love in his life felt like? For him, love was about loss and leaving and having women walk away. First his mom, then Jocelyn. Even Ashley, who he hadn't even given his whole heart to—how could he? It still belonged to Joss. But Ashley had left him too.

Why had he let himself believe that this time would be any different? That this time Jocelyn would stay?

There was always something more important than him. Not one woman had ever just put him first.

Anger and hurt and sadness churned in his stomach then made its way up to compress his chest like a vise tightening around his heart. He bit back the howl of rage he wanted to scream, and instead drove his fist into the side of the house.

***

Jocelyn's hands were shaking as she poured a glass of water and took a sip. The cool liquid soothed her parched throat, but did nothing to ease the pain in her chest.

She hung her head, her earlier confidence gone. She'd completely botched that with Mack. Why hadn't she called him last night? Or better yet, gone back over to his place and told him about the offer and the sign-ing bonus? Then he might have understood and they could have come up with a plan—together.

Her misery was a mix of sadness and frustration. She'd tried to tell him about the bonus. She wanted him to understand that she *had* to take this promo-tion—for all of them. But he was so angry—and hurt—it was like he wasn't even hearing anything she'd said.

What should she do? She wanted to forget the meeting and go after him, but that wasn't an option. Should she call him in the car on the way to Denver? Or give him more time to cool off? She wished she had someone to give her the answers.

She didn't have any close friends to vent to. She had friends, sure—she'd occasionally go for drinks with a couple of coworkers, and she had some casual acquaintances. She could drink a little wine or go to a movie with her roommates, but she had no one who really understood her, in whom she could confide and share that bond of a true deep authentic friendship. No one, except her grandmother.

Gram had always been the closest thing she had to a best friend. It had been especially tough to start a new school in her teens—friends were already chosen and it was hard to break into those tight-knit groups. But her grandmother had always been there for her. She'd even bought an iPhone so they could text and FaceTime each other.

Gram was a great listener and could always coax a smile or a laugh out of Jocelyn when she was feeling down.

But she couldn't talk to Gram about this. Because she knew she would tell her to forget the promotion and the signing bonus and to follow her heart. But her grandmother had also instilled a work ethic in Jocelyn that wouldn't let her just blow off the clients and go after Mack. She'd made a commitment, and she needed to see it through.

Didn't she?

A knock sounded on the door, and her pulse raced with hope that Mack had come back.

No such luck.

The door eased open, and Sophie poked her head inside. "Hey, there's a rental car out here waiting for you, Jocelyn. I guess they really do pick you up."

Dang. How could they be here already? She glanced up at the clock. Right on time. "Thanks Sophie. I'll be right there."

She ran down the hall and peered into Gram's office. She'd checked for the fax with the offer on it the night before and earlier that morning, but nothing had come through. The tray was still empty. Oh well, she'd just have to get the information on her phone.

Grabbing her tote bag, she hauled it over her shoulder, then pulled the suitcase behind her as she pushed past Sophie.

Sophie took a step back and held the door open, but her brows knit together in concern. "Are you leaving? What about the concert? Where are you going?"

"I'm going to Denver to meet a client. You all are going to have to handle the concert without me. Despite what everyone thinks, I still have a job, and the promotion I've been working toward hinges on this meeting going well." Her answer was snippy, which Sophie didn't deserve. She hadn't done anything other than be kind to Jocelyn.

"Are you coming back? After the meeting?"

She shook her head. "I don't think so." It felt like Mack had made it clear that he didn't care if she came back. And Gram didn't really need her anymore—she had Midge and seemed to be scooting around just fine.

"But what about Mack? Does he know you're leaving? I thought you two were getting back together."

"I thought so too, but it doesn't look like that's going to work out." A pain shot through her stomach, so sharp it threatened to double her over. But she pushed her shoulders back and walked down the porch steps, waving to the driver.

"Not work out? I don't understand." Sophie clamored down the stairs after her. "Mack's been a different guy since you've been back. He's happier than I've seen him in a long time. If you leave and don't come back, you're going to break Mack's heart."

Jocelyn offered her a one-shouldered shrug and swallowed at the burn in her throat. "Then you'll be here to pick up the pieces."

"*Me?*"

"Yes. You're so much more suited to him anyway. You're beautiful and so nice, and you love this ranch and history as much as he does."

"You love this ranch too. I've seen you this week. I might not know you that well, but you've seemed to be in your element. And I might like history, but you actually *have* a history here."

"That's all it is, my history, my past. My future and my career are back in the city." Another sting shot through her chest. But where was her life? Her heart? It felt as if she were leaving part of it here.

Sophie's perfect curls bounced as she shook her

head. "Wow. You are as obstinate as those meddling matchmaking grandmas of yours. It sounds like you've got our entire future planned out. Although I appreciate the compliments you said about me, have you ever stopped to consider that I might not be *interested* in Mack Talbot?"

Jocelyn drew up short. "No. How could you *not* be interested in Mack? He's gorgeous and kind and funny. And he has a secret romantic streak in him a mile wide. And have you seen his muscles?"

Sophie shrugged. "Yeah, but Mack's not my type. Like at all. I like blonds, and no offense, but I'm not a huge fan of beards. I'm into cowboys. And I mean *real* cowboys, the kind who grew up in 4H and know how to ride a horse." Her face took on a dreamy expression. "The kind who know how to wear a pair of Wranglers, and are comfortable with cowboy boots on their feet and a black Stetson on their head."

"That's pretty specific."

She shrugged again. "I just know what I want. And it's *not* Mack Talbot. We're good friends, and I love the guy, but not like that."

Wow. She'd had it all wrong. What else was she wrong about?

Jocelyn passed her suitcase to the rental car guy, who stowed it in the trunk then got into the passenger seat. She turned back to Sophie. "I think I misjudged you. And I'm sorry. I've got to go now, but keep an eye on Mack for me anyway, okay?"

Sophie nodded. "I will."

Jocelyn opened the driver's side door, then turned to wave to the other woman. "I hope you find that cowboy. You deserve him. Although you might want to avoid Mrs. Crandle for the next few days. I heard her talking to my grandma, and she has high hopes of setting you up with her 'nice grandson'."

Sophie groaned and slapped her head to her forehead. "Thanks for the warning. Take care, Jocelyn. I hope you find what you're hoping for."

What *was* she hoping for? Certainly not this agony of feeling like she was leaving her heart in the caretaker's cottage behind the house. Why was she working so hard to convince herself she wanted to leave, when her body was telling her in no uncertain terms that it didn't want to go?

It didn't matter now. Mack had already made his feelings clear. This job and the promotion were all she had now. She couldn't screw them up too.

A flash of brown caught her eye, and she spied Savage trotting around the side of Gram's house. He loped toward her, and she crouched to give him a hug. He licked her face as if he knew she was leaving. She swallowed as she stood and pointed to the house. "Go home, boy."

The dog planted his bottom in the driveway and let out a mournful howl.

"Go home."

The dog stood, but instead of leaving, he ran to the car and whined as he tried to climb into the front seat. Jocelyn grabbed his collar and pulled him back.

The pain of leaving the dog *and* the man *and* her grandmother ripped through her, and she choked back tears as she pleaded with the dog. "Please, buddy. No. I'm sorry, you can't come with me."

She implored Sophie to help her, and the other

woman took hold of Savage's collar and pulled him far enough out of the way for Jocelyn to get in the car.

The basset hound let out another sorrowful howl and wrenched at his collar as he tried to get back to her.

Sliding into the front seat, Jocelyn yanked the door shut. Slamming her hand in the door would have hurt less than this. She rendered the rental car guy a tearful glance. "It's complicated."

She put the car in gear and drove away, sneaking one last look at Harmony Ranch in the rearview mirror.

Chapter Nineteen

THREE HOURS LATER, JOCELYN WAS sitting at a table in an upscale pizzeria on the 16th Street Mall in downtown Denver, as she waited to meet her new clients.

The drive to Denver had been long and full of traffic. Jocelyn's thoughts had ping-ponged from the cars on the road to the heartbreak of losing Mack to the impending meeting with the coffee shop clients, Mike and Julia Carlson.

Trying to put thoughts of Mack, her grandmother, and all things Harmony Ranch out of her mind, she stopped to drop her things at her hotel and quickly freshen up. Even with the quick stop, she'd still made it to the restaurant early enough to secure a great table on the patio that delivered an amazing view of the mountains. In this world, it was all about looks and perception.

Which meant if she could paste a smile on her face and keep up a steady stream of witty conversation for the next several hours, she could give the illusion of being happy. Instead of letting them see that her heart was actually breaking on the inside, and she was terrified she'd just thrown away the best thing that ever happened to her.

A couple in their mid-forties walked up to the hostess, and Jocelyn stood and waved. She recognized them from the picture on their website, another place she had a ton of ideas to update. The woman waved back, and Jocelyn studied the couple as they made their way to the table.

Julia Carlson was dressed in jeans, a pale pink blouse, and a tailored blazer. She carried a designer handbag and wore a pair of flats that were meant to look casual, but would've carried a price tag close to one of Jocelyn's entire paychecks. Her blonde hair was cut in a trendy chin-length bob, and when she'd spotted Jocelyn and waved, her smile was open and friendly.

Mike was more casual in a golf shirt, jeans and sneakers. His brown hair was thinning on top, and he had that soft in the middle dad bod thing going on. Jocelyn noticed the way he held the patio gate for his wife and tenderly put his hand on her back as they weaved between tables. His wore an easygoing smile, and Jocelyn liked the way he joked with the hostess as she pointed them in her direction.

"You must be Jocelyn," Julia said, holding out her hand. "We're so excited to meet you."

"Thanks. Welcome to Colorado," Jocelyn said as she shook hands first with Julia, then with Mike.

Mike pulled out the chair next to him for his wife, and then settled in a seat across from Jocelyn. His gaze went to a spot above her shoulder, and a goofy smile creased his face. "Wow. Great view. Don't get me wrong. I love our view of the skyline from our apartment in New York, but this is awesome. We're so excited to be in Colorado. We love the mountains."

Score one for Jocelyn.

"I'm excited to meet you as well," she told them. "I've got so many ideas to share with you."

"We loved the campaign proposal you sent, so if they're anything like those ideas, we can't wait to hear them," Mike said, picking up a menu.

The waitress came over to take their order and by the time the food arrived, Jocelyn and the Carlsons had already bonded and were laughing and getting along like old friends. She could already tell she was going to love working with them.

She was getting everything she'd been dreaming of—an exciting new project to be involved in, a promotion, a raise, and a chance to move out of the closet and get her own bedroom.

Too bad the only place she wanted to live was in a room with a view of these mountains.

Mack flinched as his thumb touched a hot part of the steel rod he'd just brought out of the fire. *Dang.* He needed to get his mind off a certain woman and focus on his work. He hadn't burned himself on a rod in forever.

It was after dinner, and he'd been crabby all day. The only place he'd been able to find solace was the blacksmith shop, and he'd been out here the last hour working on more candleholders for the luminaries.

He pounded the rod with a hammer, taking out his frustration as he flattened the steel and twisted it to his will. Too bad he couldn't twist people to his will as easily.

He spotted the project he'd been working on the day before. *The stupid hearts.*

As a gift for Jocelyn, he'd taken several of the hearts he'd made and had been forging them together in a unique design. It was his way of showing her how she'd helped to put the pieces of his broken heart back together. At the time he'd started it, it had seemed romantic and special. Now it just seemed sappy and stupid.

He grabbed the heart project and tossed it on the anvil. He didn't even bother with sticking them in the fire, he just lifted the sledgehammer and started smashing them to bits—just like what Jocelyn had done to his heart.

How could he have been such a fool?

She'd left him. Again.

Just. *Strike.* Like. *Hit.* He. *Slam.* Knew. *Smash.* She. *Blow.* Would.

He drove the hammer into the anvil. Again and again. Pieces of the hearts, already smashed and broken, scattered and shot across the floor.

It didn't matter. He was hitting the anvil now, just for the jolt of pain it caused to shoot up his arms and across his shoulders. Sweat poured off him, and his muscles burned as each strike hit harder than the one before.

He didn't care. If his body hurt and his muscles ached then maybe he wouldn't notice how much his heart did.

His phone buzzed in his pocket, and he considered ignoring it as he struck the anvil again.

He dropped the sledgehammer. His traitorous body wanting to check the phone, his pulse quickening at the thought it could be Jocelyn. What if she was calling to say she was wrong and headed back to the ranch right now? He huffed out a laugh as he pulled his phone free.

Jocelyn admitting she was wrong? That would be the day.

He didn't recognize the number or the area code. Probably a telemarketer. But it could be a vendor or something to do with the event. He tapped the screen and held the phone to his ear as he barked out a hello.

"Yeah, hi. This is Chase Dalton. I'm looking for Mack Talbot."

"You got him," Mack answered offhandedly as he kicked a broken piece of the hearts across the floor. He almost hung up, figuring the use of his full name had to signal a sales call. Then the caller's name hit him. "Wait. Who did you say this was again?"

"Chase Dalton."

"Yeah, right, Floyd. I'm not falling for that trick again. Didn't you call me claiming to be the Colorado Lottery office a few weeks ago?"

"Sorry, I'm not sure who this Floyd fella is, but this really *is* Chase Dalton. And I heard you were having a benefit concert tomorrow night."

Okay, he'd play along with the gag. Just to see what this guy was really after. "Yeah, we are."

"Well, I was calling to offer y'all my help. I used to visit Harmony Ranch when I was a kid. I have great memories of the place, and I'd hate to see it get shut down. I'm heading through Colorado this weekend anyway, and I'd love to add my support. Do you think it might help if I came up on stage to do a short set or sing a couple songs?"

Mack pulled the phone away from his ear to check the number again. *Holy cow.* He couldn't believe it. "Is this *really* Chase Dalton?"

"Yes, sir."

Mack's legs felt a little wobbly. He sank down onto the old trunk next to his workbench. "That sounds mighty nice of you, but we're just a small outfit. We wouldn't be able to afford to have you sing even half of a song, let alone a short set."

"Oh no, I'm not asking to be paid. It would be my privilege to help out the ranch. Now, I gotta tell you though, it's just me. I don't have the band with me. But I've got my guitar, and I'd be happy to play a few songs."

Mack swallowed. An impromptu acoustic performance by Chase Dalton? Yeah, he could get behind that idea. "That would be amazing. But why? Why would you do that?"

"I don't know if you're familiar with any of my music, but I have this one song, *My Heart is Your Home*, and it's about your roots and the things that are important that define your home."

"Yeah, I'm familiar with the song. In fact, I heard you play it at the Harmony County Fair about ten years ago."

"Seriously? You can't see it, but I'm cringing over here."

"No way. You were great. My girlfriend and I heard you together, and we've both followed your career since then. In fact, we were just talking about you the other night when we heard you on the radio. *My Heart is Your Home* is kind of our song." Mack whacked his palm against his forehead. He sounded like a complete dork. "Wow. Pretend I did not just tell you that weird fact." *Shut up now.*

Chase chuckled. "It's cool, man. I'm glad to hear it. That tells me you get my music, so you know where I'm coming from. Our roots are important. And people need those places that remind them of home and family. Harmony Ranch is one of those places for me. That's why I want to help out."

"That's awesome. We'd love to have you."

"Great. You've got my number now, and I'll have my manager email you with some press release stuff, if you want to use it. I should be to Harmony Creek by about nine tomorrow, so I'll come over and hammer out the details with you sometime before lunch. But feel free to blast out on social media that I'll be there and doing a popup concert."

Social media? Shoot. Where was Joss when he needed her? "Are you sure?"

"Yeah, of course. The whole point is to get as many folks there as possible, so we can raise the money you need to rescue the ranch."

"All right. Thanks. Really. This is so great of you." *Stop rambling.*

Chase laughed again. "No problem. Happy to do it. See you tomorrow."

"Yeah, see you tomorrow." He tapped the screen to end the call and let out a whoop loud enough to make Savage raise his head from his napping spot by the door. The dog sniffed the air, yawned, and laid his head back down.

Mack couldn't believe it. He scrolled through his

contacts and had almost tapped Jocelyn's number when he remembered. His elation collapsed like a folding chair. She was the one he most wanted to share this news with, and she was the one person he couldn't call.

Shaking his head, he refused to let his blowup with Jocelyn ruin this awesome moment. He knew someone else who would be more than thrilled to hear the news. He shut down the fire as he whistled for Savage and hightailed it to Molly's.

Spying her through the screen door, he raced up the porch steps and gave a quick knock, then let himself in. The little scruffy dog jumped off Molly's lap and raced to greet him. "Hey, I'm glad you're still up. You are not going to believe who just called me."

"Pastor Jim?"

"No. Think bigger. Way bigger." He scratched the little dog's chin.

"Chris Hemsworth? I'd love it if he called me."

"Okay. Maybe not that big."

Molly tossed a throw pillow at him. "For gosh sakes, just tell me."

"Chase Dalton."

"The country singer?"

"Yep."

"The guy on the radio?"

"That's the one."

"No offense, but why would he call you? Does he need some blacksmithing work done?"

Mack shook his head. "No. Although that would have been really cool. But he was calling about you."

"Me?" She fluffed her silvery curls. "I hope you told him I'm not into younger men."

Mack laughed. "Well, not you, exactly, but the ranch. He heard about the benefit concert, and he offered to come play a few songs for it."

Molly's eyes went round. "He just called you, out of the blue, to offer to play at our concert?" She tilted her head. "Are you sure it wasn't Floyd Fischer calling you from down at the Elks Lodge? Those old guys can get up to some pretty good pranks."

He groaned at the thought of getting *Punk'd* by the geezers at the Elks Lodge. "That's what I thought at first too. But no, it was really him. I recognized his voice. I know it sounds crazy, but he said he used to come here as a kid, and he wanted to help."

She shook her head. "That's amazing."

As they'd been sitting there, the dog had run off and come back several times. Each time she'd brought something back, holding her treasure in her mouth as she sat in front of Molly with her offering. A small pile of items had collected at Molly's feet: a dog brush, a tennis ball, a slipper, a small stuffed toy, a pair of reading glasses, and a romance novel. This time she came back with a lone sock in her mouth.

"What is going on with this dog?" Mack asked.

"Isn't it adorable? She keeps racing around the house and finding the oddest assortment of things. Then she prances back and offers them to me like some kind of prize. I don't know where she's finding half this stuff. I haven't seen those readers in years." She reached down and pulled the sock from the dog's mouth, then gave her a pat on the head. "Good girl." She held the sock out to Mack. "I don't even know whose sock this is."

He winced. "Ugh."

She brought it to her nose and took a quick whiff. "It's a little dusty, but it's clean."

"Weird."

"Yes, but it's also ridiculously cute. She's been such a blessing to me. This treasure hunt has kept me entertained all day. And helped me to not think about all the other stuff going on. I haven't told Jocelyn yet, but I'm planning to keep her."

Mack shrugged and peered out the screen door to where Savage had finally caught up to him and was crashed out on the front porch, his head hanging over the top step. "I get it. They have a way of growing on you, drool and all."

Molly made a face. "And boy, can that dog of yours drool. We love him anyway though." She gazed adoringly down at the little dog. "I've decided to call her Peaches."

"Peaches?"

"Yeah. Isn't that cute? I was in the kitchen earlier cutting up a peach, and a small piece fell on the floor. You would've thought I dropped a chunk of filet mignon the way this one came racing into the kitchen and gobbled that little morsel up. Then she popped down into a perfect sit and held her paws up to beg for another bite. It was so stinking adorable. It made me laugh so hard I almost fell off my scooter. That's when I decided I was keeping her. I need more laughter like that in my life."

Mack scratched the dog's ears. "Hey, Peaches. Welcome home. Darn good thing Miss Molly didn't drop a chunk of asparagus on the floor. Who'd want to be named after that?" The dog licked his hand as if in agreement, then tore off back down the hallway.

Molly grabbed a small notebook and pen from the side table. "Now let's get back to the concert. What can we do to get the word out?"

Mack slumped back in his chair. "Chase said we could blast it on social media. Whatever that means."

"Oh dear. You know who's great at that stuff?"

"Yeah, I do. But I'm not calling her. She made it clear where her priorities lie, and they aren't with the concert. Chase said his manager was going to email me some press release stuff."

The scruffy dog came racing back into the room, a rolled up sheet of paper clamped in her teeth. She wagged her tail as she sat in front of Molly and raised her chin.

"Oh goodness. What have you brought for me this time?" Molly said, easing the paper from her mouth. She unfurled it, and her eyebrows drew together as she scanned the page. "It looks like a fax. For Jocelyn. It's got today's date on it, and it's from her company." A dawning realization crossed her face as she continued to read. "Oh dear," she said, covering her mouth with her hand. She passed the page to Mack. "I'm sorry, Mack. I think Jocelyn leaving had more to do with me than you."

He took the page, and his brow furrowed as he tried to make sense of how what he was reading had anything to do with him. Or Molly. "I don't get it. This just looks like a contract for the promotion that Jocelyn's been trying to get. We already know about this. What's the big deal?"

"Read the last paragraph."

Then he spotted it. "*Fifteen thousand dollar* bonus? Just for signing this thing?"

"Just about the amount we need to save Harmony Ranch."

"We don't need *that* much. And we've still got the concert. We haven't given up."

Molly tilted her head. "Oh, come on. You and I both know that concert isn't going to make enough money to dig me out of the hole I've created. It's a fine idea, and it will get us closer. But I think Jocelyn also knew we weren't gonna make enough. No wonder she felt like she *had* to take this job."

"But why didn't she just tell us? I mean, I guess I know why she didn't tell you. Because you'd tell her to stuff the bonus, and you wouldn't take it anyway."

"Darn tootin' I would have."

"But why didn't she tell me? That would have explained so much." Their conversation that morning replayed in his head. He cringed as he remembered his stubborn refusal to listen to what she had to say. "Aw crud. Now that I think about it, she might have actually tried to tell me. She said something about a bonus and us needing the money, but I was too focused on the fact that she was leaving and the stupid money didn't matter. This must have been what she meant when she said she had more to tell me. She said she could explain. But I cut her off."

"How did the dog find this?" Molly's expression turned pensive. "It must have rolled off the fax machine and fallen on the floor. That happens all the time."

"All the time? Do you still get a lot of faxes?"

"Well, no. Now that you mention it, I haven't got one in a while now."

"You mean since the Nineties?" The joke reminded him of Jocelyn's ribbing about his phone. Was he really stuck in the past? He'd gotten an iPhone. Didn't that count for something?

Molly ignored his remark. "This has to be it. She has to have taken the job for the signing bonus."

He scrubbed a hand through his hair, still angry at himself for not taking the time to listen to Jocelyn. "I screwed up, Molly. I let my emotions get the best of me. But dang it, it just felt like she was making excuses." He shook his head as his shoulders slumped forward. "Or maybe that's what I wanted to hear. She tried to tell me there was a good reason for why she was leaving. I just wouldn't listen. Even when she said she wanted to explain, I was too angry to hear her out."

"Angry? Or hurt?"

He shrugged. "Both, I guess."

"Come on now, Mack. You don't have to be so brave with me. I've known you since you were ten years old."

"I know. If I wasn't with my grandparents, I was with you. You practically helped raise me."

"I did help raise you, so don't try to dupe me. I know you have feelings for my granddaughter."

"Ya think?" He granted her a sheepish grin.

"So what are you gonna do about it?"

"What *can* I do about it? She already made her choice. And she didn't pick me."

"No, she picked *me*. And saving the ranch."

He sighed. "Which only makes me love her more."

"So, if you love her, go after her."

"Go after her? Like drive to Denver? Tonight?" The idea held some appeal. Except he didn't know where she was staying or how to find her. Or if she wanted to be surprised by his pounding on her hotel room door in the middle of the night.

"Well, no. That won't work. The concert is tomorrow. And we're already down Jocelyn. We need you here." She slapped the boot strapped around her foot. "I could do it if it weren't for this dang leg. But maybe instead of going to her, you could get her to come home."

"How am I supposed to do that?"

"First you have to decide if you want her to come back."

"You know I do. I've been in love with her for most of my life. Even after she broke my heart, I still couldn't get her completely out of my system."

"I know. So what's different about this time?"

"For starters, me, I guess. I'm different. Last time I was so sure Jocelyn had left because I wasn't worth staying for that I didn't even try to fight for her—I just let her go. But she's shown me that some things are worth fighting for. And that I'm worth it too. Her being here has brought back that side of me that I'd closed off after she left—the side that admits it's okay to be a little vulnerable and that I'm afraid of not being enough to make her stay. But I'm ready to face that fear, to take a chance and fight for what I want."

"Which is?"

"A life with Jocelyn. Except last time, I was a kid and I had to wait for her to come to me. Now I'm an adult, so I can actually go to her. Even if I have to go to New York to make it happen."

"You'd be willing to go to the East Coast?"

"I didn't think so. Not until this moment. But you've seen her with that marketing stuff. She really loves it. And she's good at it. I can't ask her to give that up for me."

"Isn't that her decision to make?"

"Yeah, maybe. But it doesn't seem fair to ask her to give up her dreams for me if I'm not willing to give up mine for her."

"Doesn't seem like there are a lot of jobs for black-smiths in New York City."

"No, it doesn't." He shook his head. "Who am I kidding? I can't leave the ranch. When I took over as caretaker, I made a commitment—to you, to this town."

Molly waved his concerns away. "We'll figure something out. Now what are you going to do to win her back, to show her you've changed, and that she's *worth* fighting for?"

"I think I already blew it."

"Don't be a dope. Of course you didn't. She loves you too. If you want her, figure out how to prove to her that you do. What would show Jocelyn that you've changed—not just changed your mind, but changed your mindset? You're not the same guy you were ten years ago. So don't just tell her that, *show* her she's important enough to you that you're not going to let her go again."

Chapter Twenty

MACK STRODE BACK TO THE cottage, his mind racing with thoughts of how to show Jocelyn how much she meant to him. Nothing was jumping out at him as he let himself in, then held the door as he waited for Savage to catch up. The dog followed as he walked into the living room and dropped onto the sofa. After a lengthy and semi-intrusive sniff-down of his pants, the basset let out a sigh and draped himself over Mack's feet.

"Yeah, I was with another dog. You would have known that if you would've come inside instead of stopping to take a nap on the porch. But don't worry, you'll get another chance. It sounds like she's gonna be stickin' around," he told the basset hound as he scratched his big floppy ears. "Molly already gave her a name." He knew from years of experience with the woman that once she named an animal, it was hers.

He leaned back against the cushion, wishing it were that simple with Jocelyn. Pulling out his phone, he pulled up the ranch's Facebook page just to check if she'd posted anything tonight. Although how would he know if a post had just been created or if it was one of the ones she'd scheduled to go up over the course of the weekend?

She was really good at this social media stuff. He wondered once again if it was fair of him to ask her to give that up for him. There weren't a lot of marketing jobs in Harmony Creek.

It's her decision to make, he reminded himself. And she sure wasn't going to come back to him after the way he'd acted that morning. If only he'd given her a chance to explain.

The Facebook page looked good and the announcement of the concert had gotten over a hundred likes and several comments. Jocelyn had also set up a fundraising link to the account so people could still donate to the cause even if they couldn't make it to the concert.

He clicked the button taking him to the account. His shoulders sagged as he saw the contributions so far totaled just over forty dollars. Yeah, this concert was in trouble. No wonder Jocelyn felt like she *had* to take the job to get the bonus.

But now that he knew the whole story, and with the addition of the surprise appearance of Chase Dalton, he had a chance to rescue the ranch *and* get the girl back. He brought up his photos and scrolled through the selfies Jocelyn had taken of them together.

He rubbed a hand over his chest, scrubbing against the ache that seeing her laughing face caused. He tapped the video and watched their dance for the hundredth time that week.

Hmmm. He had an idea. He wasn't sure if it was a good idea or a ridiculously lame and somewhat humiliating one—but it was an idea just the same. And it might just be enough to save the ranch and win back the girl.

He tapped the tiny letters on the screen, composing and deleting words as he tried to devise the perfect message and remember what Jocelyn had taught him about creating a post. Fifteen painstakingly long minutes later, he finished the post and read it out loud to the dog. Savage rolled over and stretched out for a belly rub, which Mack took to mean the hound approved. At least he hadn't yawned.

Mack took a deep breath then touched the word "post." Satisfied he'd done the best he could, he tossed his phone on the sofa cushion, and gave in to the dog's request.

Now all he could do was wait. He wanted to reach out, to call her, to hear her voice. But he somehow knew this was the better way to go.

This would show Jocelyn he'd changed.

And if publicly declaring his love for her on social media didn't prove he was willing to do whatever it took to get her back, then he didn't know what would.

It was close to midnight when Jocelyn finally made it back to her hotel room. She sank onto the bed, then pulled off her boots and rubbed her sore feet. She swore they must have walked from one end of downtown Denver to the other, then back again.

Mike and Julia might've been older than her, but they more energy than she did. And they were on New York time, so they should have been exhausted. But they seemed so excited about their plans and about being in Colorado, they were practically giddy. And Jocelyn couldn't help but join in on their happy mood.

Until about twenty minutes ago, when she'd finally hit a wall and begged off for the night. She'd left them in the lobby, shaking her head and calling good night even as Mike suggested they hit the hotel restaurant and order some midnight nachos.

She pushed up from the bed, summoning the last of her energy to wash her face and brush her teeth. But as she pulled her pajamas from her suitcase, the iron rose Mack had made for her slipped out and fell across her clothes. She'd forgotten she'd wrapped it in the pajama top to keep it safe.

Touching the gorgeously crafted petals, she choked back tears. The flower was beautiful, but the iron was as cold as Mack's reaction to her had been that morning. Grabbing her toiletry case and pajamas, she slammed the lid of the suitcase back down. She was too tired, and her heart was too tender, to think about Mack right now.

After completing her nighttime routine, she got out her charger and plugged it into the bedside outlet. Digging her phone from her purse, she plugged it in and was surprised to see a text from Gram which had come in hours earlier. Her phone had been buried in her bag, and she must not have heard it buzz. *Call me later*, the message read.

Jocelyn was dying to tell Gram the details of the afternoon and evening. It had all gone so well. She'd really connected with the Carlsons and was so excited about the prospect of the new job. But it was too late to call her grandmother now, and the message hadn't seemed urgent.

She also had a notification she'd been tagged in a post on Facebook. It was from the Harmony Ranch page, so she was sure it was probably something to do with the concert. There was no way she was clicking that. Not tonight.

She'd already committed to plans with Mike and Julia for the following day. They'd begged her to show them some of the sights around Denver. She couldn't face the reminder that she was missing the concert she and Mack had worked so hard on.

Turning her phone upside down, she placed it on the bedside table and turned out the light. She was so exhausted, she figured she'd be asleep before her head hit the pillow, but her brain wouldn't shut off as it replayed the events of the day. She lay awake for hours as her heart and mind debated the decisions she'd made and argued over which ones had been the right thing to do.

The next morning, Jocelyn's head was fuzzy from lack of sleep as she woke to the sound of her phone buzzing. Her eyes fluttered and she let out a groan as she reached for the phone, but still ended up missing the call. Squinting at the screen, she saw it was the third time her grandmother had tried to call.

She pushed herself up, scrubbing a hand through her hair as she redialed her grandmother. "Hi Gram. You all right?"

"Yes, I'm fine. Are you? I've called you three times already."

"Sorry. Late night. But a good one."

"Yeah?"

"Yeah. I hung out with the new clients most of the day, and night, yesterday. And I really like them. They've got some fun ideas, and they're really motivated to open a shop in Colorado. I think they'll be great to work with."

"You don't have to work so hard to convince me. I already know why you were so fired up to leave yesterday and to take this job."

"What do you mean?"

"Peaches found a copy of the contract on the floor last night."

"Who's Peaches?"

"One of the little strays."

"Oh. You found the owner?" Jocelyn's heart sank with disappointment. Not that she wasn't happy for the dog and the owner, obviously. But she'd gotten used to the cute little mutt, and wasn't ready to lose one more thing.

"Yeah, you're talking to her. No one has called about either of the dogs, so we're keeping this one. We've already bonded. But I think she misses you. She keeps going back to your bedroom and wandering through it like she's checking to see if you're back yet."

"Aww. That's so sweet." *And heartbreaking.*

"You know, you *can* come back."

"I wish I could."

"Do you really wish that? Because you *can*. That's what I'm calling to tell you. We saw the contract, and I know about the signing bonus they offered you. And I know that's the reason you feel like you *have* to take this job."

"What do you mean by *we* saw the contract? Who is 'we'?"

"Me and Mack. But that's beside the point."

Her heart skipped a beat. "Mack saw the contract? What did he say?"

"He was just as surprised as I was that you hadn't told either of us."

Jocelyn let out a frustrated sigh. "I *tried* to tell him, but he kept cutting me off."

"That's what he said. Now quit trying to change the subject and listen to your grandma. I'm trying to tell you that you don't *have* to take this job."

"Yes, I do."

"Not for me, you don't."

Jocelyn leaned her head back against the pillow and wished she'd made a cup of coffee before starting this conversation. This was exactly what she'd worried would happen. "Quit looking a gift bonus in the mouth, Gram. That money is the answer to all our problems—it's just what we need to save the ranch."

"The ranch is my problem, not yours."

"Good try, Gram. I love that place almost as much as you do."

"Be that as it may, I'm not letting you pay off the loan with that bonus."

"I don't know that we'll have that choice."

"We always have a choice. Especially in this instance. You have a lot riding on this decision. And you keep saying you *have* to take this job, but I haven't once heard you say you *want* it."

Was that true? She'd worked so hard to get this account, of course she *wanted* it. Didn't she?

"It's not that simple. I love my job, and I've had so much fun working on this account. Plus, I really like the people I just met and feel like we'd have such a great working relationship."

"But is that the relationship you *really* want?"

An image of Mack laughing as they competed in the obstacle course filled her mind, and she could almost feel his strong arm wrapped around her waist. An ache settled in her chest. "I don't know," she whispered.

"Let me ask you this," Gram said. "If it weren't for the bonus, would you still be as fired up to leave the ranch and take the job?"

"That's the question I've been avoiding asking myself."

"Okay, so I'm asking you now."

"If you had asked me two weeks ago, I would have said this promotion was everything I've wanted. I've spent the last several months working relentlessly to get it."

"But now?"

She buried her head in her hands. "But now I'm not so sure."

"Because…?"

"Because there is something I think I want even more."

"Some*thing* or some*one*?"

"Have you ever heard the term 'leading the witness'?"

"Ha. I knew it. It's Mack, right?"

"Of course it's Mack. It's always been Mack. I've never stopped caring about him and wishing things had gone differently for us. But it wasn't until the last few weeks when I've been back and hanging out with him again that I realized how *much* I still care about him." Her voice dropped to a whisper again. "How much I still love him."

"Well girl, it's taken you long enough to figure that out."

"I know. But I think Mom might have had something to do with that." She told her grandmother about the letters she and Mack both claimed they'd written to each other yet neither had ever received.

"I'm sad to say it, but that sounds like just the kind of thing your mother would do. She was determined to cut all your ties with this place. Don't be too angry with her. She just wanted you to have the kind of chances in life that she felt she never got. And she was terrified you would waste your life in this small town instead of getting to see the world like she'd wanted to."

"But that was *my* choice to make, not hers."

"That's true. Although it seems like you have a choice to make now."

"But I don't. There isn't a choice. I *have* to do this."

Gram blew out an exasperated sigh. "Not for me, you don't. Jocelyn, I would rather lose everything than have you risk losing your chance at finally finding happiness with the man you love."

"It's not that simple."

Her grandmother's voice softened. "But honey, it is. Take the ranch and the bonus out of the equation and just think about having a future with Mack in Colorado or a future with your company in New York. Which do you want more?"

That question had plagued her half the night. "My heart seems to be telling me the answer, but my head keeps fighting it."

"When is the last time you let your heart decide?"

She swallowed. "Never."

"Maybe it's time you gave your heart a chance."

There were a few obstacles in the way of that decision. "But I've already met the clients and prepared this whole campaign for them."

"So what? There will be other clients and other campaigns. If you want this job with everything in you, then by all means choose the job. But this past week I've heard you laugh more than I have in years. Don't worry about me. I will be fine. No matter what happens. But you have your whole life ahead of you. And I want *you* to make the choice of how you plan to spend it. Not me, not Mack, and certainly not your mother. Think about what *you* want that will make you happy."

"I thought it was this promotion. But now I'm not so sure." Glancing toward her suitcase, she spied the end of the iron-forged rose sticking out the side. Jocelyn knew what she really wanted. But was she willing to make the sacrifices to get it?

"I've given up so much to get this promotion, and now that it's within my grasp, it's hard to imagine letting it go."

"What's harder to imagine losing—the job or Mack?"

That question hit her like an arrow to the sternum. "Mack. Now that he's back in my life, I'm struggling to leave him again."

"That tells you something right there. And I'm not trying to sway your decision..."

Yeah, right.

"But I need to say one more thing. For Mack. If you decide it's him you want, you need to be all in. That man hasn't had an easy time of it when it comes to trusting women. So far, all the women in his life have left him. His mom, then you, then Ashley. And now you again. He needs someone to make him believe he's worth fighting for—worth staying for. So if you decide you want him, you need to prove it to him. Show him you're back for good."

She took a shuddering breath, her heart aching for the hurts Mack had experienced. "I hear you."

"Good. Because I think Mack still has a few tricks up his sleeve. Have you checked Facebook this morning?"

"Facebook? No. I only woke up to answer your call."

"You might want to check it out. What you see just might factor into your decision."

What was she talking about?

"Go get some coffee, then take a look. I love you, honey, and I'll stand by whatever decision you make."

Her grandmother was being awfully cryptic. But Jocelyn's curiosity was piqued. What could be on Facebook that could possibly help in this situation? "Thanks, Gram. For everything. I love you too. I'll call you later."

She clicked off the call and tapped the Facebook app. The first thing to come up was a post for the ranch's page that had a video attached to it. A post that she hadn't created.

Squinting at the screen, she recognized a blurry image of the pond but could recognize nothing beyond that. Her gaze went immediately to the likes and comments, and her eyes widened.

Over *a thousand* likes? And the video had been viewed several hundred times.

She read the first few lines of the post, her heart racing.

"Bring your appetite and your dancing shoes down to Harmony Creek Ranch this Saturday for Fiddles and Vittles—a benefit concert to help rescue Harmony Ranch. Special guest appearance by Chase Dalton. #PopUpConcert."

Wait. *Chase Dalton?* Was going to be at *their* concert? *What the heck?* How had Mack pulled that off? And when had he learned how to hashtag?

She kept reading, and her heart went from racing to melting.

"Jocelyn—this is for you. Forget everything I said yesterday and please come back. We'll figure it out. I love you. My heart has always been your home."

She couldn't believe Mack had posted something so personal. And she was floored at how many likes and comments his post had received.

She touched the video and the strains of "My Heart is Your Home" began to play as the camera shakily moved as if it were being set down. Two people moved into view. She gasped. It wasn't a camera, it was a phone. *Mack's phone.* And it was her and Mack on the screen.

She watched, mesmerized, as he took her in his arms and pulled her close. They swayed to the music, their bodies fitting together as if they were made for each other—like magnets, but instead of repelling each other, they were drawn together as if by a powerful force.

Her chest ached as she watched the two of them smile at each other and then laugh easily at a shared joke. Even though she remembered everything about those stolen moments by the pond, she still held her breath, waiting to see what happened next.

In the soft light of dusk, with the candles flickering off the water, Mack gazed into her eyes. Just as she had the night it happened, she felt the intensity and the promise in that gaze. Tears welled in her eyes as she watched him pull her into his embrace and tenderly hold her in his arms as they slow-danced to the song that meant so much to them.

The video came to an end and she swallowed, her throat dry.

Wiping a lone tear from her cheek, she tapped the screen and watched it again.

When it was over, she stared at her phone, remembering the night so vividly—the smell of the pond, the magic of the twinkling lights of the luminaries, and the feel of Mack's arms around her.

She was so tempted to call him, the need to hear his voice almost overwhelming, but he'd always said actions speak louder than words. So now was the time for her to act.

She closed Facebook and opened her contacts. She had an important call to make. One that could change everything.

She hoped.

Chewing the inside of her cheek, she tapped the number, then smoothed her pajama pants down as she listened to the ring.

Her boss answered on the first ring and immediately started to gush. "Jocelyn, you totally nailed it. The Carlsons have already called me, and they loved you."

Jocelyn lifted her chin as she pushed her shoulders back. "I loved them too. That's what makes this call so hard."

Chapter Twenty-One

J OCELYN HUNG UP THE PHONE, her chest already
feeling lighter. The call hadn't necessarily gone
well, but at least it was over.

Andrea had at first been stunned when she'd told
her she was staying in Colorado. Then her voice had
turned icy and she hadn't said much beyond, "I'm
sorry to hear that" and "I guess you have to do what
you have to do."

She'd tried to ask if there was a way she could work
from Colorado, but Andrea cut her off with a statement about how disappointed the clients, and the
firm, would be. And how she wasn't looking forward to
breaking the news to them.

Jocelyn had told her she was meeting the clients for
brunch, and she'd let them know her decision. Pushing up from the bed, she headed for the shower to get
ready for one of the hardest meetings of her career.

Or what was left of her career.

That night, Mack paced the area behind the stage as

one of the local bands finished up their last song. His boots kicked up dust with each step, and he snuck a quick glance at the guy leaning casually against the side of the stage, his hand resting on the neck of his guitar.

Mack tapped his fingers against his leg. He was as nervous as a long-tailed cat in a room full of rocking chairs. How was he supposed to walk out there and introduce *Chase Dalton*? The guy had played at the Grand Ole Opry, and Mack was supposed to welcome him out to a stage cobbled together from hay bales and the flatbed of Frank Ferguson's semi trailer.

At least his nerves were keeping his thoughts on the crazy busyness of the concert instead of letting him wallow in thoughts of Joss.

"I suppose you don't get nervous anymore," Mack said to the country star.

"Oh, sure I do. You should've seen me a few years back when they asked me to sing the national anthem at a Broncos game in Denver," Chase told him. "It was a good thing I decided to wear my Manning jersey, because I sweated clear through my t-shirt. I was sure my voice would crack. Then right before I walked out onto the field, Peyton Manning himself clapped me on the back and said 'You got this, Chase.' Then my nerves settled right down. I figured if the guy who had to go out in front of tens of thousands of fans and win a football game could take the time to offer me encouragement, I could sure go out and sing a song to get that game started off on the right foot." He winked. "Pun intended."

Mack laughed, a little in awe of the story. "I can totally see Manning doing that. That guy is the greatest."

"You bet he is."

"Tens of thousands of people, huh?" Mack shook his head. "I guess after that, there'd be no reason to worry about playing a small-time deal like this."

Chase craned his neck to see over the top of the trailer. "That crowd seems to be growing by the second. And I think you'd be surprised at what kind of small-time deals I've played. Remember the first time you saw me? I was singing at a county fair. I've done my share of fairs, baseball games, and rinky-dink bars when I was working my way up in the business. A particular favorite was the night I played an entire show to an empty house except for one guy asleep at the bar, and the bartender. Not one other patron came in the whole two hours I was on stage."

Mack winced. "That had to be rough."

"It was. I found out later I was performing on the same night the local high school football team was playing for the state championship. And it was the first time they'd made the playoffs in a decade. Everyone in town was at the game. It ended about the time my set finished."

"Did they win?"

Chase laughed. "Yeah, they did. By one field goal. Too bad I wasn't playing at the local diner. That place was packed. I would've done better bussing tables in the diner that night than I did playing guitar."

Mack grinned. He liked this guy. Chase was down-to-earth, and Mack was impressed that he hadn't let his quick rise to fame go to his head. He was dressed simply in jeans and a black t-shirt. He wore a black Stetson on his head, scuffed cowboy boots on his feet, and an easygoing smile on his face.

Chase had shown up that morning around nine, just like he'd said he would. Mack had been in the shop working on fixing a hinge, and Chase had been fascinated by the blacksmithing process, asking questions and studying the various tools. He'd seemed eager to tackle something, so Mack had shown him how to make a hook, one of the common projects he demonstrated in his classes. Chase had a ball heating the iron and then pounding and twisting it into shape.

He'd seemed genuinely pleased with his work and excited to take the hook with him, claiming he was going to put it up inside the front door of his house and use it to hang his hat on.

The two men had bonded over the smithing, then Mack had given him a tour of the property and introduced him to Molly. She'd made a batch of her famous mac and cheese turkey sliders and fixed up a pitcher of lemonade, and the three of them had sat on the front porch and gone over the plans for the concert. Loretta and Hank had conveniently shown up around the time Molly was pouring Chase a second cup of lemonade. Mack was pretty sure Molly had texted them.

But the country singer took it all in stride and seemed pleased to meet them. He'd been laid-back, content to drink lemonade and listen to the older folks share stories about the ranch.

After that, Mack assumed Chase had gone back to spend the afternoon in his hotel. The guy probably needed a nap. The poor guy had to be worn out after listening to his grandparents and Molly talk his ear off for an hour. But he'd been a good sport. Impressively so. No wonder he'd been so successful.

Mack had given even more props to that success

hours later, as he'd watched car after car drive onto the ranch property. More people than he could count had spilled from those cars and filled the field with blankets and lawn chairs and coolers of food. As the crowds increased, all eager to hear just a few songs from Chase, he'd had a moment of sheer terror, afraid that the country star wouldn't show back up. His panicked mind imagined this whole thing had been an elaborate setup to make him look like an idiot.

Then he realized he *was* an idiot, because nobody cared that much about him to go to all that trouble just to make him seem a fool. Besides, he could do that all on his own, thank you very much.

His cheeks burned when he thought about the video he'd posted for Jocelyn. That's the last time he'd ask his dog for advice about women. Although, posting the video had seemed like such a good idea at the time.

But he hadn't heard a word from her all day—not a text, a note, a call, not even a like or a comment on the painstakingly crafted post.

Plenty of other people had liked and commented. He couldn't believe how much attention the dang post had created. He'd held his breath the last time he'd checked it, praying as he scrolled through the comments. But there was nothing, not a single reaction, from the one person he'd written it for.

He tried to ignore the ache in his chest. He'd wanted an answer. Now he'd gotten one. Jocelyn wasn't interested. Or maybe it was simply that she wanted something else more than she wanted him. That once again, he wasn't enough to make someone stay.

He had to stop. He had a concert to run. Thinking

about Jocelyn was taking too much of his energy. And he needed all he had to get through this night.

Jocelyn is in the past. Leave her there.

The band finished their last song and began to thank the audience for coming out to hear them. That was Mack's cue. Good thing, too. Enough of this feeling sorry for himself. He had work to do. The ranch was his responsibility, and he was going to darn well do everything he could to save it.

He wiped his sweaty palms on his jeans and turned toward the stairs. This was it. *Go time.*

A firm hand clapped him on the shoulder. He turned to get an encouraging nod from Chase. "You got this, Mack."

It wasn't Peyton Manning, but it did the trick.

Mack gave the country star a thumbs-up, then scrambled up the steps and strode across the makeshift stage to take the mic. He held his arm out toward the band. "Let's give it up one more time for the Harmony Creek Crooners." He waited for the applause to die down again. "I can't thank you all enough for showing up tonight to support Harmony Ranch. This means everything to us."

He looked out over the sea of faces, shocked at the size of the audience. It seemed to have doubled since the last band had taken the stage. Hundreds of blankets covered the grass, and every vendor had a line of people. He'd been so busy worrying about how he was going to introduce Chase that he hadn't been paying attention to the crowd. But he now saw a steady stream of headlights backed up for miles along the county road that led to the ranch. So many cars were still waiting to get onto the property.

The concert was a huge success. He couldn't believe it. Even though he knew most of them had shown up to see the real star, he felt like a hero for being the one who gave them all the chance. He'd made this night happen. He and Jocelyn.

He only wished she were here to see what they'd done.

Speaking of which, he'd better get to introducing the man they'd all shown up to see. He gripped the mic tighter as he raised his voice. "And now it is my pleasure to introduce a guy who really needs no introduction. You've heard him on the radio, you've seen him on TV, and now here he is tonight on the stage at Harmony Ranch. Ladies and gentlemen, I give you..." He held his arm out. "Mr. Chase Dalton."

Applause and cheers erupted from the crowd as Chase bounded to the front of the stage, his guitar strapped around his shoulder. A huge smile creased his face as he took a quick bow, then held up his hands to settle the crowd. "Thank you so much. I'm honored to be able to play here tonight. Harmony Creek Ranch is such an amazing place. I remember visiting here as a kid. It always felt like stepping back in time to a place rich in history where things were simple, and family and hard work mattered. Molly Stone and Mack and their crew of volunteers have done an incredible job keeping that history alive for visitors like you and me. I'd love to see all of us help contribute to preserving the place that has done so much for all of us."

Mack was shocked to see Chase reach into his back pocket and pull out his wallet. He'd told the singer that he had volunteers ready to walk through the crowd with baskets, and had planned to ask for donations after Chase had sung. But he sure had never imagined the star himself would help with that task. Or give a donation. He had already done so much by just showing up and bringing in this crowd.

Chase held up his wallet. "I hope you're all opening your wallets to give tonight to help rescue this historic ranch. Mack's got volunteers ready to collect your donations. They're in period dress and carrying red baskets." He pointed to a teenage girl standing in front of the stage. She wore a yellow Victorian dress and a small blue hat, and she held a red basket. "Just like this one. Come on up here, darlin'."

The girl shrank back as she pointed to her chest. "Me?" she mouthed, her voice drowned out by the roar of the crowd. She glanced from Chase to Mack.

Mack sure as heck wasn't going to look a gift country singer in the mouth. He nodded to the girl—her name was Katy, and she'd been volunteering at the ranch since she was in middle school—as he hurried forward to help her up the stairs at the edge of the stage.

Katy stared at Mack, frozen in place as he held his hand out to her. She shook her head. "I can't. That's Chase Dalton."

Mack gave her an encouraging smile. "I know. And this is your chance to meet him. He just called you onto the stage, so get up there, girl. You're going to be the envy of every other kid in your class."

She took Mack's hand. He could feel it shaking, and he squeezed it as he helped her up the steps. She kept his hand gripped tightly in hers as she followed him the few steps across the stage.

"This is Katy," Mack told Chase when they reached him.

"Hey, Katy. Thanks for helping me out." The country singer smiled down at her, and the girl's cheeks and neck went a rosy pink as she smiled shyly back. Then she dropped Mack's hand like it was on fire as Chase put his arm around her.

The country singer turned back to the audience. "This here's Katy, and she and the other volunteers are going to be making their way through the crowds." He pulled a hundred dollar bill from his wallet and pushed it through the hole in the lid of Katy's basket. "I'm making the first contribution, and I just know you all are going to fill those baskets with money. If you don't have cash, you can still help by making a donation online." He shared the website and the instructions on how to give.

Katy beamed up at him as if he'd just invented electricity. She held the basket in the air, and the crowd went crazy.

Mack couldn't believe it. The members of the crowd were digging in their pockets and bags and holding out cash in their hands, waving it around for the volunteers to collect.

Chase gave Katy's shoulder a squeeze. "You better get down there and start collecting."

"Yes, sir." She scrambled from the stage, not bothering with Mack's help this time, and disappeared into the crowd.

"I'm so proud to be here to witness this outpouring of love. I knew this was the kind of community that helped each other out. And speaking of love, I don't know how many of you saw the post this guy put up on Facebook of him and his lady dancing to one of my songs…" He jerked a thumb toward Mack.

The crowd went wild again, whooping and hollering as they cut off Chase's next words. Which was fine with Mack. Heat was creeping up his back, and he took a few steps back, hoping to shrink off the stage. His high of seeing all the donations crashed to the ground in a burning explosion, and shame took its place. He wanted to forget about that post, and planned to delete it the second this concert was over.

"This guy has been great to me today. He introduced me to the wonderful folks who run the ranch, and even let me make something in his blacksmith shop. He told me he and his girl heard me years ago at the Harmony County Fair when I was just getting my start in music, and that 'My Heart Is Your Home' is their song. So I want to dedicate this song to them." He waved Mack over and swung his arm around his shoulder. "Can you believe this tough guy is such a romantic? Come on, Mack. Get your girl up here, and I'll do this one just for her."

Groan. This guy. He was trying to do something nice, but he had no idea what he was doing. Joss wasn't here. She was gone.

"What's her name? Jocelyn?" Chase asked.

Mack nodded. He'd told Chase earlier that Jocelyn was the one he'd been with all those years ago and that she had helped him put together this concert, so it was reasonable that he'd assume she would be there.

"Jocelyn, get up here," Chase called into the crowd.

A sick feeling churned in Mack's gut as he looked over the audience, knowing she wasn't in it. Shame burned his cheeks as the crowd went quiet, looking around to try to see her. The awkward silence seemed to last for hours.

"I'm here." Her voice called from the back of the field.

Chapter Twenty-Two

N O WAY. IT HAD TO be his imagination. Or some woman who saw how humiliated he was and was taking pity on him. Mack craned his neck to see who was yelling when he heard it again.

"I'm here!"

Shouts went up from the audience. "She's here! She's here!" The crowd split apart to let a woman through. She was waving her arm at Mack as she tried to push through the people and skirt around the blankets.

His heart swelled in his chest. It was *her*. It was really Jocelyn. He couldn't believe it. He stood frozen in place, his only movement his eyes, as he blinked as if she were a mirage that might disappear. Then his body took flight as he raced across the stage, flew down the steps and pushed his way into the crowd.

He couldn't see her, couldn't see around the hordes of people who had gathered at the front of the stage when Chase had come out. "Jocelyn!"

"Mack!"

He heard her voice and the mass of people stepped

back to let her through. Her eyes lit when she saw him, and she launched herself toward him and into his arms. He grabbed her, pulling her to him and burying his face in her neck. His hands were shaking as he clutched her back, holding her tightly against him. "I can't believe you're here," he said into her throat, inhaling the scent of her.

She held him just as firmly, handfuls of his shirt gripped in her fists.

He wanted to hold her, to kiss her, to pick her up and take her back to his cottage where they could talk. And be alone. Instead of with hundreds of people who were all watching them. How was this his life?

"Let's get those two up on the stage," Chase called out.

Mack grimaced. Would this ever end? Now that Jocelyn was here, was back, he couldn't care less about the concert. But he knew the ranch was depending on this night. And if they could pull off the money they needed, Jocelyn wouldn't feel as much pressure to take the bonus. He slid his hand down and took hers. Holding it securely, he nodded to the stage. "You okay?"

She nodded, then followed him back through the crowd and up the steps. "I can't believe you're here," he told her again as they stepped onto the stage.

She leaned in. "I can't believe *Chase Dalton* is here. How in the world did you pull this off?"

"I didn't. *He* called *me*."

Her eyes went round, but they didn't have time to say anything more as they approached Chase and Mack introduced her.

"Oh my gosh. I'm so excited to meet you," she told

him. The crowd roared as she let go of Mack's hand and threw her arms around the neck of the country singer. Then she pulled away, smoothing his shirt back in place before she pressed her fingers to her cheeks. "Sorry. I'm just so happy you're here. Wow. That hug— I practically tackled you. Was that too much?"

Chase grinned. "Nah. It was just right."

She took a step back to stand next to Mack. Her shoulder pressed against his as Chase addressed the audience. A rush of heat swirled through his chest as his knuckles brushed hers, then he felt her pinky finger twist around his. It was enough. That small connection. Enough to tell him she still cared.

Chase was sharing the origin of the song and telling a story about how he came up with it, but Mack couldn't hear a word he was saying over the rush in his ears. He peered down at Jocelyn, still amazed that she'd shown up. "What are you doing here?"

"What do you mean?" she asked, tipping her face to his. "You asked me to come."

"I know. But I didn't think you'd really do it. What about your job?"

"I quit."

He jerked back. "You *quit*? Just like that?"

She smiled and turned her hand around to entwine his fingers with hers. "Yep. Just like that."

"But you were so excited about the coffee shop account. And you love that job."

She squeezed his hand and looked deeply into his eyes, her expression earnest and sincere. "But I love *you* more."

He swallowed. She'd quit her job and come back to the ranch? For him? "Are you sure?"

She nodded, a smile curving her lips. "I've never been more sure of anything in my life. There will always be another job. But there will never be another you. Another us. This is right where I should be, and I'm staying. In Colorado, at Harmony Ranch, and with you. If you still want me."

He pulled her into a hug. "I've never stopped wanting you. I gave you my heart when I was ten years old, and it's always belonged to you."

"So this song is for Mack and Jocelyn," Chase said, turning to grin at them. "You guys are just the kind of people I write these songs for. And it looks to me like your hearts have found their homes in each other." He strummed the first chords on the guitar, and the crowd went wild.

Mack smiled down at Jocelyn as he took her in his arms. "Can I have this dance?"

She cuddled against his chest and leaned her head on his shoulder. "Yes. This dance. And every dance. For the rest of our lives."

Mack hugged her as they started to sway. "That sounds like just long enough to me."

The song ended, and Jocelyn and Mack thanked Chase and waved to the crowd as they yielded the stage to the country star. She held Mack's hand in a tight grip as he led her down the back steps of the stage.

They'd barely made it to the grass when Mack turned around, hauled her against his chest and kissed her. "I've been wanting to do that since the second I heard your voice calling from the crowd," he told her as he finally let her go.

Breathless, she peered up at him, unable to keep the smile from taking over her face. "What took you so long?"

He laughed, then his expression turned serious as he raised his hand and rested it against her cheek. "I love you, Jocelyn."

"I love you too." She pressed her cheek into his palm. "I have no idea where I'm going to live or what our life is going to look like, but I know I want my life to be with you."

"We'll figure it out. Together."

She liked the sound of that.

"Jocelyn!"

She turned toward the sound of her name being called and was shocked to see the Carlsons coming around the corner of the stage and hurrying in her direction.

She took a few steps toward them, then Julia hurled herself forward and threw her arms around Jocelyn. "I can't believe we found you."

"It was much easier once Chase called you up on stage," Mike said.

Jocelyn waved them away from the stage, and the four of them walked closer to the ranch until the sound of the music wasn't quite as loud. "What are you guys doing here?"

"Besides being huge Chase Dalton fans, we came to find you," Julia told her.

"Why?"

Julia tipped her head to give Mack an appraising once-over. "So this is the guy you threw us over for?"

A smile tugged at the corner of Jocelyn's lips. "Yes."

"I can see why. He's cute."

Mack held out his hand. "Mack Talbot."

Mike stuck out his hand and gave Mack's a firm shake. "Mike and Julia Carlson. We're the ones Jocelyn bailed on to come find you."

Mack shrugged. "I can't say I'm sorry she did."

"We're here to tell you that you don't have to," Julia said. "We put an offer in this afternoon on that second place we looked at yesterday. Then we called Andrea on our way down here and told her that we are for sure expanding into Colorado. And we also told her we don't want to work with anyone but you."

"I appreciate that, but I've already decided I'm not going back to New York. I'm staying in Colorado."

"That's perfect. You can work remotely from here, and we'll just plan to meet a couple of times a month when we're in Denver. Or we could even come up here to meet you." Julia paused to gaze around the ranch. "This place is totally amazing, by the way."

As much as Jocelyn appreciated the compliment to the ranch, she was stuck on the first part of what she'd said. "Wait. You're saying you still want me to work for you, but I can do it remotely? From here?"

"Absolutely."

"And Andrea agreed with this idea?"

"She was totally on board. In fact, she seemed a little annoyed at herself that she hadn't thought of the idea first. I think she's planning to call you tomorrow to run the concept by you."

"I'm stunned. And flattered."

"But will you do it? Will you keep your job and work on our campaign remotely?"

"You bet I will." Jocelyn peeked a glance at Mack, whose face beamed with a proud grin.

"Great." Julia gave her another quick hug. "We'll hash out the details later. But right now I want to go back and catch the last of Chase Dalton's set. I love that guy."

Jocelyn waved her on. "Go. Have fun. We'll talk tomorrow."

Mike raised a hand, then he and Julia took off back toward the stage.

Jocelyn turned back to Mack. "Can you believe that just happened?"

"Yeah, I can. Everything seems to be falling into place." He gazed out over the crowd. "Now we just have to get through tonight and see if our efforts raised enough money to rescue the ranch."

❧❦❧

"Well, that's it. That's the last of the cash donations," Jocelyn said the next morning, as she put the final stack of twenties into a pile.

It was just her, Mack, and Gram sitting around the table as they compiled the final tallies of the vendors, entrance fees, and donations. Peaches was curled in her lap, and Savage was sprawled out on the floor next to her feet. The basset hound hadn't left her side all morning. Apparently Mack and her grandmother weren't the only ones who were glad to have her back.

"So, did we make it?" Mack squinted at her over the rim of his coffee cup.

She blew out a sigh. "Not quite. We're still two thousand dollars shy, but with the donations online, we just broke ten thousand dollars."

"Ten *thousand* dollars?" Molly pressed back against her chair. "I can't believe it. I never imagined a concert that we put together in five days could bring in ten thousand dollars."

"Well, the majority of the credit goes to Chase," Mack said. "His impromptu appearance brought in hundreds more people than we'd expected. And his asking for donations really tipped the bucket in our direction."

"And your Facebook post made a huge difference too," Jocelyn told him. "The power of social media."

"And a love story," Gram added. "People love a good romance."

Jocelyn ducked her head, heat warming her cheeks. Mack's knee touched hers, and his hand brushed across her leg. Her lips curved into a coy smile.

"If you two lovebirds are done making googly eyes at each other, we should probably get all this down to the bank," Gram said.

"The bank?" Jocelyn asked, turning back to her grandmother. "Aren't they closed today?"

"Yes, but I know the bank manager, and I told him I didn't want to have all this cash out here at the ranch, so he said we could drop it off this morning, and he'd lock it up."

"Good. We're coming in with you, and I'm going to talk to him about giving you an extension on the last little bit of the loan."

"You'll do no such thing."

"It's either that, or you let me pay off the final two thousand dollars with the bonus money from my promotion."

"You don't even know when you're going to get that money. But I'm not letting you use it for me anyway.

But you can try. To talk to the bank manager, I mean. Not try to pay it."

The house phone rang as they were getting ready to leave. Jocelyn picked it up. "Hello."

"Hello, who's this?" Mrs. Crandle's voice boomed over the line.

"It's Jocelyn. Hello, Mrs. Crandle."

"No time to chitchat, dear. I could barely sleep last night. I have to know. Did you make it? Did you raise the money you need to rescue Harmony Ranch?"

Jocelyn was touched by the woman's concern. "Not quite. We're still two grand short. But we're heading down to the bank now to drop off the donations and see if we can work out some kind of arrangement with the bank manager."

"On a Sunday?" She let out a huff.

"You know small towns. I'm sure it will be a short meeting. But the loan is due tomorrow so we need to know how much more we have to scramble today."

"Well, tell Molly not to worry. I'm sure it will work out."

"Thanks, Mrs. Crandle."

Thirty minutes later, Mack, Jocelyn, and Gram's collective mouths dropped open as the bank manager sat across the desk from them and gave them some unexpected news.

"What do you mean, the rest of the loan has been taken care of?" Mack asked, the first to get his mouth to work.

The manager shrugged. "Just what I said. Someone called me this morning and made an anonymous donation of two thousand dollars, so with this deposit, the loan will be paid in full."

"But how could someone just call you out of the blue like that?" Jocelyn sputtered. "And with a donation of the exact amount we were short?"

Gram nudged her arm. "Is this you trying to pull a fast one on me? Are you the anonymous donor?"

Jocelyn shook her head. "No. I swear. It wasn't me."

Her grandmother tapped the edge of the knee scooter, then her eyes widened. "No. It couldn't be. There was only one other person who knew we were short exactly two thousand dollars." Gram squinted at the bank manager. "You don't have to *tell* me who it was, but blink twice if it was the old lady who lives next door to the ranch and whose name rhymes with handle?"

The bank manager held her gaze, but a grin tugged at the corners of his lips. "I think you know that if it were a certain Mrs. *Handle*, she wouldn't be too thrilled to find out I was the one who spilled the beans about her generosity."

Gram nodded as she tapped the side of her nose. "The secret's safe with me."

Elated, they thanked the bank manager and headed toward Mack's truck.

"We did it," Jocelyn shrieked, throwing her arms around her grandmother's shoulders.

"We sure did," Gram said. "I still can't believe it. And I can't believe Edith Crandle came through with the final donation. We've got to go over there and thank her."

"But you just told the bank manager you wouldn't give away her secret."

"Fine. We'll make up another reason to stop—we can say we're checking up on the dog. And I'll just thank her for calling this morning."

Mrs. Crandle seemed surprised to see them ten minutes later when they showed up at her door. Jocelyn wasn't sure she was going to let them in.

But there was no stopping Molly Stone when she set her mind to something, and she wheeled Midge right into the woman's living room.

"Come on in. Make yourself at home," Mrs. Crandle muttered. "You will anyway." But the woman also scooted around Gram to stand on the other side of the living room, almost as if she were blocking the hallway.

The little brown dog raced into the room, its tail wagging as it greeted each of them with a lick and a sniff. Jocelyn sat on the sofa, and the dog jumped into her lap. She laughed as she scratched the puppy's ears and it rolled over for a belly rub.

"We just wanted to stop by on our way home from the bank to tell you thanks for checking in this morning and that the loan has been paid in full. Harmony Ranch has been saved," Gram told her. "So we still get to be neighbors."

"Yippee," Mrs. Crandle said in a deadpan voice as she lowered herself into her recliner. "I'll start planning a party."

Gram waved away her sarcasm. "Oh don't be such a sourpuss. We're so excited. And we can't believe how many people pitched in to help. Do you know someone made an anonymous donation to the bank just this morning for a whopping two thousand dollars? Can you imagine? Who would do such a thoughtful thing?"

"No, I can't imagine," Mrs. Crandle murmured, as she straightened the doily covering the armrest of her chair.

"So many things really came together to make this weekend a success," Jocelyn said. "The biggest one was having the country music star, Chase Dalton, call Mack out of the blue and offer to play a few songs at the concert. Have you heard of him?"

"Oh, I think I've heard the name." Mrs. Crandle's attention was laser-focused on the doily, although Jocelyn couldn't imagine how it could get any straighter.

"We couldn't believe it," Mack said. "He really made all the difference."

Mack was interrupted by a man's voice coming from down the hallway. "Hey Grandma, I was going to run into the store. Do you need me to grab you anything?"

Jocelyn sucked in her breath as Chase Dalton stepped into the room. "*Grandma?*"

Mack's mouth fell open as his gaze darted between Chase and Mrs. Crandle. "Chase Dalton is your *grandson?*"

"Sorry, Grandma. I didn't know you had company," Chase said, offering them all a sheepish grin and a little wave. "Hey y'all."

"Edith, you little sneak," Gram said. "Are you the one who arranged for him to offer to play at the concert?"

Mrs. Crandle gave a slight shrug. "It wasn't a big deal. He was coming through Colorado for a visit anyway, so I just asked him to come a couple of days early."

"Which worked out well, because she also needed me to fix that old furnace that's been giving her trouble," Chase said, smiling at his grandmother as he rested his hand tenderly on her shoulder.

"It *was* a big deal," Gram said, taking Mrs. Crandle's hand in hers. "Having Chase play is what made the concert such a success, and him asking for donations is what earned the money to help pay the loan. We thought *he* saved us, but *you* were the one who was really behind it. *You* rescued Harmony Ranch."

A soft rose color bloomed on Mrs. Crandle's cheeks. "No—*we* rescued Harmony Ranch. All of us. We all played a part, and we did it together."

"Thank you," Jocelyn said, her eyes suddenly brimming with tears at the loving gesture Mrs. Crandle had given her grandmother. She never would have thought the neighbor she'd always viewed as a little crotchety would be the one to come through with the most generous and thoughtful offerings. "What you gave us was a real gift."

"You are the one who gave *me* a gift." Mrs. Crandle patted her thighs, and the little dog jumped down, raced across the room, and leapt into the older woman's lap. He gave her chin a quick lick before curling up on her legs. "This little guy brings me happiness every day. I named him Phil, because he *fills* me with so much joy." She put her arms protectively around the dog's body. "I'm keeping him, just so you know."

Jocelyn grinned. "Yeah, I know."

***

Later that night, Mack and Jocelyn cuddled on the porch swing as they looked out over Harmony Ranch.

The sun was just setting, and it threw a golden glow over the pond and the little cluster of buildings that made up the living history museum.

Her phone buzzed, breaking the stillness, and she pulled it from her pocket. She didn't recognize the number, so she answered with a cautious, "Hello."

"Hi there. I was calling about the dogs you found," the voice on the other end of the line said.

Jocelyn's heart practically stopped beating. *Why now?* When the dogs were just settling in?

"I was just checking to see if you had heard from their owners. I saw the posters, and they were so cute, I was going to offer to adopt them if they hadn't been claimed yet."

Jocelyn let out her breath. "Oh, that's very kind of you, but they both have been claimed, and they've found their forever homes. Thanks for calling, though. Bye." She put her phone back in her pocket and slumped back against Mack's arm. "Whew. For a second there, I thought we were going to have to give the dogs up."

Mack laughed. "As if anyone could pry those pups from either of those women's hands." He rubbed his thumb gently over her arm. "I like how you said they found their forever homes."

She smiled up at him. "That's what I've found too."

"What about New York? Will you miss it?"

"I don't think so. Not much. I've always been on my own in the city. So many people live in New York, but I've still always felt alone there."

"You're not alone anymore." He picked up her hand. "I was thinking I could fly back with you though. I could help you pack up your closet, then we could rent a truck and drive back to Colorado together. I've never been to the East Coast. It could be fun."

"I love that idea." She snuggled against him. "And I love you."

"I love you too."

Her grin turned coy. "Not that it matters, but I'd like to point out that I *did* say it first."

"Say what?"

"That I love you."

He laughed as he shook his head. "It's not a competition."

"I know. But I *still* told you first."

He pulled her against him and pressed a kiss to her lips. This was one competition he was happy to lose.

Because in the game of love, he'd already won.

Chapter Twenty-Three

Three months later…

JOCELYN STOOD AT THE BACK of the church, her arm looped through Hank's elbow, as she waited for her cue to start down the aisle toward the man she loved. The church was gorgeous, decorated in soft greens and blues and covered in sprigs of wildflowers.

Hank gave her hand an encouraging pat. He looked so sharp in his tuxedo. And so proud. He'd been thrilled when Jocelyn had asked him to be the one to give her away. "But we just got you," he'd teased in his Hank way, then tearfully told her he'd be honored.

She couldn't believe they'd pulled off a wedding in only a few months. But she'd found there wasn't much she and Mack couldn't accomplish together when they set their minds to it.

She looked out over the sea of faces who were there to celebrate with them. Emmet Scott was dressed in a new gray suit and sat next to her grandmother. Gram and Loretta were in the front row together, grasping tissues in their hands, their eyes already tear-filled. They'd enthusiastically congratulated themselves over breakfast that morning, claiming credit for their matchmaking efforts at getting her and Mack back together.

Sophie, looking beautiful in a soft pink floral dress, sat alone in an empty pew. She'd become a good friend to Jocelyn over the last few months.

Savage sat at Hank's feet, but pushed up and started down the aisle at Mack's beckoning whistle. The rings were tied in a bow around his collar. Loretta had made the basset hound a miniature tuxedo that strapped around his substantial belly. He looked more like a sad butler than a ring bearer, but Jocelyn didn't care.

It seemed like half the town had shown up to the wedding. So many people who were more like family than friends.

Jocelyn spied Edith Crandle standing at the back, taking her duties at the guestbook quite seriously.

Her eyes went round as she saw Chase Dalton sneak in the back. Edith had asked if she could bring a plus one, but she and Mack had assumed that meant she had a suitor. Chase gave his grandma a quick kiss on the cheek. She hugged him, then directed him to an almost-empty pew.

He smiled as he slid in next to Sophie. Jocelyn grinned. She couldn't help but notice the way Sophie's lips curved into a smile as she nodded to the man wearing Wranglers and cowboy boots. She sat a little taller in the seat as he took off his black Stetson and smoothed his sandy blond hair before setting the hat in the pew on his other side.

Mrs. Crandle beamed at the cute couple. Gram and Loretta must have been rubbing off on her.

Turning back to the front of the church, Jocelyn inhaled a deep breath as the organist played the first chords of the wedding march. She clutched her bouquet, the forged iron rose tucked in among the wildflowers.

She smiled at the handsome bearded blacksmith grinning at her from the front of the church. His grin turned into a laugh as he spotted Savage, who had stopped midway down the aisle to lie down and sprawl all four legs out on the satin carpet runner.

Perfect.

Her smile widened, and she laughed with the man who'd stolen her heart when she was just ten years old. She loved that they would always be bonded by their history—that they shared their past and their present.

And she couldn't wait for that to change today, as she squeezed Hank's arm and took a step toward her future.

The end...
And just the beginning...

Acknowledgments

I adore this book, and part of what made this story so much fun to write was because so many people contributed to the creation of it!

First and foremost, I have to thank my husband Todd, who not only supports every aspect of my writing career, and never stops believing in me, but also actually helped plot significant parts of this book as we traversed the trails through Garden of the Gods on our daily hikes.

Enormous thanks goes out to my editor, Stacey Donovan, for your belief in this story and for your invaluable help with this manuscript. Thanks also to Eunice Shin for finding the most perfect recipe for this book. And to the whole Hallmark staff who worked to make this book so perfect, especially the cover artist who created this amazingly gorgeous cover.

One of the neatest things about this book is that the inspiration for it came from Rock Ledge Ranch Historic Site, the real living history museum and working ranch, which sits at the base of Garden of the Gods and at the edge of my neighborhood, and is the home to many of our family's fond memories. The original idea for and many moments in the book are inspired from real experiences on the ranch. My favorite happened when I was taking a walk at the ranch one afternoon with one of my writer besties, Anne Eliot, and tossing around ideas for a new Hallmark proposal, and she stopped and looked around and said "This is it. We're walking through a Hallmark movie right now." And that's how Rescuing Harmony Ranch started. Thanks Annie. Love you, Friend.

I must thank Andy Morris, Rock Ledge Ranch's Parks Operation Administer and Blacksmith, for spending several hours teaching me about the craft of blacksmithing, how to do a double strike, and sharing facts and information about the ranch and what goes into running a festival. And yes, there really is a Jersey cow named Punkin and a muskrat couple living in the pond.

My thanks goes out to Nancy Bernard, former employee and docent at Rock Ledge Ranch, who shared important history of the ranch and made sure I got the authentic parts of the living history museum accurate. I also credit Nancy with the idea for the Boxed Lunch Social.

Special thanks to Jennifer Martinez, who has always believed in my Hallmark journey, and for her and Terry's assistance in sharing their knowledge, tips, and wonderful nickname for Midge, the marvelous knee scooter.

I have to give thanks to Leighton Mikell and Kristy Keys, for letting me steal the name and personality of Savage, their Basset hound, who was the inspiration for the scene-stealing dog in the story.

Shout-out to one of my favorite managers, Andrea Reynolds, who loves Hallmark movies, who has listened and helped with countless wacky story ideas, and who was the namesake of Jocelyn's boss.

Big thanks to my family for your support and encouragement. To my mom, who loves everything Hallmark and never doubted I would get a Hallmark deal. And for my dad and Gracie, who have always believed in me.

Huge shout-out thanks to my agent, Nicole Resciniti at The Seymour Agency, for your advice and your guidance. You are the best, and I'm so thankful you are part of my life.

Special acknowledgement goes out to the women who walk this writing journey with me every single day. The ones who make me laugh, who encourage and support, who offer great advice, plotting help and marathon sprinting runs, and who sometimes just listen. Thank you Michelle Major, Lana Williams, Anne Eliot, Kristin Miller, Ginger Scott, and Sharon Wray. XO

Big thanks goes out to my street team, Jennie's Page Turners, and for all of my readers: the people who have been with me from the start, my loyal readers, my dedicated fans, the ones who have read my stories, who have laughed and cried with me, who have fallen in love with my heroes and have clamored for more! Whether you have been with me since the first book or just discovered me with this book, know that I write these stories for you, and I can't thank you enough for reading them. Sending love, laughter, and big Colorado hugs to you all!

Turkey Sliders with Mac and Cheese

A Hallmark Original Recipe

In *Rescuing Harmony Ranch*, Jocelyn teams up with her ex-boyfriend Mack—now a strapping blacksmith—to save her grandmother Molly's living history museum. Later in the story, Molly serves her famous mac and cheese turkey sliders to Mack and a very important visitor. You can make these irresistible sandwiches for your own VIPs!

Prep Time: 30 minutes
Cook Time: 10 minutes
Serves: 8

Ingredients

- 1/2 cup heavy cream
- 8 ounces queso blanco cheese
- 2 ounces mild cheddar cheese, shredded
- 8 ounces uncooked elbow macaroni (4 cups cooked macaroni)
- 1/2cup flour
- 2 eggs, beaten
- 1 cup Japanese bread crumbs
- As needed, vegetable oil for frying
- 8 mini slider rolls, sliced for sandwiches
- 8 slices roast turkey, warm

Preparation

1. Combine heavy cream, queso blanco cheese and shredded Cheddar in a heavy saucepan; heat over low heat, stirring occasionally, until cheese is completely melted.

2. Meanwhile, cook macaroni according to package directions; drain and transfer to a large bowl.

3. Add warm cheese sauce to cooked macaroni and stir until blended. Cover and chill overnight or until completely chilled.

4. Using a small ice cream scoop or spoon, shape chilled mac & cheese into meatball-sized balls; press into pattie-shaped bites.

5. Dust each lightly with flour; shake excess. Dredge each in egg mixture; drain excess. Roll

each in breadcrumbs; shake excess. (Mac & cheese bites can be made ahead and refrigerated up to this step.)

6. To prepare mac & cheese bites: heat oil in deep fryer or deep heavy saucepan to 350°F or until oil is shimmering. Working in several smaller batches, carefully add breaded bites to oil and deep fry for 2 to 3 minutes or until light golden brown. Drain on paper towels. Repeat with remaining mac & cheese bites.

7. To prepare sliders: layer 1 slice turkey and 1 warm mac & cheese bite on bottom half of each slider roll; close each with top half of roll and press lightly to secure.

Thanks so much for reading
Rescuing Harmony Ranch. We hope you enjoyed it!

You might like these other books
from Hallmark Publishing:

Country Hearts
A Country Wedding
Love on Location
A Simple Wedding
Sunrise Cabin

For information about our new releases and
exclusive offers, sign up for our free newsletter at
hallmarkchannel.com/hallmark-publishing-newsletter

You can also connect with us here:

Facebook.com/HallmarkPublishing

Twitter.com/HallmarkPublish

About the Author

Jennie Marts is the *USA TODAY* bestselling author of award-winning books filled with love, laughter, and always a happily ever after. Readers call her books "laugh out loud" funny and the "perfect mix of romance, humor, and steam." Fic Central claimed one of her books was "the most fun I've had reading in years."

She is living her own happily ever after in the mountains of Colorado with her husband, two dogs, and a parakeet who loves to tweet to the oldies. She's addicted to Diet Coke, adores Cheetos, and believes you can't have too many books, shoes, or friends. Her books range from western romance to cozy mysteries, but they all have the charm and appeal of quirky small-town life.

Jennie loves to hear from readers. Follow her on Facebook at Jennie Marts Books, or Twitter at @JennieMarts. Visit her at www.jenniemarts.com and sign up for her newsletter to keep up with the latest news and releases.